THE
SHIP'S
REVENGE

DOUG BRODE

THE SHIPS REVENGE

Copyright © 2022 Doug Brode

Published 2022

Cover Design: Enchanted Ink Publishing
Formatting: Enchanted Ink Publishing

ISBN: 978-1-7372255-7-7 (Paperback)
ISBN: 978-1-7372255-6-0 (Hardcover)

Library of Congress Control Number: TXu-2-308-849

Alien Sky Publishing – First edition 2022

ALIEN SKY ★
PUBLISHING

For the women who have **shaped my life**:

My **mother**, Sandra,

My **wife**, Pamela,

And my **daughter**, Leia.

PART 1

RED MENACE

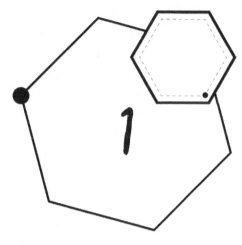

July 8, 1947

Casey Stevens didn't need to close her eyes for the nightmares to come. Winding tunnels dimmed by pulsing light; her friends running, screaming, dying. Amidst the fractured images, Casey's flesh stretched, blotched with ashen-gray patches. Blonde hair tumbled from her scalp in clumps. Her green eyes darkened to large black ovals.

I'm not human anymore.

The sound of men giggling snapped Casey from a daze. She felt their ogling eyes. Shuddering beneath a frigid shower, her exposed body still appeared healthy, normal.

For now, but for how long?

Even with an audience and no warm water, the shower was cleansing. Casey only wished the heavy spray could wash away more than blood and dirt. Fumbling for the knob, she turned the water off and saw something yellow tossed at her trembling feet. A half-dry towel. Casey spun around. Two Army guards were lingering a few feet away. Though they averted their gaze, their shoulders still shuddered with suppressed laughter.

"Go ahead," she said, wiping herself off, "get one more look." The giggling stopped. "Where are my clothes?"

"They've been confiscated, ma'am," one soldier said, his eyes studying the floor.

"I think we're past the 'ma'am' part, don't you?" She tossed the towel at them and then walked out.

Moments later she was back in a cement-lined interrogation room for round three of what seemed like an endless verbal boxing match. Sitting on a metal chair behind a desk, Casey was draped in a puffy white robe four sizes too big and nothing else. If they were trying to make her feel vulnerable, it wasn't working. Across the table, a little man in a charcoal suit awaited her answer while an armed guard lingered near a bolted door.

"Are you all hard of hearing?" Casey snapped. "I'm from *Oregon*."

"Blackwood, Oregon," the little man clarified, studying an open folder. "A town that doesn't appear on our maps."

She shrugged. "It was founded in the sixties, I think."

"But you are from nineteen . . ." He paused, searching his notes.

"Eighty-five."

"Nineteen eighty-five, yes." He pointed a thin finger at his notes to confirm. "And you're a waitress, correct?"

"Why? You planning on ordering a meal?"

"The faster we get through this—"

"The faster the next guy can walk in and ask the same questions," she finished.

"Sarcasm." He spoke the word as if it were foreign to him. "I can see you've been through a lot, Miss Stevens," the little man said with feigned sympathy. His eyes crawled over the robe and her wet hair. "Again, my apologies about the shower. We don't have any female guards here."

"Where's *here*, exactly?"

"RAAF," he replied. "Roswell Army Air Field."

She eyed his nice suit and manicured fingernails. "You're not military."

"No, no. They flew me down from Washington on the red eye." He sighed dramatically. "It's been a hell of a night."

You've got to be kidding.

"I've already told you people all I know. Twice."

"A third time won't hurt anyone," he replied. "I'd like to discuss your supposed *abduction*."

Casey burst out laughing. The little man tilted his head. "May I ask what is so funny?"

"It's just, after everything I've gone through," she said, still chuckling, "to be sitting here with a bureaucrat. It's kind of funny."

Unperturbed, he continued. "Tell me about the saucer."

The problem was, she didn't *want* to talk about the ship anymore. She'd been keeping her thoughts and feelings within a steel vault, worried that if she opened it, a floodgate of emotions might engulf her.

Arthur, I'm so sorry.

Wiping tears from her eyes, she hesitated. She'd lost her fiancé. Her home. Everything. And still, this little man was sitting across from her, waiting. Her fists clenched beneath the table, she envisioned smashing them in his beady eyes.

Thankfully, the door opened, and a soldier entered. She'd seen him at the crash site. Fixing his gaze squarely on the little man in the gray suit, he never glanced in Casey's direction.

I make him nervous, she decided. It wasn't a mere guess. His fear of her flowed out of him like a tangible, visible substance. Inwardly, he blazed with hues of bright red and orange. Outwardly, his face and voice remained flat. "The colonel wants her, sir."

The little man nodded and then turned to Casey. "We'll have to continue this later."

Prewitt. That's the little weasel's name. She'd plucked it out of his head. It was the same ability she'd had inside the ship, and it seemed she still possessed it. Casey made a mental note not to reveal anything about her abilities or the nanite technology infused in her bloodstream. If she had any hope of leaving, it was best not to make herself out to be a potential lab rat.

The guard withdrew a pair of handcuffs. Casey shot Prewitt a hard look. "Seriously?"

He shrugged. "Afraid so."

With handcuffs secured tightly around her wrists, she was led outside, down clanging steps, and toward a long stretch of airfield. The last rays of dusky sun peeked behind buildings as they crossed the tarmac. Casey couldn't remember the last time she'd seen sunlight. Not since before the abduction.

Before the monsters came.

Turning her attention to the surrounding airfield, Casey noted the warmth of the setting sun on her skin and a lingering smell of dust and manure from the surrounding hills. The heat warmed her wet skin beneath the ridiculously fluffy robe as they approached a jagged mass of broken metal and ragged corners. The ship, what was left of it, lay in a sprawled heap.

Inhaling dry air through clenched teeth, she stopped beneath the ship's massive shadow. Dozens of soldiers in olive-green uniforms unloaded rows of trucks, placing debris onto the haphazard pile of shrapnel. To her they seemed like a group of blind children trying to build a puzzle. The shape was basically right, but the pieces were a hodgepodge. The mile-wide vessel that had brought her there, trapped in the past, lay scattered across the airfield in ruins. If she had any hope of returning to her own time, she knew she'd have to find a way to put it back together.

Easier said than done, Case.

"Ms. Stevens," Colonel McKellen said, stepping forward. They'd met the night before. He was the one who had found her in the field beside the burning craft. He didn't appear any happier to see her now than he was then. Not that she could blame him. Giant flying saucers and girls who fell from the sky were probably not part of his job description. He seemed like a man who preferred to be grounded in certainty.

Like Major Reese, her mind whispered. Only, Reese was gone. So was her fiancé, Arthur. All of them were dead, and she was alone.

Shaking off the sinking feeling that accompanied those thoughts, Casey returned her focus to the haphazard mess spread across the airstrip. The center of the ship was mostly intact. At over a hundred yards across, it took up the main runway's gray concrete surface from one end of her vision to the other. As she watched the soldiers pile shrapnel onto the hull, a nursery rhyme came to mind: *All the king's horses and all the king's men couldn't put Humpty together again.*

Except, she had to find a way. It was her only chance of escaping that place. That time.

McKellen forced a smile, but she felt the tension behind his grin. It didn't take psychic ability to know that he wished that someone—anyone—else would take charge. "We've yet to find a door or a hatchway."

"There isn't one, sir," Casey replied, fidgeting in the handcuffs. The soldier had put them on too tight, but she doubted a complaint would gain her any sympathy.

"Then how the hell did you get in and out of the damn thing?"

"I thought my way out."

McKellen stepped closer. Backlit by the sun, his body was cast in darkness, like a looming statue. "That's not helpful."

"It's the truth, sir." When he didn't respond, she realized he was waiting for more. Gulping hot air, Casey let out a long, slow sigh, trying to decide how best to describe it without revealing too much. "The ship heard my thoughts."

"Heard you? How?"

"It's alive, sir," she said, meeting his eyeline. "This ship, just like those who flew it, are our descendants. It's not a machine. At least not completely."

McKellen's frown increased into something akin to a scary Halloween mask. "You're suggesting this thing's . . . human?"

Prewitt let out a squeak. Casey had forgotten he

was there. A couple of nearby soldiers traded nervous glances.

"OK," McKellen continued, gesturing toward the fractured hull. "Show me."

"It's in pieces," she said, dreading what would happen if she couldn't prove her outlandish claims. "The ship is dead, sir."

"Try."

Taking one hesitant step after the other, Casey approached the hulking, fractured vessel. She stopped twenty meters from its darkened center. The jutting angles made it look like a mouth of broken teeth, leering at her. Suppressing a shiver, she closed her eyes and tried to reach out with her senses.

Can you hear me?

No response.

She deepened her probe, pushing her inner voice outward.

Open.

An eruption of nervous gasps caused Casey to open her eyes. There was a breach in the hull. It grew slowly, spreading into a round hole. She felt her heart jackhammering in her chest as a doorway revealed itself. It had worked. The ship was still functioning. Still alive.

Casey turned back toward McKellen. She tried to smile, but it came out awkwardly. They would believe her now. But then what? Trapped in the past and held by the Army, Casey's mind raced, wondering what would become of her.

As if noticing her concern, McKellen turned to Prewitt. "Take those cuffs off her."

Prewitt paled. "Sir?"

"This lady just became the US military's most valuable asset."

The little man fidgeted uneasily. "But, sir—"

"And for Christ's sake," McKellen interjected, "someone get her some damn clothes."

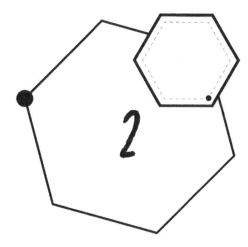

November 4, 1957

Harold Stone arrived at an unmarked military instal-
lation in the Nevada desert one month after Russia
launched their Sputnik satellite and began an arms race
into outer space. It was Monday morning, and he was
reporting for duty as a biochemical research assistant.
Tapped by the US government in his final year at Stan-
ford, this was his first job right out of school. Several top
labs had already offered him positions across the western
hemisphere, but this was the one that had captured his
interest. Not because of the pay—the government paid
almost half what the private sector positions offered. It
was the letter he'd received. It consisted of a single sen-
tence that made the wheel in his mind's eye spin wildly:
"Help us save humanity from our future."

What an odd proposition, he'd thought. *And so vague.*
Yet, coming from the Department of Defense, it had a
certain weight that he couldn't ignore. It was the "from

our future" part that immediately caught his attention. Considering the current political climate, he assumed it had something to do with America's burgeoning space program, though how that might apply to biochemistry remained a mystery to him. After all, with the Russians having launched the world's first satellite into orbit, every American knew they were in a race to catch up. It was the day of the scientists and engineers now, he figured. *Our country needs us.*

The phrase "from our future" continued to bounce around in his mind as if the invitation were offering far more than simply beating the USSR. Whoever had written the note knew precisely how to capture his interest because Harold was also a closet futurist, though not in any sort of hocus-pocus, mumbo-jumbo sense. Within his own scientific research, he'd often taken a long view, more interested in where space travel and technology might take humankind in a hundred years, three hundred years, or longer rather than in the next two to ten years. To Harold, science was a means to discover what lay beyond tomorrow.

From our future. He played with the term once again as his driver slowed to a halt before a lonesome gate where a soldier stood watch. Harold scanned the lone stretch of road, surrounded by miles of empty desert.

If this is where the future lies, he thought with a chuckle, *no wonder no one has found it.*

"Sign here, here, and here," a young sergeant, Davis, said at the front desk. They were standing at a counter just inside the main gate in front of an airfield from which Harold could hear planes taking off.

Harold thumbed a thick stack of papers. The first page was a government non-disclosure form. The second page was the same. So was the third. He flipped through a dozen more.

"These NDAs appear to be identical," Harold said.

"Each goes to a different office, sir," Sgt. Davis replied. "Now, please raise your right hand. Do you, Doctor Harold Stone, solemnly swear that you will reveal nothing you see or hear on this base for as long as you live?"

"I do."

"In the eventuality of a security breach, do you agree to waive all legal counsel, knowing that, if found guilty, you will face immediate imprisonment of no less than one hundred years?"

Harold's raised arm wavered. One hundred years? Had he heard that correctly?

"And, uh, if I don't agree?"

"You'll be escorted back to the train station, sir. No harm, no foul."

Harold glanced down at the stack of forms. What was he getting himself into? As alarm bells rang in his mind, so did another realization—something super top secret lay waiting for him on this base. The future?

He raised his arm higher. "I swear."

After signing all the documents without reading a single page, Harold followed the soldier toward a nondescript brown building near the front of the base. The soldier led him to his room on the third floor. It contained a table and chair, a lamp, and a bed. A small window was set into the wall to his right. Harold heard jet planes roaring outside. *Home sweet home*, he thought.

"Doctor Stevens will be by to give you the grand tour," Davis said.

"Stevens. Is he my boss?"

"*She* runs your team, yes, sir."

Harold raised his eyebrows. "A woman?"

Davis nodded. His skin paling, he avoided Harold's gaze, as if the subject made him uncomfortable. "Colonel McKellen oversees the base and operations, but Doctor Stevens handles the civvies. Scientists like you. I'm sure she'll be along soon."

With that he turned to leave.

"Wait," Harold said. "What's this place called?"

"Groom Lake, sir. Named after the salt flat to our east." Davis pointed out the window toward a dry white lakebed that stretched beyond the airstrip. "But the bigwigs up in Washington have another name for it: Area 51."

After Sgt. Davis left, Harold unpacked, placing ten days' worth of clothes in the closet. Shirts hanging on the right, trousers on the left. Underwear and socks in the lower corner, beside an extra pair of shoes.

Scanning the bottom of his suitcase, he saw that one last item remained: a cross hanging from a chain. His mother, it seemed, hadn't wanted her boy to go off to the wolf's den unprotected. Harold sighed, then closed the suitcase and shoved it under the bed.

He stood up and paced for a moment, then pulled the case back out and grabbed the cross. Pushing out a long, slow huff, he dangled the chain over the desk lamp. The cross swayed, catching the sunlight.

There you go, Mother.

Returning the suitcase beneath the bed, he took a final appraisal of the closet. Everything was in its proper place. Satisfied, he perused his tiny room, noting there wasn't a phone. He wondered when he'd be able to call home. He imagined his mother pacing around the house, scowling as she awaited his call. Grinning inwardly, Harold decided he wasn't in any rush to find a phone after all.

Plopping into the chair behind the desk, he watched trucks drive by. A plane roared past, rattling the room's contents. Glancing at his watch, he realized he'd only been waiting twenty minutes. It was 3:00 p.m. *Or,* he corrected, *1500 hours. When in Rome . . .*

Standing, he glanced around, trying to decide how best to occupy himself. With nothing to do, he stretched out on the cot, trying to relax. It had been Harold's first cross-country trip, and he couldn't recall the last time he'd slept. As he tossed and turned, the bed squeaked beneath him until he finally drifted off to sleep.

By the time there was a soft knock at Harold's door, the sun had dimmed, and shadows were pooling across the tiny gray room. Blinking his eyes awake, Harold was startled to find a woman leaning over him. Blonde hair dangled from a haphazard bun, and her once-white lab coat was covered in stains of various colors.

"Sorry to have kept you waiting, Harry," she said, offering a firm handshake. "I'm Doctor Stevens." Harold noted that she used his first name but not her own. Her way of setting up their roles, he assumed.

"Actually," he said, standing and stretching, "I prefer Harold."

"Harry makes you sound mysterious," she replied. "Dangerous, like a dime-store detective."

He smoothed the creases along his pressed shirt. "Which is precisely why I prefer Harold."

"Whatever you say, Harry." She shot him a quick wink. "Come on, let me show you around."

Dr. Stevens led him down the stairs and outside toward a cherry-red Chevy convertible. Surrounded by the base's simple structures and somber earth tones, the vehicle appeared garish. He assumed that was the point. Clambering behind the steering wheel, she revved the engine, suppressing a giggle. As Harold sat in the passenger seat, hearing the motor roar, he wished the car had a roof. Without another word, they were off in a cloud of dust, streaking across the runway before jerking left and heading toward the large white salt flats in the distance.

"Top of your class!" she shouted over the rushing wind and the engine's roar. "Impressive."

"Th-thanks," Harold stammered, gripping the door. He glanced at the base behind them and the open desert in front. "Where are we going?"

"Your new home away from home for the next few years," she said with a Cheshire grin.

"Years?" His voice was pitched higher than he'd meant it to be.

"Something wrong?"

"No, ma'am. I just wasn't sure how long this position was for!" he shouted over the wind. "The letter I received was rather vague."

"Got you here, though, didn't it?" She shook his shoulder, as if hoping to loosen him up. "And *ma'am* makes me sound like an old woman. *Doctor* is fine. Or *Casey* in a pinch."

"I noticed there was no phone in my room, Doctor. I assume because of secrecy around whatever we're working on," he said, shielding his eyes from the swirling sand. "Does my position at least include holidays and weekend trips?"

She laughed. "If you're anything like I think you are, Harry, you'll never want to leave."

As they neared the edge of the salt flats, the convertible whipped left again, barreling straight toward a distant brown hill. Through the dirty windshield, the hill grew into a small mountain. Still, Casey didn't slow their approach. As they raced toward the looming mound of dusty earth, Harold was about to plead for her to stop when a giant doorway, twenty yards across, sprang open like a wound in the mountainside. Rising in front of them, the entrance revealed pitch darkness beyond.

"Dear lord," he exclaimed. "A camouflaged door."

"If you think that's something, Harry," she said, chuckling, "wait till you see what's inside."

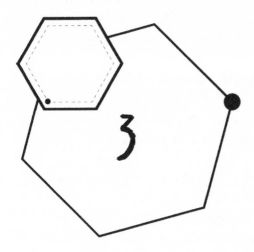

3

The origins of Area 51 were as mysterious as the programs it contained. Officially opened in 1955 for development of the Lockheed U-2 reconnaissance aircraft, the land had already secretly been in use by the government for several years prior. Abandoned diamond mines in the mountains had initially drawn Casey and her team there. When the Air Force later used the surface above to test recon planes, it helped maintain their secrecy. Even in its fractured form, the ship was almost a mile in diameter, which meant they needed somewhere enormous to hide the damned thing. Despite popular belief, however, it wasn't aliens or anything otherworldly that they were keeping secret. It was exactly the opposite.

The ship's terrestrial origins had urged government secrecy. Beings from another world, folks could handle. Bug-eyed descendants with human DNA? Not so much.

Even the military higher-ups still called the ship "alien." Casey supposed it helped them sleep at night.

Leading Harold through the underground "hangar," as they called it, she watched his eyes dart about like a dog trying to keep track of a busy squirrel. This, she knew, was the *oohs* and *ahs* phase. They always started out that way. Her last assistant was Miles, a bright young man from Minnesota. Casey had liked him, especially because he was a smart black scientist in a place that had never seen—or even considered—such a thing before. Still, his fate had proven to be the same as all the others. He made it almost two years before curiosity got the better of him. Waiting until dark, after everyone had left the hangar, Miles snuck inside the ship. He never came out. Not alive, anyway.

Pausing at the iron-gated elevator, Casey silently prayed that this new assistant wouldn't be so reckless. Though academically brilliant, Harold's psychological profile also suggested he was more cautious than Miles. Fearful, prudish even, due to his strong religious upbringing, Casey assumed those beliefs might keep him wary of exploring too much too fast. Caution, she surmised, would be the key to Harold's survival. At least she hoped it would.

"Good evening, Doctor Stevens," a guard said, opening the door.

"Hey there, Mike," she replied, ushering Harold inside.

The guard nodded, smiling. "Where to?"

"Out of town."

His face flattening, the guard slammed the gate without another word. When the elevator began its descent, she turned to Harold. "His name's not really Mike."

"What is it?" Harold asked.

"No idea. The soldiers inside this hangar have their identities hidden, so we just call them all 'Mike.' It's kind of a running joke." Harold tried to fake a laugh, but it didn't work. Casey shrugged. "When you work in a hole in the ground for twelve hours a day, you find humor where it's available."

They continued their descent without further comment, passing level after level filled with giant crates and stacked boxes. The place looked more like a storehouse than a hangar. Harold pointed at a line of dusty train tracks running across the second sublevel.

"You have a train down here?" he asked excitedly.

"Used to," she said. "We haven't needed one in years. Cargo trains were used when we first built this place, to transport equipment."

"Must have been a lot of equipment."

She chuckled. *Just wait, Sparky.* "Behind the tracks is a series of lifts, stretching over a mile wide. It's quite a feat of engineering, or so I've been told." She shrugged. "Not really my area of expertise."

"May I ask what is?"

"I hold doctorates in biology, physics, and chemistry."

His jaw slackened as he studied her youthful face. "All *three*?"

"I'm a quick learner."

As the elevator slid into shadow, the air turned frigid. Descending to level ten, they came upon a hallway with two rows of multiple glassed-in rooms. On the left, frosted glass, blanketed in clouds of white, obstructed their view. Through the haze, blurred technicians worked in parkas and winter wear, fiddling with a thirteen-foot-long metal tube.

"Now," she said, pausing the elevator, "here's where things get interesting. Research and Development. The labs on the left we call the Fridge."

"Is that a weapon?" he asked, indicating the long metallic tube.

"Not yet," she said with a huff. Five years into development, and the experiment still barely worked half the time. "You're familiar with Bose-Einstein condensate?"

"A state of matter in which separate atoms or subatomic particles are cooled to near zero-degree temperatures."

"What are you, a textbook?" Casey snapped. "Down here, imagination pays the bills."

Harold peered through the frosted surface, studying the tube's size and shape. "You're attempting to turn something gaseous into a solid," he said. "Something quite large, I'd say. Organic, possibly?"

"There ya go, Harry." Casey applauded. Pointing across the hall, she drew his attention toward another lab. Its windows were clear at room temperature, with cement blocks lined up throughout. "This one we call the Well. Short for gravity well."

Inside, a soldier held a bolt-action Smith & Wesson, modified with metallic tubing along its casing. As the weapon fired, a bullet zipped around a cement block, twisted in midair, and then exploded into another block behind it.

Harold gasped. "That . . . that's not possible! General relativity prohibits—"

"Gravity, like time, can be bent," she assured him, pushing the button, and resuming their descent. "Einstein's equations state as much."

"But he was speaking *theoretically* about black holes and space-time."

"In here we make the theoretical *practical*."

"How?"

"Funny you should ask . . ."

The elevator clanged to a halt. Casey opened the door. "Last stop."

Harold followed her through a bowl-shaped chamber deep in the earth, stretching out farther than they could see. In the distance, shadows formed odd angles.

Hearing him gasp, Casey looked back. "You feel it?"

Harold paused, glancing about. He touched his shoulders, as if expecting something to be resting upon them, but found nothing.

"Yeah," he said, spinning around. "It's like, I don't know . . . a weight."

"A weight," Casey repeated. "I suppose that's as good a description as any." She waved him on, toward the blanketing darkness. "Everyone feels it the first time."

Harold followed, his pace flagging as a hulking shadow slowly took shape. Piece by fractured piece, the ship came into view. Casey watched his reaction; it was the same as all the others. Still, she loved this part. Harold's jaw unhinged, his eyes wide and his hands trembling as he mumbled to himself. Casey couldn't make out the words, but she assumed it was something like, *Holy shit!* Or, more probably considering his religious upbringing, *My god! I don't believe it!*

"Not too close," she cautioned, stopping his approach. "This thing has teeth."

"A flying saucer," he said with a crazed giggle. "Unbelievable."

"But *not* alien," Casey clarified.

Harold paled. She could practically see the wheels spinning in his mind. "*We* made this?"

"Not us. Try again." She was testing him, wanting to see how quickly he could gather the information and—

"Help us save humanity *from our future*," Harold whispered, quoting the letter she'd sent him. "It's from Earth," he exclaimed, his voice rising to an excited squeal. "In the far future."

She nodded, impressed. "A million years, give or take."

He squinted, scanning the wreckage. "How do we get in?"

"You don't." Casey's voice flattened. "Everyone who's tried has gone insane—or died."

"Nobody's been inside?"

Casey bit her lip. "The ship allows me to enter, but I rarely do."

"Allows you," he repeated, pacing in front of the ship. "So, it's sentient."

He's quick. Gesturing for him to follow, Casey walked away. "There's more."

Harold hesitated, not wanting to leave. "Nothing could possibly top this."

Casey's emerald eyes sparkled. "Hold that thought."

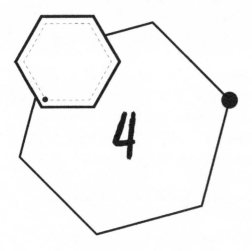

4

Black eyes glared back from the center of a bulbous head covered in rubbery gray skin. The creature's body was thin to the point of anorexia, its rib cage and shoulder bones protruding. Seemingly lifeless, it floated in a tank of clear liquid, both grotesque and startlingly familiar. Harold had seen this form before in various artist sketches and Hollywood movies. Though apparently dead, its very existence triggered Harold's basest instinct to run. This was something to be feared, his primordial self whispered. The warning grew incessant. Reflexively, he took a step back.

Casey stood unflinching beside him. "An empty husk, nothing more."

"No sexual organs," Harold whispered, his eyes trailing down the thing.

"It's a clone," she replied. "A carbon copy grown in sacks, each identical to the other."

The implications horrified him. Grimy fingers crept up his spine as he attempted to remain detached, scientific. "So, this is what becomes of us."

"Not quite." Casey headed through steel doors, away from the floating monster and its blank black eyes. Relieved to put some distance between himself and the creature, Harold hurried after her into a larger chamber.

Though the ceiling and jagged walls were made of the same brown rock as the previous rooms, metallic paneling and glass brightened the environment. Harold sighed, having not realized until then that he'd been holding his breath. Ahead, two researchers, a man and a woman in their mid-thirties, looked away from a glass container and nodded in his direction. The woman, he noted, had a subtle bulge along her tummy—about four months pregnant, he guessed. Harold smiled back with an awkward wave, glad to see other people down there. *With the monsters*, his brain moaned.

"The cloned bodies are to the seekers what a sweater or jeans might be to us," Casey said as she approached the researchers. "Clothes to be used and discarded."

"Seekers?"

"Just something I call them," she replied with a shrug. "To my knowledge they don't actually have a name."

Seekers. The word bounced around his skull. *What are they seeking?* Before he could ask, Casey stopped in front of the researchers.

"Ruthie, Max, meet our new assistant, Harry. He has a PhD in chemistry and did undergrad work in physics and molecular biology."

"It's Harold, actually," he mumbled, shaking their hands.

"Max and Ruthie were married just last year," Casey continued. "So, if you see them sneak off into a closet, *don't follow*."

Harold forced himself to chuckle. Doctor Stevens' brand of humor didn't click with him, but he felt pressure to respond correctly. He hoped she didn't see through his false laughter. One look at those sharp green eyes of hers, however, and he knew that she knew.

"Can I ask what you're working on?" he asked the others, wanting to change the subject.

"I'm a biologist, and Ruthie's a chemist," Max said, squeezing his wife's shoulder with pride. "Originally, we started with the clone you saw out front, but lately, we've been leaning toward our crimson friend here."

Ruthie moved next to a ten-foot-tall glass container. Stepping beside her, Harold struggled to keep his eyes from glancing down at her swollen belly. He wondered if he should ask about her pregnancy, whether it would be polite or not. Social graces had never been his strength.

Returning his attention to the case, he saw a red mist billow behind the glass. Harold leaned closer. The mist seemed to curl forward, strands of it reaching out like vaporous tentacles. A trick of the eye, he assumed.

"Knock on the glass," Max said, chuckling.

Off Harold's hesitation, Ruthie assured him with a nudge. "It's OK. I promise."

He rapped the glass lightly with his knuckles.

The vapor lunged, smashing against the clear surface with thick, heavy weight. Shocked, Harold stumbled backwards. The others laughed. It seemed that Doctor Stevens wasn't the only one with an odd sense of humor.

"Wh-what the hell is it?" Harold stammered.

"That," Casey said, approaching the mist, "is what becomes of humanity."

Forcing himself to step closer, Harold peered at the vapor, watching it twist and curl about with animated life. How could physical beings be reduced to a gaseous substance? The concept repulsed him even more than the misshapen gray creature in the other room. At least that had still resembled something akin to a human.

"And it's . . ." He paused to swallow. "Conscious?"

"Yes," Casey replied with a crooked smile, "and hungry like the wolf."

An odd turn of phrase, he thought. Still, Harold now understood the need for all the secrecy. He doubted anyone was ready to see this, to know what became of humankind. Certainly not his mother or his hometown congregation. An image sprang to mind of his mother's round face, her pale, flabby skin glowing red with anger as she railed on about the end of days. She often called the scientific community a "wolf's den" that she believed wanted to replace God with a bunch of fancy equations. As Harold observed the red mist, he wondered if she was right.

Slanting his gaze sideways, Harold glimpsed the exit door. With a heavy exhale, he struggled to slow his rapid breathing and keep his feet firmly planted in place. After all, this was the very future knowledge he'd sought his entire life. There it was, right there, swirling behind glass. The future . . .

Touching the glass again, gentler this time, he watched the vapor swirl about as if matching his response. It created smoky fingers, offering an outline of a red hand. Stunned, Harold knew there was no going back, not for him and, potentially, not for humankind.

Casey approached the glass, the crimson light reflecting off her beautiful features. "We think their gray bodies deteriorated over time," she said, "until they evolved into this."

"But vapor *dissolves*," Harold protested. "How does it keep its gaseous state intact?"

"It can't," Casey replied. "That's why it needs a physical host."

Max chuckled. "So, if the glass breaks—don't inhale."

The others laughed uneasily. Harold couldn't bring himself to join in.

Midnight had come and gone by the time Harold returned to his tiny room, a changed man. Exhausted, he didn't bother to hit the light switch. Clambering into bed, he kicked off his shoes and lay down, fully clothed. His mind whirling, Harold attempted to process everything he'd seen and learned. The implications were astounding—and more than a little unnerving. Yet, science was the language of the future, and now more than ever, Harold wanted to be a part of that conversation. Lying in bed, beaming, he imagined himself being written about one day in scientific journals and history books, his biography placed neatly between names like Oppenheimer, Plank, and Einstein. A smile creased his lips, broadening with his imagination.

In the surrounding darkness, a glimmer caught his eye, disturbing his wandering dreams.

The cross his mother had given him was hanging from the desk lamp. Sitting up, Harold was reminded that he hadn't said his prayers before bed. Huffing loudly, he no longer saw the point. Not after tonight. The future, he decided, didn't come from Bible stories or prayers. Instead, it was right there, buried beneath the earth, waiting for all of its wonders to be discovered. Perhaps, by him.

Grabbing the small golden cross, Harold shoved it into a drawer and slammed it shut.

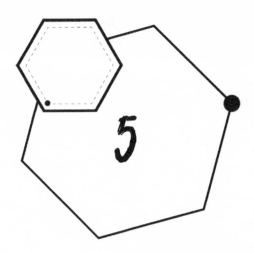

5

A few months later

In 1958, contrary to popular belief, Area 51 was not solely an Air Force base. Instead, it was a joint operation with a bunch of fingers plunged into the proverbial pie. The CIA and the Air Force oversaw Lockheed's aerial reconnaissance programs above ground while the Army handled security and logistics for the secret hangar below. With so many agencies sharing the same plot of land, with none of them knowing what the others were doing, it was amazing that it ran as smoothly as it did. That was thanks in no small measure to the base commander who oversaw the whole damn quagmire, Colonel Thomas McKellen.

Having been repositioned from the Army Air Forces to the Air Force proper in September 1949, McKellen was the right man for the job—whether he wanted to be or not.

And at the moment, he sure as hell didn't.

Leaning over a balcony railing, McKellen watched as Sgt. Davis led a parade of suits toward his office below. *G-men. The worst kind of visitors.* Not that the CIA or Lockheed executives were a barrel of laughs, but at least they didn't hold the purse strings. The procession strolling up the runway as if they owned the place, on the other hand, did, which made this meeting particularly tricky. McKellen knew what they wanted. He also knew they'd leave disappointed. Situations like these needed to be handled just right. His mind turning, he wondered how his old man had dealt with the Washington boys. To quote *The Pirates of Penzance*, his father had been "the very model of a modern major-general." A tough act to follow.

Buttoning his uniform jacket, McKellen straightened his posture as he practiced his smile: polite but revealing no teeth. Returning to his office, he shut the balcony door and then sat squarely behind his desk. Finally, he lit a cigar for good measure.

Hearing stomping footsteps climb the staircase outside, McKellen smoked and waited until he heard a rap at his door.

"Come."

Davis entered alone, closing the door behind him.

"How do they seem?" McKellen asked.

"Anxious, sir. Like their balls are on fire."

"Wonderful," McKellen replied, his voice dripping with sarcasm. His eyes fell to a newspaper on his desk. The headline told the whole story: "U. S. prepares launch of its first satellite, Explorer. Will America catch up to Russia?"

"Catch up," McKellen mumbled.

"Sir?"

McKellen showed him the front page. "This is why our Washington friends are all in a tizzy."

"I don't follow, sir," Davis replied. "You think the launch might go bad?"

"You know who Tom Courtney is, son?"

"The runner, you mean? He won gold a couple years back."

"Yep," McKellen said, nodding. "And do you remember who came in second?"

Davis drew a blank.

"America *doesn't* run second, Davis," McKellen said. "Or play catch up."

"Yes, sir!" Davis sucked in his gut and straightened his back, practically beaming.

McKellen had orchestrated the conversation on purpose. He needed to feel in his power right about then. *The very model of a modern major-general,* he hummed in his mind, cracking a smile.

"Show our guests in, Sergeant."

Over time, Harold had begun to think of the top-secret base as a home of sorts. Keeping a daily routine helped: a morning jog around the base, "shit and shower," as the soldiers liked to say, breakfast, work twelve or thirteen hours, then off to bed. At first he'd dutifully written letters home every weekend, apologizing profusely to his mother for having missed Christmas. But as the weeks turned to months, his letters grew less frequent. Spending more and more time in the underground lab, day and night, soon became an abstract concept while the outside world now seemed more like a momentary distraction. He worked whenever Dr. Stevens, Ruthie, and Max worked.

During his rare free time, he'd drop by Research and Development. His favorite lab to visit was engineering, up on level ten, the one they called the Well. The guys up there had even let him try one of their modified Smith & Wesson rifles over a few extended lunch breaks. Firing several shots, his bullets flew around the cement obstacles, striking a target hidden behind the moving blocks. The engineers called them "zig-zag bullets," but for the longest time the projectiles only turned one way or the other. Harold joked that the bullets were more *zig* than *zag*. Still, the men kept at it day after day, week after week. No one was happier than Harold when they finally got one of the prototypes to zig *and* zag, twisting around two obstacles before the bullet hit its mark.

And then, of course, there was the source of all these incredible achievements. The ship.

Harold walked past it every morning and at the end of every shift. Impossible to ignore, the thing hung there in the outer hall, suspended on beams and cables like a limp, fractured origami sculpture. Its dark silhouette seemingly watched everyone and everything around it. Harold still felt its presence, like an invisible weight, as if someone or something were leaning over his shoulder. No matter how much room he gave the enormous craft as he walked by, Harold always detected a lingering sensation akin to a hot breath brushing against his ear and neck. The closeness and overbearing natures of its presence could never be ignored, and he soon understood why none of the engineers studied it anymore. Both awesome and frightening, the ship, for lack of a better word, gave him the willies.

Instead, his focus turned to the mysterious, gaseous red mist. Safely trapped within a glass container, his fear of it had diminished over time. Even the horrendous implications of humans becoming a gaseous form eventually became a commonplace concept. After all, evolution had taken on many wondrous forms over billions of years, so why should the future not hold as many wonders?

Also, it was not entirely gaseous, he soon learned. It was, in fact, composed of 30 percent biological DNA and 50 percent methane, with the remaining 20 percent composed of tiny crystalline computers, called nanites. It seemed that in the future, man and machine had joined in some fashion, and the crimson vapor was the unlikely offspring of that union. Each nanite was independent while also connected to the whole, which was how it was able to separate and infuse with a gray body or, potentially, the ship itself. Dr. Stevens had even hinted at the notion that the mist had, at some point, taken over human beings. *Possession*. Harold could only imagine what his mother would say. "The devil in red mist" or something to that effect. Despite its uncanny implications, by the time Harold had learned of potential possession by a vaporous entity, he'd seen and learned so much that this new revelation also seemed commonplace. Another piece of the chemical-engineering puzzle of the mist that fit well with the whole. It even made sense, in a fashion. Man and machine combined to adapt to any host or environment, whether it

walked on two legs, four, or even flew about in a metallic hull. It was, in essence, a perfect evolution, able to
adapt to nearly any environment.

On the other hand, while the machine mist became
more known to him, Dr. Stevens—Casey, as he was eventually allowed to call her—was progressively becoming
more of an enigma. First, there was her office, which no
one, not even Max or Ruthie, had ever seen. The door
remained locked all hours of the day, whether she was
inside her office or not. Harold would often find himself
strolling past, trying to make out any sounds that might
escape or detect evidence of light beneath the doorframe. If a top-secret project was taking place in there,
it sure was quiet.

As they worked seemingly endless hours together,
she occasionally let a tidbit slip here and there regarding
possible future events, things that had yet to occur—a
war in Southeast Asia, for example, and a series of assas-
sinations. No details, merely vague hints. At first, Harold
just assumed she had an overzealous imagination. Who
could blame her, considering all the strange technology
at their disposal?

Then one night near the end of his shift, visitors
came, and everything changed.

Colonel McKellen, an intimidatingly large gray-
haired figure with a burly mustache and a sturdy build
to match, had come down to the lab flanked by men in
suits. G-men, Harold assumed. The colonel strolled in,
glancing about with mild interest as if he saw gray bodies and living red mist every day. The government men,
however, grew paler every time their heads twisted this
way and that, discovering fresh horrors on every side.

Harold, for his part, kept his gaze down, studying the microscopic DNA from the red mist. Max and Ruthie, he noted, also kept to the corners. In the back, Casey emerged from her office, shoving her hands in her coat pockets. McKellen shot her a plastic grin.

"Colonel," Casey said, "what brings you down to my neck of the woods?"

Harold peeked up from his microscope. Across the room, Max and Ruthie did the same. Between them, Casey and McKellen stared each other down.

McKellen squared his shoulders. "These men are from Washington."

"You don't say," Casey replied.

"They're hoping you're able to offer something to give us an edge over the Reds."

"What kind of edge?"

"With the space program." McKellen's mustache drooped. "Don't play games."

Casey rolled her eyes, suddenly appearing more interested in the equipment around her. Checking readouts from a printer, she huffed. "We've been down this road before, Colonel. The ship won't fly."

"Maybe not, but surely you have something down here that can give us a leg up."

Casey tossed the papers aside. "I already told you, there's nothing to worry about. We beat them when in counts. To the moon."

Having completely forgotten about his DNA sample, Harold's ears pricked. *The moon?*

"Yes," one of the G-men interjected, "but you haven't told us how."

"No idea," she replied, lowering her voice as if suddenly aware that others were listening. "I was only five years old when it happened."

The argument continued for several more minutes, though Harold's swirling thoughts drowned out the voices. His mind spinning, he began to place imaginary puzzle pieces together. The ship. The gray beings. The red mist. All of it from the future. And Casey? Where and *when* had she come from? One point suddenly became clear: the greatest mystery at Area 51 wasn't a spaceship or bug-eyed monsters. Instead, it was the blonde-haired, green-eyed, thirtysomething woman working right beside him.

As McKellen led the disgruntled G-men out, Harold looked up from his studies, eyeing Casey. Did she hold the answers to all his questions? Was the very future he'd been seeking standing right there in front of him? For the first time, Harold found himself noticing the angular lines of her face, the way her hair draped along her shoulders. He even allowed himself a quick glance down toward the fullness of her breasts. Beautiful and brilliant, Casey was unlike any other woman on Earth. How had he not seen it before?

She's everything your mother warned you about, a voice hissed at the back of his mind. *The proverbial forbidden fruit.*

Harold jolted upright. The slurred hiss didn't sound like his own thoughts. It was as if someone or something had whispered just inside his ear, but no one was standing beside him.

You want her, don't you, Harold? I can help.

Catching his absent stare, Casey turned toward him, curious. Harold went back to his microscope. Fingers trembling over the controls, he tried to stay focused on his work.

Thankfully, the hissing inner voice went silent.

For the moment.

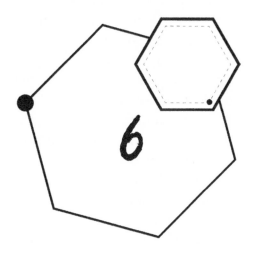

The day before the ship vanished, Casey noticed something out of the ordinary. It was still early by her reckoning, not even 0800 hours, when she exited the elevator, making her way across the dark, quiet hangar. Some might have called it "empty," but she knew better.

The hairs on the back of her neck sprang up as she felt the ship observe her approach. Her high heels click-clacking along the stone surface, she busied herself with a mental checklist of the day's experiments. Ruthie and Max would be preparing a fresh sample from the seeker mist while Harold would be creating graphs based on the protein fluctuations raised by various conditions. She had originally hoped he would assist with her own studies, but over the last few weeks, that had proven problematic. Harold's growing fascination with her, possibly an attraction even, was becoming a distraction. It was her own fault, really. She'd reviewed his psych evaluation before offering him the position. Now Casey berated herself for not having seen the possibility of his interest sooner. The son of a widowed, overbearing mother, raised in a stifling Christian environment, Harold seemed sexually repressed even by 1950s standards. Coupled with his sudden awareness that Casey had come from the future, it was merely a matter of time before his growing attraction became impossible to ignore. For now, Casey only sensed his feelings, bubbling just beneath the surface of his awkward, ever-present smile. But it was there, sure enough. Casey knew she would have to deal with it sooner rather than later.

Where's a high-priced prostitute when you need one?

Suddenly, her heels splashed in something wet. Casey stopped. A trail of black ooze snaked along the normally stone-dry rock floor. Kneeling, she scooped a droplet of liquid between her fingertips and smelled it. It had no scent. *Not gasoline, at least,* she thought. Following the watery trail, she found herself approaching the ship, spotting a pool of dark liquid dripping from its fractured hull.

What's the matter, old girl, sprung a leak?

Thrusting her senses outward, she listened for a response, but the ship remained quietly dormant. Pacing along the liquid's edge, Casey's interest grew. Something had changed. And change, she'd learned, was never good.

Bending low, her skirt tightened around her thighs as she struggled to see beneath the vessel's dark hull. A brief, fiery flash of emotion erupted behind her, surveying her bent-over posture. Casey spun. Of course. Harold. His lips were curled back into an awkward grin.

Here we go, Casey thought.

"Everything OK?" he asked, as if trying to be helpful.

Casey's emerald eyes narrowed. "Don't you have a graph to be working on?" Her tone came out sharper than she'd intended. Swallowing audibly, Harold scurried off to the laboratory.

Yep, she decided, watching him leave, something would have to be done. *Pronto.*

Behind her the constant *drip-drip-drip* from the hull continued unabated.

Harold's vision blurred as he stared at the graph. The test conditions might have changed, but the results hadn't. Somehow, the methane in the red mist wasn't dissolving under prolonged exposure to oxygen. Instead, it was hardening, solidifying into tiny black pebbles. He'd never seen anything like it. No one had. It wasn't possible. *Gaseous elements simply don't work this way,* he told himself over and over. And yet, for whatever reason, the red mist, when left outside its container for too long, transformed into a solid. Perhaps the mixture of DNA with nanites affected the methane's properties, but how? And why?

Huffing, he plopped into his chair and rubbed his bleary eyes. Glancing at the clock, he saw that it was already past four in the afternoon, and he still hadn't eaten lunch. His stomach growling, he decided to take a break.

Heading down the singular hallway, he passed Max and Ruthie snuggling at their desks. Max whispered something in her ear that made Ruthie giggle with a high-pitched squeal. *A regular lover's paradise,* Harold thought.

The door opened, and Casey entered. Abruptly, his eyes found the floor. His heart catching in his throat, he held his breath until she passed. Exhaling as he exited into the hangar, Harold sighed. His fascination with Casey seemed to be growing every day, along with his apprehension. What could he possibly say? *"Hi. I hear you're from the future. Have I told you how lovely you look today?"* Even in the privacy of his mind, it sounded ridiculous.

Don't use words, a voice whispered at the back of his skull. Harold's footsteps faltered. **Take her**, the voice urged. **Make her love you.**

Harold lingered in place, glancing about. No one else was in the hangar. The air grew chill.

Shivering, he continued toward the elevator until his feet splashed in something wet. Peering down, Harold found a trail of dark ooze snaking along the hangar floor. Having noticed the liquid hours earlier, he was surprised no one had cleaned it up yet. His eyes swiveling in their sockets, he followed the curling trail back to its source: the hulking ship. The black thing loomed above him like a fractured monolith. Something pressed against his spine and shoulders with invisible weight. The chill became frigid.

Harold rushed to the elevator, unable to exhale until he'd climbed inside and safely locked its grated door. His sweaty fingers marked the elevator's button as he pounded on it to go up. It was all an imagined fear, he assured himself. The thing—the ship—couldn't simply reach out and grab him. It couldn't drag Harold along the rocky floor, kicking and screaming, pulling him inside its jagged teeth-like frame. No, he was safe. As long as he didn't go inside.

With a lurch, the elevator rose. Sighing, his head cleared as the space between him and the ship widened.

It's all in my mind, he thought. *It can't hurt me unless I go inside. Everything's fine as long as I don't . . .*

Below, shadows pooled around the ship, seemingly moving with a life of their own.

Shuddering, Harold made a mental note to stop by his room and dig out his mother's cross.

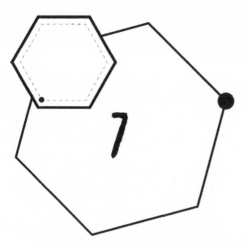

Indianapolis, 1950

*T*his could be the worst idea in the entire history of bad
ideas.

Casey had been parked outside a Woolworth's department store for over an hour, the stolen black Buick's
engine running as cigarette smoke billowed out the driver's window. Fidgeting behind the wheel, Casey finished
her third cigarette since arriving. Whoever owned the
car had left half a pack in the glove compartment. The
smoke burned the back of her throat as she exhaled. Casey wasn't a smoker, but she had decided on the trip up
that it might be a good time to start.

Feeling woozy, she kept her eyes glued to the store-
front window, looking past sale signs and new dishwash-
ers as a young blonde receptionist rang up another customer. Casey still couldn't make out the details of the
woman's face. For that she'd have to get out of the car and
go inside, which, so far at least, she'd resisted.

Through the windshield she saw blinking Christmas lights strewn about low-rise brick buildings, painting shops and lampposts in red and green. Snow cascaded about, dulling the lights in a white blur. Thankfully, the car's heater worked just fine, keeping the vehicle a balmy ninety degrees. Having made her way from New Mexico to Indianapolis in under twenty-four hours, Casey had only stopped for burgers and gas. Now, after her mad dash across the country, she just sat there.

By the time the young blonde girl rang up her last customer, it was a quarter to eight. Almost closing time. *Move it or lose it, Case.*

Exhaling one last, long stream of smoke, she crushed her cigarette and turned the engine off. It took another few moments before she opened the door. Once outside, the winter air snapped some urgency into her. Severely underdressed in a pinstriped skirt and white button-down, she hadn't had time to find a coat before making her escape from the RAAF base. The biting chill was the least of her concerns, though. Now that she'd finally gotten herself out of the car, she had to summon the courage to enter the store. Despite the cold, sweat beaded across Casey's back, crawling upwards. Wiping her palms against her skirt, she eyed the cashier. Though she was still too far away to see much detail, she assumed the twenty-year-old's eyes were green, just like Casey's. After all this time, she'd found the woman who'd died giving birth to her. A woman she'd fantasized about since she was a child.

Her mother.

When she was a little girl, Casey kept a picture of her mother on her bedside table. When she was frightened, she'd cry to the picture, pray to it, plead with it. After staring at that photo for so many years, Casey had created a mental image of what her mother's personality would be like. In her imagination, they'd talked every night after her father had come in and . . . done things. Awful things. But those nightmares were gone now. Casey had faced those demons and won. Now, staring through the department store window, Casey noted the difference between the picture and the person inside. The woman in the picture had been in her thirties, her eyes dark, her smile a thin, crooked barely visible line. The girl at the counter had a bounce in her step and a wide smile as she waved gleefully at various customers. "Bubbly" was the word that came to mind. Casey couldn't help thinking that this young girl should enjoy as much life as possible. *While there's still time.* Time was, indeed, a factor, Casey reminded herself. The government cronies would be close behind. None of them had proven particularly cunning thus far, but there were only so many places that Casey could have run off to, and they'd figure it out eventually.

Still, her feet remained rooted on the frozen concrete. She couldn't seem to gather the courage to reach out and open the door. All this way, and Casey still found herself suddenly wishing she hadn't come. The ship had warned her against this, multiple times. Just as the military couldn't hide their thoughts from her, including her mother's whereabouts, she hadn't been able to hide her feelings from the ship. However, the problem remained. If she went inside the store and met her mother, what would happen? Some sort of paradox where all of time and space went ass up? What would that even look like? Casey was currently studying biology, physics, and temporal mechanics with the best professors in the country, yet no one knew what would happen if someone from the future met their parents in the past. Casey was the only one able to test such a hypothesis. Staring through the frosted glass, her legs went numb. With a *ding,* the front door opened, and an elderly man held it open for Casey. Fate, it seemed, had made the choice for her. Casey caught the door and took one step in.

And then stopped.

Her mother glanced over from the register, offering a smile. Casey wanted to return it, but her mouth suddenly seemed as numb and as useless as her legs. Stumbling back outside into the frigid wind, she closed the door.

She couldn't do it. All this time Casey had spent trying to find her mother, all the chances she'd taken breaking out of the RAAF military base, and yet now she had lost her will.

Casey climbed back into the Buick, firing up the engine. *Time to go home,* she decided. Her stomach turned at the idea of calling a military base in the desert "home," but it was all she had now. This place wasn't her home, and the young woman inside that store wasn't her mother—at least not yet. Suppressing a shiver, Casey put the Buick into reverse and tilted her rearview mirror.

In the reflection, black eyes stared back, boring into her like rats crawling through a hole. A scream died in her throat as wet fingers reached out from the backseat, yanking her into shadow.

Casey jolted awake in her office, her skin covered in gray patches and her body trembling at an accelerated rate. The tiny cot shook beneath her, thumping loudly, threatening to break into pieces. Taking a deep breath, she huddled into a fetal position and searched inwardly for the nanites within her bloodstream. The seeker's so-called "cure" was an infection she had to fight to keep at bay. It had been years since she'd experienced an episode and never this bad. At least not since before the Roswell crash. Her thoughts searched for an explanation, but she quickly shut it down, focusing on the job at hand. Survival.

Taking deep, slow breaths, she concentrated first on her rapid-fire heart rate, bringing it down to a constant, steady beat. Then she turned her attention to the nanites swirling within her bloodstream. She felt the microscopic machines vibrating. After a few more breaths, their motion slowed until, finally, her body stopped trembling, and her skin returned to normal. The nanites had gone dormant once again. Exhausted, she collapsed into a heap, covered in sweat. Salty tears stung her eyes. The discomfort helped her regain focus. Her dream had been true, mostly. The stolen car, the trip to Indianapolis, the glimpse of her mother. Even the gnawing sense of cowardice she'd felt twisting in her stomach as she fled. All of it had happened.

Except for the thing in the backseat. The seeker.

A new idea crystalized in her mind as her thoughts slowed along with her heartbeat. She wasn't alone. Someone or something had telepathically touched her. It wasn't the ship. After a decade of communicating with it off and on, she knew it's touch better than she might a lover's embrace—or a pedophile's. Ghostly fingers groped her mind, rummaging through her thoughts like a pervert in her underwear drawer. Casey pulled a mental door between herself and the intruder, hoping to block it—a seeker, she assumed. It had to be. Gulping air, she struggled not to hyperventilate. She needed to stay calm. In control.

The thing was close.

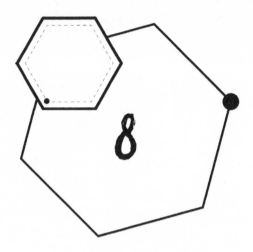

8

Colonel McKellen sat behind his pinewood desk, knee deep in paperwork. Despite it being almost 0300 hours, sleep still seemed another stack of papers away. People would be amazed, McKellen thought, at how much bureaucracy government conspiracies required. Filling out requisition forms in triplicate, his knuckles whitened around the fountain pen, as if pressing harder might make the act of signing go faster. Exhaling loudly, he rubbed his throbbing temples in an attempt to stay focused. The words blurred on the page. Flipping to the next form on his docket, he found that month's research budget for Casey's team. Eyeing the exorbitant amount at the bottom of the page, he burst out laughing. This was his job now. Taking care of her.

And the joke's on me.

For a decade, McKellen had been charged with getting Dr. Stevens whatever she needed. *Doctor* Stevens. Even the title annoyed him. He'd been responsible for that too, under orders, of course. It became almost immediately apparent after the crash that Casey had the ability to consume information at a vastly accelerated rate, presumably because of her time on the ship. As a result, McKellen had been tasked with bringing in the brightest professors to teach Casey physics, biology, and chemistry. She'd wanted to learn even more, but at some point the higher-ups saw the light and decided that giving the crazy future woman too much knowledge might eventually bite them in the proverbial ass. He only wished they'd come to that conclusion before she'd received her first diploma. Not that she'd won any kind of jackpot. She was trapped there right beside him in the oozing black tar.

McKellen sighed. At least he could retire, he reminded himself. Casey, however, would never be allowed to leave. Even if she died someday, they'd probably keep her remains underground for study. Nope, no escape, not for him or for her. It was about the only damn thing they had in common. But it was enough to work together and get the job done. They wouldn't be sending each other lovey-dovey letters anytime soon, but they got on alright. *Like cell mates in a prison*, he thought before returning to the stack of forms awaiting his signature.

Flipping past the top sheet for Casey's monthly financial report, he read through the breakdown. Pages and pages of numbers. Research and development had spent more than a million just that month alone. *That's what you get when you give a woman a blank check,* he quipped. A new image came to mind: the poor, nervous clerk who would have to find a way to hide all these expenditures. The thought warmed McKellen's heart. At least someone's job was worse than his.

Suddenly, alarms screeched.

Shoving his wandering thoughts aside, McKellen opened his drawer and withdrew a pistol. Even before he'd gotten to his feet, Lieutenant Colonel Cafferty, his second in command, was at the door. They shared a look, both men having already surmised where the alarm had originated: the lowest level of the secret underground hangar. The place they rarely spoke about but which often took up most of their concerns. The underground hangar with the broken ship and the distorted gray body. Sublevel twenty, Out of Town. It seemed that babysitting duty wasn't done for the night.

God help me.

Area 51 was not simply built in the middle of nowhere to keep civilians out. It was to keep potential dangers in. Somewhere off base, McKellen knew, a little red button was connected to a nuclear weapon, just in case things went tits up. It was that knowledge that made him hesitant to get on the horn and request outside support before he investigated the emergency. An alarm from the hangar could mean a lot of things, none of them good. Having only sounded twice before, both incidents involved civilian deaths due to the ship acting up. The damn thing seemed to have a taste for scientists. Though seemingly broken beyond repair, the craft was known to have little hissy fits from time to time. It reminded McKellen of an ex-wife who'd drop by to ruin her ex-husband's day. It might get bad, but unless it was catastrophic, he wasn't going to be calling anyone from the outside.

Following Cafferty to a jeep, they raced across the desert toward the mountain. On the runway, two planes readied for takeoff while tanks flanked McKellen on either side. It took less than five minutes for the entire base to be up and ready for anything. Leading the charge across open terrain, wind slashing his face, McKellen felt like a soldier again.

Maybe tonight might not be so bad after all. If nothing else, this sure as hell beats paperwork.

Ahead, the mountain's hidden door opened before them. Tanks positioned themselves around it while McKellen and Cafferty skidded to a stop and then hopped out and led a squad on foot inside.

At the end of the tunnel, a metal elevator came up to meet them. Casey stepped out. McKellen sighed, relieved. If shit had been truly awful, his soldiers inside the hangar would have locked it all down by now. Whatever was happening wasn't a containment issue. Most probably, the ship had gotten itself another tasty scientist. Tragic but not catastrophic. He regretted that fleeting thought as soon as it came to mind. Whoever had died had been under his charge.

Frowning, he approached Casey under the overhead lamp's yellow light. Her skin was pale. More than pale, actually. "Blank" was the word that came to mind. Like a thin, ghostly sheet of paper. No color in her cheeks, her eyes sunken. If he didn't know better, he'd say she looked sick. But in ten years he'd never seen Casey catch so much as the common cold. It was another oddity in a long list of anomalies he'd kept note of. Still, something was obviously wrong with her.

"Report."

"There's been a breach, sir," Casey replied. "A seeker. At least one, maybe more."

Even her voice had lost its life. Usually, it had that cocksure, know-it-all drawl that made McKellen's stomach turn sour. Now, hearing the deadness in her lowered voice, he found himself missing it.

A seeker? Here?

They'd never seen a live one before. The thing in the watery tank below had been dead when they found it.

"On the lower level?" he asked, keeping his expression stoic for the sake of her and his men.

She shook her head. "I don't think so."

"I'm not following." He tried to keep the irritation out of his tone, but at that hour, it was a losing battle. "Where's the threat?"

Her eyes shifted, along with her feet, and her crossed arms. "I'm not sure."

"But you sounded the alarm."

Again, she fidgeted. He'd seen that reaction before. She was hiding something. Or a lot of somethings. He'd known it for as long as he'd known her. Whatever it was, she kept it close to her chest. McKellen's best guess was that she was some kind of psychic. He never asked, and she never told, but he'd seen evidence of it now and again, as if she could pluck a stray thought out of his head and say it aloud. On the few occasions he'd seen it, though, she had been just as quick to hide it and play ignorant. This time, however, whatever abilities she had seemed to have gone haywire.

"It's here somewhere," Casey said. When he pushed for more information, she clamped down. Still, the paleness in her complexion and the tightness in her voice spoke volumes. Whatever she'd seen or felt, she believed the threat was real. If anyone else had sounded the alarm because of a simple feeling, he'd have thrown them in the brig. But not her. Instead, he nodded and turned to Cafferty.

"Search the base, top to bottom."

Weapons at the ready, the squad spread out. Casey uncrossed her arms, sighing. "Thanks."

"For what?"

"Trusting me."

Offering a crooked grin, McKellen sighed inwardly. Resentment roiled his gut. He suddenly wondered how much babysitters made per hour. Maybe, McKellen thought, he should add that title to his resume. *Leader of men. Winner of wars. Babysitter to crazy women.* He pushed the bile back down and kept his tone friendly. "Whatever you say, Doc."

She scowled. Eyes narrowed, burrowing into him. Had she heard his thoughts? As if in silent reply, she spun and hit the elevator call button. For the umpteenth time that night, McKellen reminded himself that retirement was still a viable option—for him.

"Where are you going?"

"To check on the ship," she said, her voice flat.

Yep, he decided, *she heard*.

Casey stepped into the elevator. "Come find me when the screaming starts."

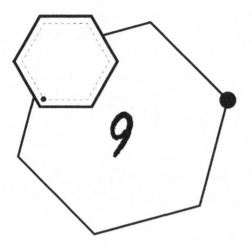

9

Drenched in sweat, Harold thrashed in his sleep until a shrill klaxon alarm woke him with a scream. The noise was so loud, he tumbled from his cot, not fully waking until the rock floor was at eye level. Having worked late, he'd been too tired to drive back to his room, so he decided to spend the night in the hangar. Wiping tears from his eyes, his fingers trembled. Though the dream was already forgotten, Harold had the distinct impression that he'd been trapped within something. Buried alive. Immediately, his mind drifted to the ship. Had it been in his dream as well? Overhead, the screeching alarm only added to his mounting anxiety.

Thankfully, he could hear Max and Ruthie in the lab outside, their voices mounting over the incessant noise. He couldn't tell if they were panicked or annoyed. Probably both. Hobbling through the door, he scrambled to put on his shoes and lab coat.

In the main laboratory, Max and Ruthie rushed around, haphazardly shoving equipment into cabinets.

"What's happening?" Harold asked over the blaring alarm.

Unwilling to pause, Ruthie continued to put away vials. "Help us secure everything!"

"Someone hit the containment alarm!" Max shouted over his shoulder.

Scanning the exit, Harold's feet didn't budge. "Shouldn't we get out?"

"Our priority is containment," Max snapped, "not survival,"

His stomach turning, Harold shifted his attention to the red mist floating within the glass case. He sighed with relief. At least that hadn't been breached. Though still a relative newbie, Harold had learned enough to know that even a small amount of that stuff was deadly. Worse than deadly, it made whoever it possessed into something else. Something not human.

His head woozy from the alarm's shrill tone, his mind drifted back to his mother. The lab didn't seem like home anymore. It was more akin to an underground cage. Lingering in place, it took significant effort to propel his legs forward and begin grabbing notes and equipment.

I didn't sign up for this. Not by a long shot.

While Harold worked, the alarm's ear-piercing scream blocked out any further internal argument. Ruthie handed him a stack of boxes, gesturing toward a locker. By the time everything had been secured, Harold's eardrums were throbbing painfully due to the incessant alarm. They sealed the gray body's chamber last. Inside, the thing floated peacefully while the world went mad around it. Before slamming the door and locking it, he met the thing's lifeless black gaze, and a foreboding shiver raced up his nerve endings. He suddenly dreaded ever seeing the ghastly thing again.

Rejoining the others, he found Max pacing while Ruthie sat, absently rubbing her stomach. Max approached her, shouting over the alarm. "You alright?"

"Never better, hon!" she yelled with a crooked smile. "Loud noises never hurt anyone."

"We can't just stay down here," Harold grumbled, plugging his ears.

"Don't worry," Ruthie assured him. "Someone will come check on us."

Trembling, Harold started for the door. "I'd rather wait somewhere quieter."

"Hold on." Max grabbed his arm. "You can't go."

"Watch me," Harold said, breaking free.

Exchanging a knowing smile, Max and Ruthie sat and waited as Harold raced toward the door. He yanked the handle. It didn't budge. Scrambling, Harold rummaged through his coat pockets until he found his keys. Shakily placing a key into the lock, he twisted, first to the left and then to the right. The door still didn't open.

"It's bolted from the outside!" Max shouted. "We're in lockdown."

Harold spun around, his jaw gaping. "How do we get out?"

"We don't. These labs are underground for a reason, kid. No one leaves here until the threat is over."

Ruthie nodded, clutching Max's arms, which were wrapped tightly around her. "No matter the cost."

Harold crossed his shaking arms and paced back and forth, trying to keep his legs from wobbling. He'd never claimed to be a hero, and he certainly wasn't planning on becoming one that night. The constant ear-piercing noise frazzled his nerves to no end. Like a caged animal, he paced the long white hallway, absently counting his footsteps while monsters lingered on either side. To his right a gray husk floated uneasily in a liquid tank. To his left a slithering red mist snaked about with a life of its own. Ahead, Casey's closed office lingered. Only God knew what waited inside there.

Harold sighed, though the sound of his exasperation was drowned out by the klaxon. His eyes glued to the floor, he didn't notice Max's approach until he walked right into him.

"Don't be too hard on yourself, kid!" Max shouted, slapping his shoulder. "You stayed and helped when you *thought* you could run."

"So," Harold said, loud enough to wake the dead, "we just wait?"

Before Max or Ruthie could answer, the alarm turned off. The silence was so sudden, it threw Harold off balance. His eardrums throbbed in his skull as the hangar door opened at last. Soldiers entered and scanned the room, their weapons raised.

"Glad to see you, boys," Max said, grinning from ear to ear.

The soldiers spread out, investigating the entire lab until one of them announced it was all clear.

Arching her back, Ruthie stood. "What happened?"

"Doctor Stevens set off a containment alarm," the lead soldier said.

Harold and the other scientists exchanged curious glances. They all seemed to be thinking the same thing: *Why didn't she warn us something was wrong?*

"We'll need to sweep the labs," the soldier continued, the reluctance in his voice clear.

Following Max's signal, Harold used his keys to unlock each lab, one after the other. When he opened the door with the gray clone inside, the soldiers gasped. These men had never been down there before, and they would be ordered to forget everything they'd seen. Not that they would, of course. No one could. Like Harold, these men would now be taking the secrets of Area 51 to their grave. That brought up another question that had been tickling the back of Harold's mind for months now. Just how *did* they expect to keep this all secret? Eventually, someone would tell the world. Not him, Harold reminded himself, thinking about all those forms he'd signed when he first came, but someone. The truth couldn't possibly stay buried down there forever.

Finally, the soldiers stopped at the last door on the right. Harold held up his key ring and shrugged. "This is Doctor Stevens' office. No one has a key except her."

"We'll wait." The lead soldier huffed, long and slow, as if trying to steady his nerves.

"I'll get her," Harold volunteered. Ruthie nodded, offering a sly grin. He squirmed under her knowing gaze. Had his growing interest in their boss been that obvious? Still, it wasn't attraction that drew him down the hallway at a rapid pace. Harold couldn't imagine Casey would ever let the soldiers inside her office, but if she did, he wanted to make sure he got a peek. His fear was suddenly replaced by growing anticipation. After all this time, he was going to find out what Casey had hidden in her office.

Keeping his focus on his burning curiosity, he didn't want to admit that he was also worried about her. Casey valued her privacy. Whatever had caused her to sound the alarm, Harold knew it had to be bad. Horrible, even. His pace quickening along with his heart rate, he exited the labs, running across the enormous main hangar toward the distant elevator.

Spotting something out of the corner of his eye, his back straightened, and his feet stumbled to a halt. A voluminous silhouette loomed beside him. The ship. Broken and fractured with jagged edges twisted every which way, it appeared to be watching him. At its center, a round door lay open. Now *that* hadn't been there before.

He heard the sound of shuffling feet inside. Had Casey gone into the ship? Hesitating outside the door, he noted a faint green light pulsing from within, both ominous and strangely inviting. Although he'd been frightened by the ship mere hours ago, now his fascination returned. What lay inside? What did the future actually look like? To see it, to touch it, suddenly seemed worth any risk.

Despite his growing excitement, Harold couldn't seem to will his legs to move. The warnings about what had happened to those who had gone in before crept back to the top of his mind. Some went insane, Casey had told him. Others died. Except for her. Why?

Because I invited her, a voice whispered at the back of his mind. This time he was certain it wasn't his imagination. *Come in, Harold.*

Unable to move forward and yet unwilling to turn back, he simply stood there, wavering in place. The light within the ship grew brighter.

Come in, the voice urged.

Harold's right foot inched closer.

Come.

One step.

Come.

Another step.

Come.

Before Harold realized it, he was walking up the ramp.

Come.

Harold found himself, at last, standing within the ship's entrance. After months of fear and wonder, fascination and dread, he was finally inside. Standing at the future's very doorway. So overwhelmed by the experience, he failed to notice the voice had disappeared.

A winding tunnel with slick gray walls pulsed with a faint glow before him. The pulsing walls reminded him of lungs breathing. Slow and rhythmic. *Alive*, his mind whispered. *H. G. Wells, eat your heart out.*

"Casey!" Harold shouted, continuing down the tunnel. The echo of his cry dimmed oddly in the distance, as if the sound of his voice had been muted somewhere up ahead. "Doctor Stevens! Can you hear me?"

As he made his way through the craft from one million years in the future, his fingers danced along the pulsing walls. They felt moist, not metallic, more akin to skin that was hardened, like moist scabs. Even more surprising, the ship's structure didn't appear nearly as damaged on the inside as it did on the outside.

The sound of his footfalls grew distorted, as if the noise took a moment longer than it should to reverberate each time his feet hit the floor. The sound was all wrong in that place. Despite the floor feeling wet and slippery, the volume of his footsteps seemed more akin to boots clanging on metal. Pausing, he suppressed a shiver as he listened to the thundering echo of his footfalls behind him. Still, no ghostly apparitions or bogeymen were in sight. He almost chuckled at the ridiculous notion. As if there would be.

Turning another corner, Harold found himself staring at a dead end. The tunnel stopped at another illuminated gray wall. The ship's layout and structure seemed to make as much sense as the sounds that reverberated within it.

Struggling to keep calm, Harold went back the way he had come, or so he thought. As he turned the corner, however, he started to doubt it was the same tunnel as before. The walls looked the same, but they curved in the opposite direction. He was sure the tunnel had slanted left, but now it curved sharply to the right. Perhaps he was only imagining it. After all, walls didn't simply move. The farther he walked, though, the more different each of the plain gray-walled corridors appeared. With each new tunnel, he felt more and more alone. Isolated.

An old Bible story about Jonah being swallowed by a whale came to mind. Absently, his fingers scrambled toward his collar, finding the cross that his mother had given to him. The symbol, however, offered no relief. With the image of Jonah and the whale fresh in his thoughts, his fast walk turned into a full-out run. Heading down one corridor, then another, he no longer concerned himself with trying to retrace his steps. Instead, he simply ran. His legs pumping faster, he still hoped to catch up to Casey, if she was even in there. But each turn only led to another winding pathway. And the lights, he noticed, began to dim.

Fire cranked up his legs, causing him to stumble. Winded, he keeled over, clutching his shaking knees as he struggled to catch his breath. Without any doors or markings, it was impossible to tell one tunnel from the next, and none of them, it seemed, led to an exit. Harold was lost. Trapped. Worse, the temperature had dropped. Shivering, he wished he could trade his rumpled lab coat for a parka. The fainter the wall lights became, the colder it grew. Harold could see his breath in a clouded mist.

My God, he thought, feeling the cross dig into his palm as he clutched it, *how'd it get so cold in here?*

His momentary bravery wilted as he abandoned all hope of finding Casey. Instead, he focused on finding a way out.

Before he could renew his frantic pace, his feet faltered as a new eruption of sound brushed against his eardrums. A moaning breath, gentle and feminine. Sexual. Still a virgin, Harold had always imagined what a woman's intimate moans might sound like. In his romanticized imaging, they had been precisely like those now echoing around him. Noting a hardening in his trousers, he blushed. Rubbing sweat from his face, he tried to block out the moans and calm himself as the temperature continued to drop.

Taking a quick breather to find his bearings, he leaned against the moist, curved wall. Light pulsed warmly on his back, a slight relief from the sudden frigidity. The sensation caused his arms and legs to tingle.

Breathing a haggard, frosty breath, he pushed himself farther back into the wall's warm, wet embrace. So desperate for its heat, it took a moment before he noted the way the surface moved alluringly about him. Its fleshy surface curved into a pair of breasts, brushing against his body. Turning toward it, he discovered a faint feminine form seemingly writhing behind the wall's light. The silhouetted woman's arms stretched, pushing against the wall from the other side like it was made of an elastic fabric, embracing him. Harold knew he should run or scream for help, but the naked body beneath the surface was so intimately inviting. His penis ached. His mouth watered.

Until, at last, the wall engulfed him.

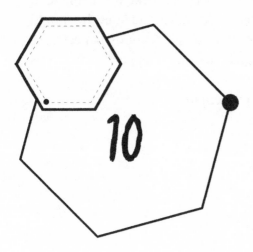

10

Casey lingered impatiently at the heart of the ship beneath an enormous red sphere that twisted and turned, revealing multiple layers, seemingly infinitely. It was called a hypersphere, a fourth-dimension representation of a sphere. It was the source of the ship's power and the means by which it had once traveled through time and space. Her skin prickled at the mere sight of it; she hated the damn thing. The hypersphere was also the source of everything that Casey had lost. Her fiancé, their planned family together, her home. Instead, because of this thing spinning above her, she was trapped in the past with nowhere to go, no one to love, and no children to bear. Though still able to conceive, the nanites in Casey's blood would pass to her children and her children's children. That had been the seeker's plan, to use her to genetically alter human DNA over generations in order to secure the seekers' future survival.

Having mourned Arthur, the first few years of her self-imposed abstinence had been relatively easy, but as the years progressed, her basest urges bubbled to the surface. On a military base surrounded by healthy potential suitors, it became a constant distraction that eventually grew into resentment. Several men had made advances over the years, and the more handsome and charming they proved to be, the more forceful her rejection. With Casey labeled as an ice queen, most soldiers now kept their distance. Locking herself in her office deep underground, Casey had made herself an outcast, all because of the hypersphere. Even after years of research, she had no idea how the damn thing worked. Glaring at the swirling red orb, her fingers clenched into fists, and her heart pounded as the sphere continued to swirl silently.

The most powerful object on Earth seemed to be playing dead.

Coward, she hissed in her mind, knowing it could hear her. Still, it did not reply. She'd been standing there for over twenty minutes, and yet the spinning globe hadn't reacted. Casey could guess why. It had felt the presence of a seeker as well. But, unlike her, it wanted to be found. She assumed it had been waiting for this moment. What was time to a seemingly immortal craft to which past and future were interchangeable?

"Seems they've finally found you," she said.

Not me. You, a slithering voice teased at the back of her mind. Casey smiled. "There you are," she said, a note of triumph in her voice.

Before she could egg it on further, a figure appeared beneath the sphere. Her father, dressed in a plaid shirt and jeans. A pale imitation of the real flesh-and-blood monster she'd endured as a child. He offered a sympathetic smile. "You look tired."

"And you look like a man who's been dead for over a decade," she replied, knowing the phantom image was simply a projection created by the ship. "Back to your old parlor tricks? Jesus, you really must be upset."

"You won't escape this time, honey bun," her father promised.

"I defeated the seekers before. I can do it again."

His grin flattened. "You have too much faith in your abilities."

"No, I have too *little* faith in yours."

Either way, the ship had confirmed what Casey already knew. The seekers were there, somewhere on the base, and they were coming for her. Waving a hand, she manipulated the curved walls into a straight line, creating a direct path for herself.

Ahead, she glimpsed something covered in a wedge of shadow. A limp figure was lying on the floor. Casey stumbled to a halt. Harold. He must have followed her in.

Checking for a pulse, she felt a vein throbbing weakly beneath her fingertips. He was still alive. Closing her eyes and taking a deep breath, she tapped into the dormant nanites throughout her body. Feeling her muscles tighten, she lifted Harold with ease and fled the ship in a blur.

Entering Harold's mind, Casey was assaulted by sexual feminine moans and the sounds of pained ecstasy. As she pushed further, flickers of light came into view, like a movie projector finding its focus, revealing splashes of red and gold. The gleaming light was distorted, eventually solidifying into a wondrous recreation of ancient Rome. Sometime around the era of Emperor Caligula, she imagined.

Lithe, naked bodies writhed, chained to marble columns. The sound of a whip and gasped screams echoed from a chamber to her right. To her left was a golden throne. Sitting upon it while being orally gratified by a slave woman was the scrawny, naked form of her assistant, Harold. If the situation weren't so dire, Casey would have laughed—or puked. But the longer the young man remained under the ship's control, the less likely it was that he could escape. Eventually, Harold would go mad. She'd seen it before, more than once.

Glancing down at her own body, she found herself, thankfully, dressed. It seemed she was still able to retain some control over herself in his mindscape. Hopefully, she had enough power to pull Harold away from the ship's control before it was too late.

His eyes were shut, lost in a lustful daze. Shuddering to a climax, Harold pushed the slave woman's head aside and blinked up at the tall blonde in a lab coat. If he recognized Casey, it didn't show. Sipping from a golden goblet, he smirked at her. "Strip for me."

"In your dreams," Casey said as she yanked Harold off the throne, shaking him. "Dammit, Harold! Wake up!"

He merely laughed. Casey needed a new tactic. While the thought of probing deeper into his mind revolted her, she needed something akin to a bucket of ice water to awaken his consciousness. Something cruel, hurtful. With a heavy sigh, she pushed deeper into Harold's swirling thoughts. The Roman Empire receded, melting away.

A cold breeze created goosebumps along Casey's imaginary flesh. She found herself at the foot of a long wooden staircase in a darkened house. No warmth there, no joy. A baby cried from an unseen room while heavy footfalls thundered upstairs. Overhead, a lamp swayed due to the ruckus.

Following the noise, Casey climbed the stairs, which creaked under her weight. As if in response to her approach, the baby's shrill cry ceased. Peering over the banister, she searched for whoever had made the thundering footfalls upstairs, but no one came into view. A short corridor was lined with windows draped in velvet curtains that blocked out the sunlight. Following the sound of sniffles, Casey stopped at the first closed bedroom door. Opening it, she found a young boy, perhaps thirteen years old, crouched on the floor with his pants down. The wails she'd heard hadn't come from a baby; it was a young boy. Harold. His sweater was raised over his shoulders, exposing slashes across his back. Beside him a book on Roman art was open to images of statues and paintings of naked women.

Casey blinked, trying to comprehend what she was seeing. The boy pulled his pants up and wiped his right hand.

Jesus, she thought, *jerking off to an art book? That's all sorts of weird.*

As she eyed his wounded back, it was obvious that someone had beaten him. Pieces clicking into place in her mind's eye, Casey was reminded of her own abuse at her father's hand.

The thundering footsteps returned. Casey stepped aside from the doorway as a gray-haired woman stormed in, carrying a ruler. Blood dripped along its metal edge. She grabbed the book.

"Colossians 3:5: 'Put to death whatever belongs to your earthly nature,'" she quoted, acid in her voice, "sexual immorality, impunity, lust, and evil desires!" Lifting a cigarette lighter, she ignited a flame and held it to the book.

"It . . . it's a schoolbook," Harold stuttered.

"All the worse," she said, tossing the burning book into a trash can. Casey watched, flabbergasted, her heart swelling with sympathy for the poor boy.

"John 2:16: 'For everything in this world—*lust* of the flesh, *lust* of the eyes, and the *pride* of life—comes not from the Father but from the *world*,'" his mother said, her nostrils flaring.

Raising the ruler, she swiped him once more across the chest for good measure. A red mark blazed beneath his neck. Harold whimpered but otherwise remained mute.

"'The world,'" she said, her voice lowering to a raspy growl, "the world with its art and so-called sciences, that's the *evil of men*." Sighing sadly, she dropped the ruler, sending it clattering to the floor, and then left.

Wiping his eyes, Harold shuddered, his gaze fixed on the burning book.

Casey knew what had to be done, but she was revolted by the thought of it. Holding a breath within lungs that didn't exist, Casey focused once again on the Roman throne room.

In a flash she was back at the throne, glaring down at the petulant emperor as he molested another naked slave. The ridiculous fantasy made more sense to her now; the abused often fantasized about having control over others. Casey understood that better than most. Having risen from an abused little girl to a scientific leader and the government's most prized asset, she'd enjoyed the power that came with her position. But right now, Harold needed to lose control. He needed to be a small, vulnerable child again. Grinding imaginary teeth, Casey leaned over the naked young man.

"There you are," she said.

Emperor Harold turned, half interested, a woman's bare breast in one hand and his goblet in the other. "Are you going to strip for me now?"

"Get up, you nasty, disgusting little thing!" Casey shouted.

Harold paled. "Wh-what?"

"You heard me, young man," she said, grabbing his wrist and yanking him to his feet. "I bet this is what you think about when you're tugging your little meat. But you don't really want to punish these women, do you?" She brought his face close to hers. "You want to be punished because deep down you know you deserve it."

She clenched her fist, and a wooden ruler with a metal edge appeared in her hand, summoned from his memory. She hit him with it over and over again, first on the shoulders, then the back. When he spun around, trying to shield himself, she slashed the ruler across his nose, drawing blood. His eyes widened at the gory mess. Watching herself beat the young man, slashing him across the skull and back with the ruler, her imaginary insides retched at the sight, but she pressed on.

"You pathetic little thing," Casey spat. "Get up before your mother sees the evil you've wrought!" The words pouring from Casey's mouth made her hate herself. It brought back memories of her own father that she'd hoped to keep buried. This time, though, *she* was the monster.

Tears filled Harold's eyes as he cradled his nose, staring up at her in horror. The spell broken, he glanced about as if waking from a dream. "Casey?"

The world dissolved around them. Naked women vanished. Marble columns receded. It was over. Casey knelt beside him in the growing void, offering her open hand.

"Come on, Harold," she whispered. "It's OK."

Weeping, Harold nodded and took her hand. His fingers trembled in hers. She saw the fear and pain she'd caused in his eyes and hoped he'd forgive her. Stone-faced, Casey cursed inwardly. She knew precisely how he felt. Like a victim.

Daddy would be so proud.

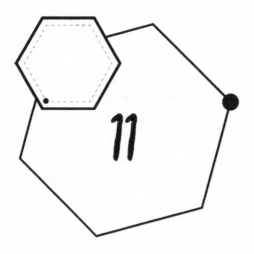

11

Harold awoke on the hangar floor. Rubbing his nose, he expected to find blood caked on his face and lips, but there wasn't any. It had just been a dream. He rolled over, eyeing the ship at the hangar's far end. It hung in a fractured silhouette like a gaping, smiling mouth with broken teeth jutting out every which way. *The damnable thing is grinning at me.* A shadow crossed over him. Moments later, Casey's shallow breathing was in his ear. Unable to summon the courage to meet her gaze, he lowered his head and studied the stone floor. He couldn't imagine what she thought of him now.

When Casey spoke, though, her voice had lost its anger. It sounded drained, monotone. "The ship fucks with your mind," she whispered. "It wasn't your fault."

Ignoring her offered hand, Harold rose to his feet. His head was throbbing, and his knees didn't seem to want to keep him upright. Sighing, he forced his back to straighten as figures rushed forward across the vast hangar. Max and Ruthie approached, followed closely by armed soldiers.

"There you two are," Ruthie said. "We were worried."

Max gave Harold a once-over. "You alright there, kid?"

"I'm not a kid," Harold snapped. He already felt vulnerable enough.

"He just means you look pale," Ruthie soothed.

"Like shit, actually," Max said, correcting her.

Harold could practically feel Casey's tension rising beside him. He assumed she was concerned about what he might say, such as mentioning the fact that his boss could somehow enter people's minds. She needn't have worried though; Harold planned to take the entire episode to his grave. Instead, he shrugged and let out a fake yawn. "Just tired, I guess."

"Doctor Stevens," the lead soldier interjected, "we need to check your lab."

"There's nothing of interest in there, I assure you," she replied.

Harold noted the fear in her voice. He assumed that to others it sounded like an icy snarl, but he knew better. How he knew remained a mystery, one he didn't wish to solve.

"Colonel's orders, ma'am," the soldier persisted. "My apologies for the inconvenience."

"It's not a matter of convenience, Major," she said, glancing at his rank insignia. "You and your men don't have clearance to go in there." Her voice was steady. Harold assumed she felt like she had the upper hand.

Then a familiar baritone echoed through the domed hangar. "Is there a problem?" Colonel McKellen came off the elevator and strode over to them. On most days he looked to be about sixty years old, but with the lines on his face drawn into a shadowy scowl, he seemed to have aged several more decades.

If Casey noticed, she revealed no sign of it. Her arms crossed, and her back grew rigid. "May I remind you, Colonel, that we had an agreement. My office is to remain off limits for private research."

"And might I remind *you* who it was who sounded the alarm?" he replied with a drawn-out sigh. "Now, we've searched this area high and low, and no bogeymen or bug-eyed monsters popped out, so the only place left to look is your lab." He smiled as if he were enjoying this. A lot. "Come on," he continued, "cough up the keys." He stepped closer. "Now, please, *Doctor* Stevens."

The two stood their ground, glaring. For a moment, Harold thought Casey wouldn't back down. Then she withdrew a keychain with a pink rabbit's foot on it from her pocket.

McKellen's smile broadened. "Thank you."

No one spoke as they headed back to the labs. As he passed by the ship, Harold's feet faltered. Drawing closer to the dark, broken beast, he wondered if perhaps it had *tasted* him in some way and might want more. *Like a metallic vampire,* he imagined.

"It's alright," Casey whispered, breaking his train of thought. "Stay close."

Finally meeting her gaze, those sharp green eyes staring back suddenly frightened him more than the ship. Her beauty had lost its attraction. Could she be a seeker? Maybe she was something even worse.

As they entered the lab's antechamber, it occurred to Harold that an hour earlier he'd have given anything to peek inside Casey's office. Now it was the last place he wanted to be. Harold decided he'd seen enough. More than enough to last a lifetime. All he wanted at that moment was to run away and never look back. But, like a good little boy, he silently followed along.

Making their way past lab doors and various monstrosities, they stopped at the end of the hall. The last door on the right was Casey's office. Seemingly as eager as Harold to get this night over and done with, McKellen quickly unlocked the door. Flipping a light switch, he paused, staring at something inside. Harold thought he heard a soft groan escape the colonel's lips. Following close behind, Max and Ruthie gasped as they entered. Harold lingered outside until the last of the soldiers had filed in. Lumbering behind, Harold kept his focus on the tiled floor as he entered. Dancing amidst pools of shadow, a bluish glimmer reflected along the floor's surface. Noting the drawn breaths and grim silence, curiosity got the better of him. Harold looked up, and there it was: Casey's secret.

A giant glass cylinder containing a floating seeker body. Instead of gray, however, its skin color fluctuated between red and black, as if its flesh were mercurial. Its eyes were also different, not black but white. Red veins crawled along their surface. The thing was horrible to witness. Whatever Harold had expected to find in Casey's office, no matter how outlandish his imagination had made it out to be, this was worse. Much worse.

"Dear lord," McKellen said, voicing what Harold was thinking. "What . . . what in the living hell is that?"

Harold watched Casey fidget. Her fingernails incessantly scratched her wrists as she paced in front of the container of liquid. Whatever this thing was, she obviously hadn't been prepared for it to be discovered. Clearing her throat, Casey lifted her head and met the eyes of her waiting audience.

"I call it the Prime," she said.

Before McKellen could ask a follow-up question, Max jumped in. "Where'd you get it?"

"Same place we got the first one," she said, shrugging. "From the ship."

McKellen turned on her. He and Casey stared each other down, the Prime suspended between them. "There was only one viable body, the pilot."

"I was able to repair one of the others."

"Why?" McKellen shouted. "Since when are you, of all people, in the business of saving these damn things?"

"I'm not," Casey snapped, her face contorting with anger. "This could be the means to destroy them."

McKellen paused, tilting his head, his interest piqued. "Explain."

"It's a variant," Casey replied. "Think of the seekers not so much as offspring of man and machine but rather like a disease created from the remnants of both. A *conscious* disease."

"And this variant is the cure?" McKellen asked.

"Possibly." Casey walked around the tank, liquid reflections dancing on her face. "We may not be able to destroy the seekers in their gaseous form, but when they slip into a body . . ."

"They become vulnerable," McKellen finished. A small smile creased his face.

"Hold on," Ruthie said, shaking her head so fast that Harold thought it might pop off. "You can't just 'cure' an entire race from existence."

Casey's expression flattened. "Why not?"

No one responded. Harold watched all this play out in stunned silence. One thing seemed clear to him, though: whatever she was trying to cure, it wasn't some future race a million years from now. Recalling how Casey had been able to enter his thoughts, he assumed there must be a connection. As he stared at the looming black-and-red shape, Harold grew cold, worried that the cure might be worse than any disease.

A phone rang, breaking the silence. Casey answered it, then handed the receiver to the colonel. "It's for you."

While McKellen listened, Harold's eyes swept the room, trying to discern the others' reactions. Their faces crinkled, the soldiers' disgust was plain to see. Ruthie and Max were off in a corner, whispering. Casey watched them as if awaiting their response. Harold, meanwhile, couldn't hide his horror any better than the soldiers. Unable to imagine why anyone, especially Casey, would wish to create something more hideous than the originals, Harold's mind felt numb. While he still considered her outwardly beautiful, his fascination with her future knowledge had dulled his attraction considerably. Like a magic potion that had finally worn off, he observed her now with detached dread. Maybe his mother had been right about the evils of men—and women. Absently, his fingers clutched the cross that hung from his neck.

"Copy," McKellen said into the phone, breaking the silent tension. "Get crash crews on the tarmac, and tell medical to prepare for possible injuries." He paused, eyeing Casey, then returned his attention to the phone. "Surround the perimeter with everything we've got. Birds in the air, tanks on the ground."

That got everyone's attention. He slammed the receiver down and headed for the door. "I'll expect a report tomorrow about . . ." He stopped and waved at the creature. "About whatever this thing is."

"I was right, wasn't I?" Casey asked, nodding toward the phone. "They're here."

McKellen stopped in the doorway, framed by fluorescent light. "Calm yourself, doc. It ain't a flying saucer." His tone softened. "Naval bomber coming in hot. Their radio's out."

Casey moved closer, her voice rising to a fevered pitch. "Were you expecting them?"

"No," he admitted, holding her concerned gaze, then he spun around and left.

After the soldiers followed, Harold finally found his voice. "I thought planes needed special clearance to land here."

Casey's eyes hardened. "They do."

Behind her, Ruthie and Max lingered, still whispering. He couldn't tell if they were horrified or intrigued by the Prime, or both. Harold stormed out. He knew precisely how he felt.

He never wanted to see the damn thing again.

Or Casey.

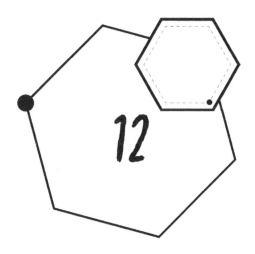

12

By the time Ruthie and Max had finally vacated her office, Casey was exhausted. She hated having to justify herself. No one knew the danger the seekers posed more than her. Max seemed enthusiastic but not Ruthie. *Squeaky clean Ruthie.* She had called Casey unethical, even dangerous.

Easy for you to say, Casey thought. *You can have children.*

It was after 5:30 in the morning, and it sure as hell felt like it. Slouching behind her desk, Casey glanced at the Prime, floating lifelessly in a chemical vat. It was gruesome, she admitted, but that was merely a byproduct of having tried several versions of the antidote on it. She wasn't Doctor Frankenstein, going crazy in her lab while trying to make monsters, Casey assured herself. The floating thing was simply a "flesh suit" to be studied. While its vital organs were functional, it contained no seeker mist and no soul, so where was the harm? If Casey succeeded in destroying the nanites in the seekers, she might also be able to kill the ones inside herself. The key was to do it without shutting down anything else in the body, vital organs like the heart, kidneys, brain function . . . *Me*, she added, chuckling.

The seekers had taken so much from her that Casey just hoped she could eventually take something back.

Ironically, Ruthie had been the inspiration for Casey's experiments. Her pregnancy had spurred Casey into action, hoping to find a cure. While able to conceive herself, Casey didn't dare. The seekers had made sure of that when they injected her with nanites to save themselves and doom humanity. It was as if humans had traveled back in time to alter primates in the hope of saving themselves from some future ailment. We'd do it, she conceded, but that didn't make it any more right from the primates' perspective. And, unfortunately, in this scenario, Casey was the Prime primate. That's where she'd gotten the experiment's name, the Prime seeker. Casey was simply turning the tables, which seemed fair.

So far, however, she'd yet to find an actual cure. For all the damage she'd inflicted on the Prime, its body appeared to grow stronger with each dosage. She worried that by injecting such a wide variety of serums into the thing's system, she might have made it even more resilient. Still, the empty husk was harmless, she assured herself. A shell, nothing more.

Flipping off the light switch, the room reflected liquid lines in darkened corners. Too tired to drag herself topside and drive back to her room, she pulled out a cot.

It was an old companion. Her eyes shut the moment her head hit the pillow.

Above her, the Prime loomed, lifeless.

In her dreams, Casey's mother returned. This time Casey knew it wasn't real, though it didn't stop her from wanting to soak in every detail. She noted the similarities between them. Her mother had the same color of hair, the same emerald eyes, even the same crooked grin. They sat and talked about boys and clothes and all the stupid, simple subjects Casey was never able to speak about in the real world. There was no mention of spaceships or monsters, nothing to terrify, threaten, or break the spell of that wonderful dream. Sitting beside her mother, Casey felt safe, as if she were finally home. She never wanted to wake up.

When she did, the earth shook with a violent upheaval.

An earthquake, she assumed, her eyes snapping open in the pitch blackness. Scrambling out of the cot, she reached for the light switch, but when she flicked it, nothing happened. A veil of black remained, so dark she couldn't see within an inch of her nose, another reminder of just how far below ground level they were trapped.

Shaking off her grogginess, Casey blindly searched for a flashlight. Rummaging in the supply closet, she knocked over various small boxes. Something metal clanged to the floor. Following the sound's source, her fingers stopped over a weighty metallic cylinder. A flashlight. She pressed the button, and the flashlight blazed to life, pushing the shadows aside. For the first time since she'd awoken, Casey sighed, releasing a long-held breath. Pulling her pants on and slipping into faded sneakers, she left her lab coat behind and opened the door, heading through the labs.

As she stepped into the hangar, the vast, open space swallowed her flashlight's beam like a whale might consume a guppy, as if it were nothing of consequence. Careful not to trip, she inched forward. At such moments, Casey wished for something from her own time, circa 1985. Even the smallest flashlights from that era were brighter than the weighty, oversized thing she was carrying.

Thankfully, she knew the hangar and its connecting labs well enough to make her way half-blind through the blackened maze. Her larger concern was if a moronic technician had left stray equipment somewhere that it wasn't supposed to be. Trapped in utter darkness a mile underground was one thing; limping along with a broken ankle would be another. Outside of a few wayward cables and cords, however, the floor proved to be unobstructed.

Pausing for a moment, she expanded her focus outward, searching for potential danger, but she didn't sense anything amiss.

No monsters in the dark, Case, she assured herself. *Not this time.*

"Doctor Stevens," Max called from the blackness. Casey turned, following his voice. He and Ruthie were standing in the doorway to a closet. Ruthie was wiping sleep from her eyes, but her husband seemed more alert.

"What the hell was that?" he asked, his concern obvious in his tone. "The entire mountain shook."

Having not sensed any danger, Casey shrugged. "Earthquake?"

Max shook his head. "Strong enough to knock out a military-grade generator?"

Casey stopped, considering his words. Max was right. The hangar had backups upon backups. The lights shouldn't have been taken out quite so easily. Not that she'd paid much attention to that sort of thing, but a young engineer once told her about the carved-out mountain's basic setup. He had been trying to impress her. He was attractive too, with thick black hair and dark eyes, an intelligent brooding type wrapped in a strong, presumably vigorous young body. Momentary urges weren't worth the risk, though, she'd decided. Instead, Casey had the young man transferred off base. *Steven*, she remembered with a pang of guilt. *That was his name.*

"Doctor," Ruthie said, snapping Casey out of her wandering thoughts. "Where's Harold?"

Sweeping her flashlight over to the third and final supply closet, Casey opened the door. In the corner was a tiny cot. It was empty.

"He must have gone back up to the base to get some shut-eye," Max said. "Wish we had."

Casey closed the door and put the light under her chin, so they could see her relaxed grin. "I'm sure someone's working on it upstairs, just give them—"

Her voice died in her throat as a loud metallic crinkling sound cut through the darkness.

Again, Casey stretched out with her senses, and again she felt no danger. Keeping her focus on the surrounding darkness, she realized she didn't sense anything at all, not even Max and Ruthie. Somehow, her inner eye was as blind as the rest of her. Ice trickled up her back, climbing up her neck to the base of her skull. Something was wrong.

The metallic crinkling sound grew louder, followed by grinding noises that set her teeth on edge.

In the distance, blue and white sparks shimmered. Casey led their approach. Max grabbed his wife's hand, pulling her behind. It didn't take long for them to find the source of the reverberating noises. Gray and black hull plating flew through the air, snapping into place, their dents and bends straightened into a polished sheen. Casey gasped. With each step she took, her heart rate increased, thundering in her chest.

Overhead, red emergency lights blinked on, flooding the hangar in a crimson bath, revealing the cavernous structure and the hulking metal beast before them. Only it wasn't the wreckage it had been mere hours earlier. The side paneling was whole, and half the underside was covered with a patchwork of metal. Hung from countless cables, the suspended origami-like structure continued to grow larger, its fractured surface smoothing itself into straight lines. More metal fragments spun off a heap below, twisted in midair, then snapped into position on the vessel's hull. As soon as each piece clicked into place, a spark ignited, welding it shut, until the seam vanished. Casey heard the others gasping beside her, but she found it hard to even breathe, let alone make a noise. Watching, dumbstruck, her flashlight bounced back and forth while her eyes bulged from their sockets. She couldn't believe what was happening.

After all this time, the ship was rebuilding itself. With each new panel or wire or jagged sliver that went into it, the hull grew a little brighter and larger.

Casey tried to communicate with it, over and over, until her thoughts became a scream, but the ship ignored her pleas. Max finally broke her concentration.

"Backup generator must have kicked in," he said, relieved. "Elevator's coming down."

"Thank God," Ruthie said, sighing. "Whatever this ship is doing, I don't think we want to be the only ones down here when it finishes."

Staring awestruck at the healing, hulking vessel, it took a moment for Max and Ruthie's words to register in Casey's mind. Once they did, she spun her flashlight in her hands, tilting it up toward the descending elevator. *Soldiers?* she wondered. *McKellen, perhaps?*

She looked back and forth between the approaching elevator and the ship. Max and Ruthie raced to the lowering platform, eager to go up top. Part of Casey agreed, and yet, something seemed off. Why was the ship blocking her senses? Why had the mountain shook moments earlier?

"The unidentified plane," she whispered, the jigsaw of events snapping into place.

Ruthie didn't seem to hear, her attention fixed on the lowering elevator and potential escape. Max, however, did. He stopped and turned back. "What?"

Casey paced, eyeing the elevator. Her mind racing, she tried to decipher why the ship would have blocked her abilities after all this time. *Because it's been waiting for this moment*, she realized. *It doesn't want me to know what's happening above ground.* Spinning, Casey watched the elevator's approach with narrowing eyes. *Or what's in that elevator.*

She turned to Max. "What if that shaking before wasn't an earthquake?"

He paused, considering it. "You think the plane crashed *into* the mountain?"

Casey's flashlight resumed its scan of the healing ship. A few more fresh pieces coated its underbelly. "I think something's woken our friend up," she said, tilting the beam up to the slowly descending elevator. "And it's not alone."

Her stomach twisting, Casey drew a step back. Then two more. Max pulled Ruthie's arm, following. Ruthie's expectant smile vanished. "What are you doing? We need to leave!"

"Not that way, babe," Max said. "I think Casey's right. Better safe than sorry."

Ruthie pointed at the ship, her voice turning shrill. "We're not safe down here with that thing repairing itself." She waved frantically at the elevator. "Help's coming. For Christ's sake, just wait one more minute."

Casey tried again to sense anyone, or anything, inside the approaching elevator, but all she found was a blank spot in her inner vision. *If the ship is blinding me, it must have a purpose,* she decided. *And maybe that purpose is coming down right now.*

Spinning around, she raced toward the labs. "Run!"

Ruthie hesitated, but Max picked her up and followed.

"Put me down!" Ruthie screamed. Behind them the elevator came to a stop, the door opening with a *clang.*

Casey held the lab door open for them. Once they were through, she was about to shut the door, but curiosity got the better of her. Sneaking a quick peek, Casey glanced back toward the elevator. A figure emerged, drenched in floodlights.

Harold.

Oh, Jesus, thank you!

Casey relaxed, stepping halfway out the lab door, waving. Turning toward her, his body twitched and convulsed. His feet slid haphazardly against the floor, like a newborn trying to find its footing. Pulsing veins crisscrossed his blank expression as he slid another step toward her. Harold's eyes blazed bright red.

Casey gasped with immediate recognition. She'd seen such a thing before. The seekers were indeed back, only this time she seemingly had no ability to protect herself.

The thing drew closer, its footing growing more precise with each step. Arms outstretched, red lines were revealed across its pale skin. Its mouth opened with a silent scream. Above it, red orbs shone in deep sockets.

Inhuman eyes, Casey's mind protested. She slammed the lab door, fumbling with the lock until she heard it click. As she ran down the hall, she heard metal crunch behind her as the thing that had been Harold pounded on the door.

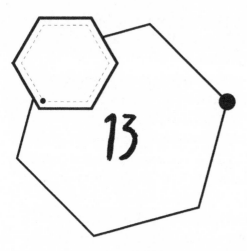

13

Moments earlier

"Everyone and everything has a splinter point," Mc-Kellen's father had told him before the war, back when Hitler's armies seemed nearly invincible. All the Allied armies had to do, his father assured him, was find Germany's splinter point. As it turned out, D-Day was that point. Not the end but the beginning of the end, the point where the tide of war shifted, and the cracks in the Nazis' armor were laid bare. As he stared up at the C-124 cargo plane's rapid descent through the dusky clouds, McKellen couldn't help but feel like he was staring at another splinter point. Perhaps his own.

The knot in his stomach grew larger the closer the cargo plane's blinking lights drew. It was diving so rapidly toward the earth that the C-124 appeared to be in a free fall. But it wasn't, McKellen knew. He could still see its belly while the plane's nose was tilted only slightly downward. If anything, it seemed as if the plane might do a belly flop right on top of their heads. McKellen's mind churned. *The whole thing's damn peculiar.*

Surrounding the colonel, emergency crews rushed about, preparing for any contingency. Behind them, tanks rolled into position, flanked by tired-looking soldiers, still yawning away sleep as they hustled into position. McKellen had already sent up two planes to try to make contact over radio and using hand signals, but neither had received a reply. The pilots reported that they had seen two men in the cargo carrier's cockpit, but they either were unable or unwilling to return the signals. McKellen was still hoping for a simple, non-hostile explanation, but the closer the giant plane came, the faster those hopes vanished.

Eyeing the soldiers flanking the runway, McKellen found himself absently fingering the 9mm in his holster. He usually wore it only for show, projecting a steadfast image of the tireless old war horse to his men, or so he hoped. Rubbing the handgrip between his fingertips, he wondered if it was even loaded. It had been years since he'd drawn his weapon, let alone fired the damn thing. Unclasping the buckle, he withdrew the pistol and checked its clip. Feeling the gun's weight in his palm, it seemed heavier than he remembered. His eyes drifted up toward the behemoth plunging toward them. There had to be a reasonable explanation, he assured himself, though that inner hope was wavering like a candle in a strong breeze.

As soldiers whispered nervously around him, McKellen holstered his weapon, then squared his shoulders and turned, offering a reassuringly stoic nod. The grumbling chatter quieted. Men fell in line. Waiting. Above them all, the C-124's engines roared louder.

Closer.

McKellen's radio squawked; it was the control tower: "Sir, the C-124's landing gear hasn't been deployed!" a man said through static, "Repeat, landing gear is *not* down."

With a thundering shriek, the giant cargo plane buzzed overhead. Flying past McKellen and his strategically located barrier of tanks and personnel, it continued past the runway, heading over the salt flats. Spinning around to track the plane, McKellen realized too late that the airstrip was not the plane's destination. It was headed for the mountain ridge, plunging toward the hidden hangar.

"Shoot it down!" he shouted into his radio.

A burst of static was followed by a hesitant voice. "Sir?"

"Open fire! Now!" McKellen sprinted across the tarmac, waving to the now-useless barricade of men. "Get to the hangar!"

Cafferty pulled up in a jeep. McKellen jumped in, eyeing his two planes as they slowly turned, trying to line up a shot. It was too late.

The C-124 barreled into the mountainside. The rocky ridge blazed red just before the sound of the crash reached McKellen's eardrums. The ground shook violently enough to jerk the jeep's steering wheel, sending their vehicle careening. Struggling to regain control, Cafferty yanked the wheel to the left and kept the pedal down, now less than half a mile from the raging inferno on the mountain. The plane appeared to have crashed directly into the camouflaged entrance. Dead center. Someone, it seemed, knew precisely where to strike.

Flanked by several other vehicles, with tanks following slowly—too slowly—McKellen was the first on the scene. His 9mm was in his hand before he sprang out of the jeep. Keeping his distance from the raging fire, he tried to peer through billowing black smoke into the fractured plane's hull. Were there any survivors? If not, what was the point of the attack? McKellen felt his knees buckle beneath him, and his back slouched as he tried to determine precisely what he was facing. He grabbed the radio off his belt and held it to his lips. "Control tower, tell our birds to sweep the area. If this is a diversion, I don't wanna get caught with our pants down. Again," he added sourly.

Stumbling along the fire's edge, he chewed the inside of his cheek until he tasted blood. Maybe Casey had been right. Still, he thought, trying to console himself, it seemed like an altogether human attack. No big-eyed monsters or flying saucers.

Clouds of swirling dust announced the arrival of tanks and trucks. Screaming orders, McKellen had them create a perimeter around the blazing hillside while fire-fighting teams rushed in with hoses. His mind whirled. The sooner he could determine what sort of attack he was dealing with, the sooner he could form a plan for how to defend against it. For the moment he was forced to stand idle, like a useless lump, waiting until the fire crews knocked down the raging flames.

As the fire turned into steam beneath the water's onslaught, the plane's twisted wreckage came into view. Beyond the shattered plane's bent and broken metallic skeleton, the mountain's hidden two-foot-thick steel barrier wobbled. Cracks spiderwebbed from the explosion, revealing darkness beyond. The hangar had been breached.

By the time the fire was finally doused to smoldering ruins, McKellen had received an all-clear signal from his planes in the air. No other threats were in the area. Instead of relief, it only made McKellen's stomach tighten further. If this wasn't a diversion, and there weren't any other incoming attacks, then the hangar had indeed been the target. The C-124 seemed to have accomplished its mission, whatever that might be, and now McKellen was playing catch up.

After the firefighting teams withdrew, soldiers fidgeted anxiously just beyond the smoldering wreckage. Taking a gulp of burning air into his lungs, McKellen held it before giving the go-ahead with a silent nod. Off his signal, Cafferty led an infantry squad toward the burnt plane's blackened hull. Considering the twisted, bent husk, full of jagged edges and tight spaces, the fewer men who went in, the better. Still, McKellen thought, allowing himself a slight sigh, whoever was inside had to be dead. Perhaps the danger was over.

Maybe this isn't my splinter point. Just maybe . . .

The squad, wearing gas masks, entered through the plane's rear, leaping through a blanket of black-and-gray smoke. The craft's gaping hole seemed to swallow them as the soldiers vanished from view.

McKellen fingered his radio, eager to hear a report from inside the wreckage. Seconds ticked by, turning to long, frozen minutes without any word. He began to pace. The worst part of command was being forced to wait for others to do the jobs that he would have rather done himself. When a report didn't return promptly enough for his liking, he brought the radio to his mouth, ready to demand a report. Before he could initialize the transmitter, though, figures appeared, blinking in and out of view through the smoky haze. After counting all eight of his men, McKellen released a long, slow breath. His muscles relaxed, and his arms fell to his sides.

The men were carrying two stretchers, the bodies on them wrapped in thermal blankets. Once clear of the smoke, they placed the stretchers on the ground, then unwrapped the blankets, revealing the two bodies. It was clear from what remained of their uniforms that they had been naval airmen, but their features were burnt beyond recognition. While standing over them, what struck McKellen the most was not the condition of the bodies but, rather, the way they were posed. Their arms were draped to the side, their mouths closed. If not for the blistered flesh and smoldering bones, they would have appeared to be sleeping.

He waved a medic over. "How did these men die?"

Tilting his head, the medic offered a blank expression. "Sir?"

"Humor me," McKellen replied. "Check for bullet wounds."

Cafferty approached. "What is it, Colonel?"

"Look at their faces," McKellen said.

Cafferty leaned over the medic as he worked. It took Cafferty a moment to figure it out, but he finally got there. "If they died in a fire or a crash that they saw coming, they should have been screaming."

McKellen nodded solemnly. His stomach souring, he tasted acid at the back of his throat. Even though the sun wasn't up yet, trickles of sweat dripped in his eyes and down his spine. He'd seen a lot of weird shit over the last few years but nothing like this. He only knew two things for certain: this crash was no accident, and things were about to get a whole lot worse.

While the medic continued to examine the blackened remains, McKellen pulled Cafferty aside, keeping his voice to a low grumble. "Get back to the base and call this in. We're going to need a containment unit." Pausing, he took a deep breath. "And tell 'em to put Peggy on standby."

Cafferty was too professional to show his surprise openly. Still, McKellen had served with him long enough to be able to read the subtle creases forming around his eyes. "Peggy" was the code name for the nuke in Texas pointed directly at Area 51, a final backup in case something ever went seriously wrong in Dr. Stevens' labs. It was another in a long list of reasons why the base had been built so far from civilization.

Cafferty nodded, his mouth drooping. "You really think we're at that point?"

A splinter point? McKellen wondered.

Before he could answer, he heard the medic screech. Stumbling back from the bodies, the medic pitched forward, his hands gripping his knees. Everyone turned to look. McKellen's jaw tightened, and his eyes narrowed to slits as his worst nightmare became real.

On the stretchers, the dead had begun to move.

Boney rib cages wrapped in tight, blackened flesh and melted uniforms bulged as if something were pushing beneath the surface, trying to escape the pilots' corpses. The protrusion grew larger, becoming bulbous as the ribs struggling to contain it snapped and crackled like twigs. McKellen took a step back, waving for his men to retreat. The corpses trembled violently, spasming, before an enormous red explosion burst from their chests, engulfing the surrounding soldiers in a swirling red mist.

Oh God, was all McKellen had time to think as half of his men were consumed by the crimson cloud. Thrusting out vaporous appendages, the mist swarmed through the soldiers, vanishing into their mouths and noses. A few struggled to remain standing against the onslaught. Most, however, crumbled, clutching their faces.

Casey was right, he thought, cursing. The seekers had arrived, and nothing seemed able to obstruct their path. Certainly not guns and tanks.

McKellen saw a gaseous form closing in on him as he impotently fingered his pistol. Desperate, he fired off several rounds, but the mist continued to draw closer. All he could do was watch helplessly as the red death slowly draped over him.

Before the noxious vapor could enter his lungs, however, Cafferty knocked him aside. "Go, Colonel!"

Bowled over by the surprise blow, McKellen tumbled into the dust just as Cafferty took the red smoke inside himself.

No! McKellen screamed in his mind, but too many years of training stopped him from hesitating in doing what had to be done. McKellen retreated.

Seeking new prey, the mist separated into tentacle-like streams, piercing the surrounding tanks. Within the metal husks, men's screams rose before fading to a quiet din.

Leaping into his jeep, McKellen hit the gas. Yanking the wheel around, he bolted through a cloud of dust and rocks, racing back toward the base. As he fled for dear life, McKellen decided that he had, at last, faced his own personal D-Day.

His splinter point.

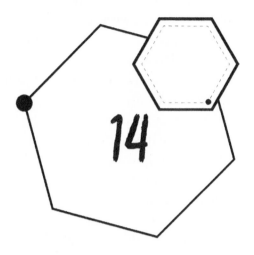

14

*K*a-junk.
　　Ka-junk. Ka-junk. Ka-junk . . .

The elevator's metallic frame shuddered as it ascended at a rapid pace. The rhythmic thumping reminded Harold of a fist rapping against the lid of a coffin.

Ka-junk. Ka-junk.

Feeling pressure push against his stomach as the elevator rose, he still wanted the damn thing to go faster. Harold needed out. Now. He was done with Area 51, Casey, bug-eyed creatures, and, most of all, with the creepy haunted ship that had invaded and violated his mind.

Pacing like a caged animal, he silently counted the floors. Eleven, ten, nine . . . Almost there. And then what? Getting back to his room was not the problem. Going out the front gate and escaping this madhouse, that wouldn't be so easy. He'd signed a contract. A whole stack of them. Granted, none of them mentioned spaceships that could mess with his mind or red-and-black creatures with blank white eyes. Still, he doubted the military would simply let him up and leave. Would it be considered desertion? He was a civilian, after all, not a soldier. Surely, he could quit and leave whenever he wanted to, right?

Pushing his mind beyond the initial escape, he tried to calculate how far the lonesome road that had brought him here might be. Twenty miles? Thirty? Too far to walk, that much was certain. *Maybe I should speak to the colonel*, he thought. While the overbearing mustached man intimidated Harold to no end, at least he couldn't get inside Harold's head. Not like Casey. Or that damnable ship.

A mish-mash of thoughts cascaded on top of each other, thundering in his skull. At the fifth floor, almost topside, the elevator halted, and Harold's world went black.

I didn't get out in time, he thought, staring into the pitch darkness. He reminded himself that he was literally buried deep underground with no escape. The image of knuckles rapping against the inside of a coffin lid returned. So consumed with planning his escape from the base, he'd never stopped to consider that he might not be able to even leave the hangar. Though it wasn't a hangar, he thought, not really. It was more like a prison. An underground prison with only one exit.

Pacing in the small square of darkness, he imagined the monsters below coming back to life. Raging, clawing their way out of their glass containers, let loose, and Harold trapped inside with them. He should have gotten out sooner. Months earlier, when he first arrived. He'd been as blind then as he was now. Only, instead of pitch blackness, he'd been blinded by the sheer wonderment of it all. Wonderment. The thought tasted like acid in his mouth now. More like stupidity. His mother's voice bubbled above his mind's noisy din: *Smarty-pants people don't see what's clear as day to the average Joe. Better to be smart-average than stupid-smart.* And that, Harold now realized, was precisely what he'd been. Stupid-smart.

As he tried to peer through the blanket of darkness, every tiny noise seemed amplified. A distant rumbling commotion from seemingly everywhere echoed around him. Above the reverberation, the elevator creaked and whined, suspended over an invisible chasm. Harold's chest tightened, his breathing transforming into shallow gulps. Crumpling to his knees, his fingers found the cross around his neck as his mind screamed. *Stupid-smart, Harold! Stupid-smart!*

A soft sound, like a whispering wind, drifted down from above, drawing his attention to the elevator's unseen ceiling. In the blackness, a red glow formed, mere feet in front of him. It took a moment for his eyes to adjust to the new sight, but once they did, Harold's feet slid backwards, pushing himself against the farthest wall within the cramped elevator. Blinking rapidly, he prayed the glow was merely the result of his overactive imagination, but it kept coming. Coils of red smoke slithered around him. There was nowhere for Harold to run. Having heard the stories about how the seekers could control people, he shut his mouth and plugged his nose. Kneeling in the corner, his body shook nervously as he waited for whatever might come next. Would there be pain?

As if in reply to his unspoken question, the darkness gave way to a bright light while feminine moans lingered in his ear, and invisible fingers probed his groin. There was no pain; instead, the mist offered paradise. Roman columns erected in his mind's eye. Below, naked feminine forms writhed, eager for his embrace.

If not for his earlier encounter with the ship and Casey, Harold would have languished blissfully, trapped in that fantasy world until there was nothing left of him. However, the magic trick had already been revealed, and the dream held much less sway this time. The naked figures lying prone and waiting at his feet held no power over his base needs now that he understood it was merely a dream. The sexual conquests on offer suddenly seemed dull and pointless. Instead, focusing his thoughts on how he'd gotten there, he remembered the elevator and the red mist. *It must have taken control of me*, Harold thought. But what was it doing with his body while he was stuck in the dream state?

Feeling curiously detached, his consciousness drifted upwards until the Roman columns vanished, and a red light appeared, flashing before him. At first he thought it was another dream, until he noted that he could see the elevator door open and feel his legs propelling him forward. He was back in the hangar.

At a distance, he glimpsed Casey lingering in the doorway to the lab.

His feet rushed forward, toward her, his arms outstretched. When Casey slammed the door in his face, he pounded against it. He wanted to consume her, to make her like himself. The sensation was not all that different from the longing he'd felt for Casey over the past few weeks, like a hunger. Had his desire for her truly been of his own volition? Recalling the hissing voice in his skull from earlier, his thoughts turned to the ship. Perhaps his attraction to Casey had been real enough, but the ship had amplified those feelings. But why? To what end?

Returning his awareness to the present, Harold tried to consider the facts as clinically as possible. The seeker had taken his body, yet somehow it didn't seem to notice Harold's consciousness was fully aware inside. He tried to stop his legs from moving, to no avail. Then his back grew rigid, and his feet spun, turning his attention toward the ship's hulking, red-lit silhouette. As he approached it, he could see the emergency lights blazing above and smell the earthy dust around him. Yet, beyond his base senses, he had no control over where he went or what he did.

Harold attempted to peer into the seeker's thoughts. When he did, however, all he saw was blackness. Either the creature lacked coherent thought, or it was somehow blocking him.

As he drew closer to the ship, Harold saw pieces of shrapnel spin through the air and clamp onto the metallic hull, like puzzle pieces slotting into place. The ship seemed larger, he thought, before correcting himself. *Not larger—fuller.* The horrid thing was rebuilding itself.

Then, to his horror, Harold watched as a curved doorway appeared, and his body entered without hesitation. He was a puppet on a string, being led once again through corridors of pulsing luminance. This time, however, the walk was short, ending in a domed chamber and stopping directly beneath an enormous crimson sphere. It whirled overhead, pulsing with shafts of red light. *A beating heart,* he thought. It was the most fantastical thing he'd ever witnessed, and yet, all he wanted now was to look away and run like hell. Sadly, that wasn't an option.

A voice crawled behind his eyes, burrowing deep into his thoughts like a rattlesnake slithering through rocks. *Are you my new pilot?*

"Yes," Harold heard himself say, though the words were not his own. He was simply a voyeur. The seeker continued. "We have been stranded here and must return to the tower."

The tower? For a moment, Harold's trickling fear gave way to an incessant scientific curiosity. Even after everything he'd been through, his curiosity still drew him forward in anticipation of what he might learn. As he did, his mother's rebukes rose again at the back of his thoughts. *See? Stupid-smart.* Ignoring the warning, Harold's attention remained focused on the conversation between the beings so unlike himself.

The tower is gone, the ship replied, *along with all that we have built.*

Harold felt a distinct physical reaction, as if battery acid were eating away at his tongue. The seeker was afraid, he realized.

"Explain," the creature ordered.

In silent reply, a flash of images swarmed Harold's mind, a cacophony of sights and sounds too rapid for him to discern one from the other. Each image overlapped with the last at a rapid pace. Still, within the haze, a few fractured visions became clear: Casey writhing within a metallic pod while dozens of tiny syringes stabbed her from every angle, each needle filling her bloodstream with microscopic nanoprobes. Harold witnessed her transformation on a molecular level. Her body chemistry altered, Casey's pink flesh turned ashen gray before snapping back to its natural state. Her screaming breath against the glass pod turned her world to fog.

It wasn't torture, Harold realized; it was a medical procedure, a cure for the seekers whose biology had broken down over millennia. They were, Harold assumed, attempting to reverse-engineer their own cure by infecting the past with a machine virus—at least that had been the hope.

Another series of images revealed explosions and giant beams tumbling into a vast ocean. Though difficult to discern what he was seeing, Harold could sense the emotions tumbling through him along with the haphazard picture show. Casey had betrayed them, destroyed their last remaining stronghold sometime in the distant future.

Harold watched as the last remnants of life on Earth lay dying, murdered by Casey.

Then she'd fled here, to the past, and all this time the ship had waited. Now, at last, it had been found by a new pilot.

The picture show dissolved behind Harold's eyelids, and the inner voice returned.

She can still save us.

Harold felt himself nod in agreement.

We must correct the timeline.

Again, his head bobbed before he turned back and headed out of the domed chamber. Harold felt the warmth from the sphere's glow diminish as he exited the ship and set out to hunt down Casey and the cure she carried within her.

Unable to do anything but watch this horror show play out, part of him wanted to simply hide in his makeshift fantasy paradise, but that was only a small part. A larger part of him wanted to find a way to fight this thing inside him, to stop it before it could locate Casey. But how?

Lumbering across the hangar, he returned to the lab door, only this time his fists didn't pound uselessly against the metal. Instead, he felt the seeker accessing his memories, plucking images and thoughts as one might a daisy from a garden. Fingers fumbling inside his lab coat pocket, the seeker withdrew a key.

No! Harold's mind shouted as the key slid inside the door, activating unseen tumblers. The lock clicked open. Harold's silent screams intensified, begging.

If the creature heard his pleas, however, it didn't reply.

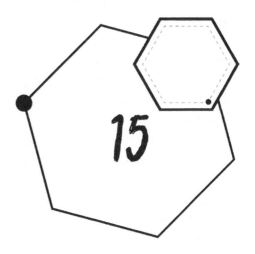

15

Casey's heart lurched upward in her chest. The once-straight hallway now seemed to warp and bend like an abstract painting around her. She gasped for air as her legs became like rubber bands, bending beneath her. Searching for Ruthie and Max, she scanned the glass laboratory doors as she raced along the corridor. It wasn't until Casey reached the last door on the right, her office, that she realized Harold had ceased pounding on the door behind her. Casey doubted that the thing possessing him had given up the search quite so easily. He, or *it*, she corrected herself, would return. Soon.

The respite gave her a moment to bend over and steady her shallow breathing. Stopping didn't slow her whirling thoughts, however. If anything, it only made the reality of what was happening more apparent. Once again, Casey found herself being chased through a dark corridor with a thing that had once been human close behind. Despite all her research, studying, and planning, Casey was back where she'd started ten years prior: running in the dark from red-eyed monsters. *Running*. That was the worst part. After obtaining her abilities and defeating the ship the last time, she had sworn she would never have to run again. Not from the ship. Not from anything. Yet, there she was.

Casey cursed, trying to figure out how to escape the seekers. Her stomach churning, she forced her body to straighten up. Exhaling, she let out her breath in a long, slow stream of hot air. Calming herself as best as she could without the nanites' help, her heart rate slowed enough so that at least the thundering in her eardrums faded to a quiet din. Powers or no powers, she wasn't the frightened young girl she used to be.

I can face this, she told herself defiantly. *I can face them*.

Breaking her train of thought, a soft whisper, like a whimper, emanated from behind her office door. "Casey?"

Ruthie's familiar voice made Casey sigh with relief. Entering, she found Max cradling his wife in the back of the room, hidden behind the Prime's floating husk.

Ruthie peeked out, her eyes wide. "How is the ship repairing itself after all this time?"

"I don't know," Casey admitted. "But we have bigger problems."

"Like what?" Max asked.

"Seekers," she said. "One of them took Harold, possessed him. It's right outside the lab."

Ruthie fidgeted, her voice quivering. "And he's trying to get in here?"

Casey nodded absently, her thoughts wandering. If the seekers had gotten to Harold, what about all the soldiers stationed above? Had they been infected as well? If so, there would be no escape. Noting Ruthie's pale expression, Casey decided not to voice her concerns. Instead, she swallowed air through her clenched teeth and turned to Max. "You need to get out of here."

"You just said Harold was right outside," Ruthie said.

Max nodded in understanding. "The emergency stairs."

"Yes," Casey replied. "Move slowly. I don't know how many of those things have taken over our people."

Max pulled Ruthie toward the door, but she stopped, turning to Casey. "Aren't you coming?"

"I'll be right behind you," Casey assured her.

Max shook his head. "We need to stick together."

"It's after *me*, not you," Casey said. "Take her. Go."

Ruthie hesitated. Max pulled at her, but her feet remained planted, unwilling to budge.

"Hold on," Ruthie said. "We can't just leave her."

Max pulled harder, forcing Ruthie toward the door. His best chance at saving his wife and unborn child was following Casey's order, even though that meant leaving Casey behind. Opening the door, Max glanced back at Casey. "Don't take long."

"I won't," Casey said, struggling to smile. "This isn't my first rodeo."

As soon as the door shut behind them, her smile vanished. Yes, she'd been hunted in the dark by these monsters before, but back then she'd had enhanced abilities. Now she had nothing.

A loud *click* at the other end of the hall signaled the seeker's return.

Her heart quivered. The thing was inside the labs.

Casey had spent years hoping to find a way to destroy the nanites infecting her, but at that moment, she would have traded just about anything to reactivate them. Without the nanites and the enhanced speed they offered, she was powerless to stop the seekers. Still, the sound of shattering glass a few doors down propelled her into action.

She scanned the office for a weapon, anything. Trapped in another dark room with another monster stalking her, she couldn't shake a sense of inevitability. Her mind whirling, her eyes drifted over the Prime's black-and-red body looming ominously in the tank. A patchwork of multi-colored scars were evidence of various tests. Approaching it, she pressed her nose against the glass, searched the cadaver for the most damaged area. As she stared, an idea formed in her mind. The Prime's right arm was stained black, scars from lesions along the wrist.

Outside in the hall, another explosion of glass announced Harold's approach. Stealing a final glance at the wound along the Prime's wrist, Casey checked once more to make sure it was indeed the darkest blotch along the creature's red-and-black skin. Gazing through the liquid at the disfigured form covered with countless scars and wounds, it was difficult to discern precisely which was the most damaged area. Thundering footfalls outside, however, forced her to a conclusion.

Casey ran to her desk and flipped through her notes, trying to read them beneath the red emergency lights. The words were blurry, and she found her own handwriting nearly impossible to decipher. She hadn't expected to review them in such a situation. By the fourth folder, Casey found what she was looking for:

Dated 9/12/57. Right arm: test #9. Dosage: 50 CCs of variant strand 4.

Scurrying to her cabinet, Casey flung the metal doors open. Too late to stop them, they clanged ear-piercingly loud. *Shit!* Outside, the smashing glass stopped. Had it heard her? Casey held her breath, her fingers fumbling desperately as she scrambled through vials, searching for the one labeled "Variant Strand #4."

The footsteps grew louder, the thing that had been Harold drawing closer.

Unwilling to stop to glance at the door, her trembling hands knocked vials aside in her desperate search. Midway through her search of the second shelf from the bottom, Casey stopped at a tiny vial. She'd found it. Variant #4. Inside, purple liquid swirled about, containing augmented nanites from her own blood. Her hope was that if she injected Harold with it, her nanites would spread through the healthy nanites and multiply like a cancer. How fast or effective it might prove to be remained unknown. Still, it was the only chance she had.

Snatching a syringe, her fingers shook so violently that the first few drops spilled on the floor. Catching her breath, she halted, waiting for her hands to stop shaking enough to extract the dosage.

At the door a crimson shadow crossed behind smoky glass. A rasping breath followed, announcing the thing's arrival. Biting her lip, Casey tipped the needle into the vial and methodically withdrew the purple fluid, desperate not to spill another drop. Once the syringe was full, she ducked behind the doorway and waited.

Seconds seemed like hours. Her breath sounded like a locomotive chugging in her ears, thundering so loudly that she swore the creature could hear it. Clutching the needle like a dagger, tears welled in her eyes. As she desperately blinked them away, the door burst open.

PART II

ABOMINATION

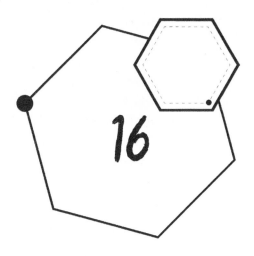

16

Harold Stone was a silent passenger in his own body. He observed himself shuffling along the hall, eyes scanning left to right, glimpsing darkened labs, but he held no sway over what his body did or where it went. Hesitating before the encased gray clone, he felt the seeker's excitement ignite within him like a sparkling flame. Strands of red vapor escaped his nose and lips in eager anticipation of the new, stronger body. The closer the strands drew to the clone, however, the more Harold sensed the seeker's growing fascination turn to bitter disappointment. Damaged beyond repair, the clone was useless. The smoky tendrils withdrew, returning through Harold's mouth and nose before the seeker moved on.

A clanging noise rang through the hall, emanating from Casey's office. *Damn*, he cursed, as his body moved even faster. Then, just as quickly as it had started, the seeker stopped, turned, and peered into the third lab on the left. Inside, swirling red mist was trapped in a clear container. It thumped loudly against the container's glass walls, agitated and eager to escape.

Harold watched himself open the lab door and approach the gaseous substance. His fists clenched, he punched the glass case over and over until spiderwebbed cracks appeared and spread. With a hissing gush, the crimson vapor escaped. Harold noted glass shards sticking out of his knuckles, blood dripping to the floor. From this vantage point, though, he couldn't tell if the seeker had punctured a vein. Harold wanted to rage and scream, hoping to warn the creature that slow blood loss would mean his eventual death, but he couldn't make a sound. All he could do was watch the newly escaped red mist swirl about before vanishing up his nose and into his mouth.

A new sensation filled him; something familiar like . . . a great weight. The same feeling he'd experienced the first time he'd seen the ship all those months ago. Now he understood what the weight was. Another consciousness pressed against his own. Only this time the weight was much greater, for there were now two of them writhing within him. Though he couldn't make out any words, he sensed the communication between the two seekers. There was a distinct burst of emotion, not too dissimilar from the way siblings or other family members might feel embracing each other. Was it love? Perhaps not the way a human might experience it, but it seemed like a close approximation. With a flash of recognition and a warmth gathering about, the two beings intertwined within him, pushing Harold further downward, as if he had been shoved from the passenger seat to the backseat. Squashed between the two intermingled creatures slithering around his skull, Harold felt invisible walls close in, shutting out even more of his dwindling senses.

A loud crash from Casey's office broke the seekers' revelry. Spinning around, the creatures' attention was drawn back toward the hallway, and Harold's body lurched forward. Toward Casey. Harold wished he could at least offer a warning. Something, anything to let her know he was coming. But it was too late. He, or rather, they, were at her door.

Harold's blood-drenched fingers wrapped around the doorknob, turning it. Stepping into fractured light, they hesitated at the entrance. Harold's eyes danced around the room, finding the cabinet open with a disarray of vials spilled about. Behind it, though, something else grabbed the seekers' attention: a disfigured black-and-red clone body. The Prime.

As the seekers examined this new discovery, Harold felt their swirling emotions boil, rising within him like a wave smashing against a beachhead. Morbid disgust turned to rage, then dissolved, upon closer inspection of the body, into a fresh spark of hope. Momentarily distracted, the seekers didn't notice a blur of shadowy movement at the edge of Harold's vision, but he did.

Casey lunged, stabbing him in the neck. Harold welcomed the attack as a fiery sensation ran through his nerve endings, blazing up his spine and burning his skull. It was the first physical sensation he'd felt since the first seeker had taken control. The pain, while awful, was also delicious, like a burst of light in an endless, pooling dark. Collapsing to the floor, Harold heard the seekers scream with his own voice. Glancing up, they found Casey looming above, a syringe clutched in her shaky fingers. Below her terrified eyes, a victorious, cocky grin creased Casey's lips.

Spasming on the floor, Harold felt the sensations of his physical form return. His sleeping limbs awoke while a thousand tiny needles stabbed every inch of him. The feeling in his nerve endings came back to him in a rush of agony. Escaping the pain, a swirl of red mist puffed out of his nose and mouth. But it was only the second seeker that had left, he realized, before his perception once again dimmed. While Casey's injection had expelled one of the creatures, the other remained, fighting to retain control of Harold's body. Lurching upwards, it swatted Casey aside with a backhanded blow. Flung across the office, she crashed behind the desk in a heap.

Harold's body started toward her, only to stop, as if pulled back toward the encased Prime. The fleeing seeker swirled around it longingly. Harold sensed the mist's desperation. It desired this new body. Groaning inwardly, Harold watched in horror as his already bloody fist smashed repeatedly at the tank's glass surface. His wound deepening, Harold thought he heard bones break before the creature controlling him finally relented. Flesh and blood weren't strong enough to destroy the tank. Scanning the haphazard office, his eyes fell on a metal chair. Grabbing it, the creature swung high and hard, shattering the cylindrical tube with a single blow.

The Prime spilled outward in a tangled mass of darkened flesh and splashing liquid. Hitting the floor with a wet, squishy *smack*, the sound made Harold want to retch. The pungent formaldehyde odor assailing his nostrils caused his head to swim.

The disembodied red mist swirled around the lifeless figure like a serpent circling its prey before pouring into the clone's mouth. For a moment, there was no movement. Then a twitch. And another. With a grotesque lurch, the thing's white eyes blinked open. Arms blotched with red and black pushed itself up as the creature struggled to stand in the slippery liquid. Harold watched his own arms reach forward, steadying the creature. The thing tilted horrifyingly close, leering down at him.

Feeling the clone's scaly, sickly wet skin against his fingertips, Harold noted that a faint tinge of sensory perception still lingered from Casey's shot. Perhaps there was still a chance to regain control of his faculties.

Through his peripheral vision, he glimpsed Casey crawling out from behind the desk. It was now or never. Struggling to focus beyond the ghastly creature before him and the one inside, Harold pushed his consciousness as far forward as possible. Able to feel his skin and the bile-like liquid burn his nose, the world's outward sensations grew enticingly closer. Then he felt a fire along his wrist from his bloody wound. Air filled his blazing lungs. The onrush of tactile sensations was so immediate and violent that he almost withdrew back into his deep, dark cave. But he didn't. He couldn't. Not now. Not when he was so close. Focusing instead on Casey, Harold forced his mouth to open and his tongue to work.

"Run, Casey!"

Whipping around, she met his gaze with a mixture of shock and sadness. As he stared into her emerald eyes, Harold's affection reemerged in a rush of swelling emotions. Fear and anger vanished, replaced by a desire to protect her.

Harold felt the seeker's invisible fingers groping inwardly, trying to regain control. Knowing this was only a momentary victory, Harold issued one more warning. "Go . . . now!"

Like a rubber band snapping, the seeker's ghostly fingers snatched him from his flesh-and-bone body and flung him back into the dark cave of his skull as the thing once again regained control. It was too late to stop her, though. Casey bolted out the door. Instead of giving chase, the seeker held the weakened clone upright. The grotesque thing flailed in Harold's arms, struggling to stand on its own volition.

Outside, they heard the emergency staircase door slam shut. Both he and the seekers knew where she'd gone. For now, though, the Prime needed to gain its strength. The feeling of horror gone, Harold instead watched events unfold with a new sense of confidence that he hadn't possessed moments earlier. These creatures were not invincible. They could be beaten. Perhaps, he hoped, from the inside. Somehow, Harold felt as if he'd regained a sliver of his humanity. Whatever Casey had injected him with had had an effect. How long it would last, he didn't know.

Beside him the Prime reared upwards, gaining its footing before marching clumsily toward the door. The seeker who had hijacked Harold's body followed silently. All Harold could do was observe himself walk out the doorway and approach the stairs, powerless to stop it. Yet, for the first time since this invasive nightmare began, Harold felt a pang of hope.

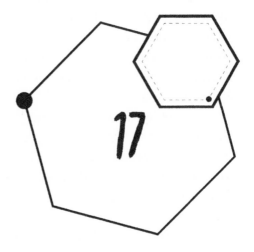

17

Jerking the steering wheel, Colonel McKellen skidded the jeep to a halt, spewing a cloud of dust in his wake. During the mad dash back to the base proper, he'd attempted to reach the command tower over the radio, to no avail. The receiver spit out only static. Bolting up the stairs to the main complex building, he prayed the seekers hadn't arrived before him. Having driven at breakneck speed, no one seemed to have followed. Still, the base appeared deserted; no airmen or soldiers stood outside to greet him. Despite the area being placed on high alert, the tarmac was empty. Even the planes in the sky were gone. McKellen ground his teeth, rubbing his sweaty palms against his pant legs. This was all wrong. Turning back to the entrance, his meaty fingers hovered over the doorknob. Frightened by what sort of horrors might await him, he held his 9mm at the ready before thrusting the door open.

Silent darkness greeted him. An empty reception room with carpeted floors and tiled walls stared back. No dead bodies or blood-covered horrors. Yet, the quiet stillness of it all pushed his blood pressure even higher. Stealing a final glance at the barren tarmac outside, Mc-Kellen entered.

Weapon quivering slightly in his hands, he swept the vacant room. Crossing to the reception desk, McKellen checked the phone. As he'd feared, the line was dead. The radio and the landline were out, half the base was possessed by vapor-like creatures from the future, and the other half was MIA. Heat rising to his face, he felt the reception room shrink around him. McKellen was thinking about pinching himself just to make certain this wasn't some sort of twisted lucid dream when the front door sprang open behind him. Airmen and soldiers poured in, flanking him, Army and Air Force personnel alike.

The gang's all here, he thought with a sigh of relief. "Is the base secure?"

In silent reply, the soldiers raised their rifles. The color drained from McKellen's usually stoic expression as he looked at the array of muzzles facing him. Once again, he wondered if he was dreaming. For a long, drawn-out breath, McKellen struggled to speak.

Shouldering his way through the door, Sergeant Davis appeared. His face covered with beads of sweat, he cleared his throat. "Please drop your weapon, sir."

The colonel didn't waver, keeping his pistol raised. Scanning the airmen and the soldiers' faces, McKellen knew them all by name. These were *his* men, had been for years, their loyalty unquestionable. Yet, their rifles were aimed dead center at his chest, fingers on the triggers. The men's anxiety was obvious, but their eyes did not glow red, nor did they show any signs of seeker possession. Whatever this was, it was an entirely human conflict, which only made this sudden standoff that much more inconceivable.

"Please, sir," Sergeant Davis repeated, "drop your weapon."

His teeth clenched and muscles throbbing along his jawline, McKellen's finger fidgeted on his pistol's trigger. He saw the fear in Davis's eyes, but that didn't make the moment any easier. Even if McKellen got off a few shots, he couldn't take them all down. And he didn't want to.

Military police appeared behind him, rushing down from the second floor. Weighing his limited options, McKellen finally removed his finger from the trigger and raised his arms in supplication before placing the weapon on the reception counter.

His shoulders relaxing, Sgt. Davis lowered his rifle slightly. "Step away from the counter please, sir."

"We're under attack, Sergeant," McKellen snapped, unwilling to move. "What the hell are you doing?"

Two guards rushed up beside him, grabbing his arms. McKellen shrugged them off, never taking his eyes off Sgt. Davis. "I asked you a question, son."

Davis nodded for the guards to back away, a mixture of charged emotions washing his pale complexion. When he spoke again, his voice had lost its energy. "Following orders, sir."

"Whose orders?"

Sighing, Davis headed up a staircase. "This way please, sir."

Eager for answers, McKellen finally capitulated. Veins popped along his neck as he lumbered up the stairs, his feet stomping heavily beneath him. His eyes bored into the back of Davis's skull. "I'll have your head for this, Sergeant," he growled.

Davis didn't reply.

Davis led him up to the top third floor and down the hall to McKellen's office. His mind racing, his palms were covered in sweat, and his head was throbbing, but his concern had nothing to do with the armed men leading him along the hallway. McKellen's thoughts were back in the hangar with Cafferty and all the men who had been consumed and controlled by the red mist. He needed to get back to stop the seekers before they got down to the ship and Casey. Instead, he was stuck up there in a damnable office complex, surrounded and unarmed. *Playing fucking games.*

Davis opened the office door. Inside, a dark figure sat behind McKellen's desk, his feet propped up as he smoked a cigarette. Whoever it was had made himself at home. McKellen stormed past Davis to the desk. His sudden action took the guards by surprise, their weapons snapping to attention.

The figure turned on the desk lamp, revealing a little man in his fifties dressed in a suit and tie. McKellen recognized him, though it took a moment to recall his name after so many years.

The little man smiled, an icy expression. "Colonel, it's been a long time."

"Prewitt." McKellen's throat tightened with recognition. It was the weaselly bureaucrat who had been sent by Washington after the Roswell crash. They hadn't seen each other in the ten years since, but there was no forgetting him. "What the fuck do you think you're doing?"

"I would have assumed that much was obvious, Colonel," Prewitt said. "I'm relieving you of your duty."

McKellen leaned over the desk, his face flushed and his fists clenched. "You don't have any authority here!"

Prewitt gestured toward the guards in the doorway. "All evidence to the contrary, I'm afraid." He nodded to Davis. "That will be all, Sergeant. Please station two men outside. I'll call you if I need you."

Davis nodded. The colonel glared at him. "What's he got on you, son?" he asked, his voice softening. "What the hell makes a career man turn against his own commander?"

"It's my career I'm thinking of, sir," Davis said, his eyes dropping to the floor. "We all are." He walked out, his head sagging.

"Don't be too hard on them," Prewitt said. "After all, they were never really *your* men." He smirked in response to McKellen's silent glare. "Did you really think Washington would just let you oversee a CIA, Air Force, and Army joint venture of this magnitude without contingencies in place?"

When the door clicked shut, McKellen's face creased with a grim smile. "And do *you* really think I can't choke the life out of you before they get back in here?"

"I think, Colonel, that you are a man who follows orders."

"Not yours," McKellen spat. "This base is under attack, and you're just sitting there—at my desk—playing games."

Prewitt let out a long, disappointed sigh. "You must have known they'd come here eventually," he replied in a tone that sounded like he was speaking to a simple child.

"What are you going on about?"

"The seekers, as Miss Stevens is so fond of calling them." Prewitt glanced out the window toward the smoke rising from the crashed plane. "Luckily, I was close enough to get here in time."

"You're not *in time*," McKellen roared. "They've breached the hangar!"

"Miss Stevens is quite safe, I assure you," Prewitt said. "We have a team in there now, searching for her." He stood up and stretched, pacing behind the desk. The way he moved reminded McKellen of a sickly feline.

"What about the ship?" McKellen asked through clenched teeth.

"You've had it for, what is it now, ten years?" Prewitt continued to watch the distant, billowing smoke filter upwards toward the first hints of sunlight. "And yet, you've learned nothing. Nor will you, I imagine." He turned, meeting the colonel's hardened gaze, a soldier's glare that made most men wet themselves, but it seemed to have no effect on the little man. His confidence, McKellen noted, made him appear taller than he was. "Advanced sciences are all well and good, but I'm afraid that in this case, whatever marvels that ship contains are too far beyond our comprehension to ascertain."

"Wait," McKellen said, his fists quivering at his sides. "You're letting them take it?"

"Colonel, as I'm sure you are aware, our greatest threat is not some distant evolutionary step that humankind may or may not take centuries from now."

McKellen felt ice curl up his scalp. The answer suddenly seemed obvious. "Communism,"

Prewitt nodded. "If the USSR continues to beat us into space, then what happens a million years, or even in fifty years, from now will be of little consequence."

McKellen staggered as understanding dawned on him. He collapsed into a chair, the air wheezing out of his lungs. The reality of Prewitt's words pushed him farther into his seat. "But my men . . ."

"Would you or would you not sacrifice every single person on this base to win the Cold War?"

McKellen didn't answer; he didn't need to. Defeating the USSR was obviously more important than any single life. Even his. Still, he shook his head. "The seekers won't help us."

"Yes, they will," Prewitt assured him. "After all, we have something they want."

McKellen looked up. "The ship?"

"No," Prewitt replied, shaking his head. "Your glorified waitress."

McKellen's face wrinkled in surprise. "Casey?"

Prewitt chuckled. "Ten years and she still hasn't told you the truth."

"What truth?"

"They altered her, changed her in some way. They made her like them."

McKellen nodded. He'd suspected as much. "How do you know this?"

Prewitt sighed dramatically as he crushed out his cigarette. "Because, Colonel, while you've been dillydallying about with spaceships and bug-eyed gray bodies, I've been planning what to do when they return." Prewitt came out from behind the desk and leaned over McKellen in his chair. "You deal in warfare, Colonel. I, on the other hand, deal in contingencies." His self-assured grin broadened. "At the end of the day, our victory over communism, and our government's future, will be assured."

McKellen struggled to make eye contact. He hated that the little weasel might be right. "By *betraying* our own men," he said, his voice breaking.

"And," Prewitt added, "one woman."

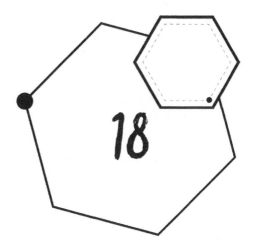

18

Three hundred and twenty-two stairs. That was how many Casey counted before her mind gave up, along with her legs. Her lungs on fire, she bent over, desperate to catch her breath. Overhead, spinning red lights flickered, creating revolving shadows that looked like blood repeatedly being wiped on and off the narrow walls in fractured chunks. The image made her mind and body snap back into gear. Groaning, Casey lumbered onto step 323, pushing forward.

It took another twelve flights before Casey finally stopped, leaning against a steel door. Frigid tendrils of ice snaking up her back told her she'd arrived at her destination. Floor ten, Research and Development. With the lab's base temperature hovering at around zero degrees, she would need to get in and get to the parkas hanging inside as soon as possible.

When she flung the door open, frozen air hit her like a slap across the face. The burning in her chest from the hike up there made the cold air entering her lungs that much worse.

The door whooshed shut behind her, sealing her inside. With no time to wait, Casey bolted for the clothes racks. Thankful that the parkas were still in place, she grabbed one off the rack, along with some thick winter pants. The fabric was so cold to the touch that Casey had trouble maintaining her grip as she slid into the parka. The pants were next. Kicking off her sneakers, she slid the pants on. The frozen floor knifed into her sock-covered feet, reminding her of the last time she'd been hunted by monsters in the dark. Skipping into the cloudy lab, she put her shoes back on in mid-hop. Her hands bunched into fists, she found gloves clipped to the parka and put them on too.

By the time she was fully clothed, her heart lifted at the sounds of familiar voices ahead. Inching around an ice-covered corner, she found Max and Ruthie dressed in similar winter gear, leaning over a workstation. Ruthie turned large gears while Max struggled to activate the elongated metal piping that stretched throughout the laboratory. Watching the two shout back and forth as they fiddled with knobs and levers, Casey was reminded of a joke that her fiancé, Arthur, used to tell: *How many physicists does it take to turn on a lightbulb? Answer: one. Two to do it, minus one to renormalize the wave function.* At the time she hadn't understood it. Now that she did, it still wasn't funny. A pang shot through her chest as Casey pushed the memory of Arthur aside. Observing Max grow more frustrated over the metal tube, she couldn't help but wish the seekers had at least attacked during the day when the engineers were on duty.

Ruthie lowered her parka's hood, catching sight of Casey. "I didn't think I'd see you again," Ruthie said, smiling gleefully as a stream of frost spewed from her lips.

Forcing a crooked grin to her lips, Casey struggled to match Ruthie's enthusiasm. "You're not getting a promotion that easily, Ruth."

Max peeked out from behind the tube, his coat covered in grease stains. He didn't bother to attempt a smile. "What happened?"

Casey approached, eyeing the machine and the gears. "The seekers got Harold. Probably a lot more people up top too."

"So, they'll be coming from both directions," Max said, his eyes flicking from the emergency staircase in the back to the elevator at the far end. He was pragmatic, which Casey admired. It had also prevented her from dwelling on poor Harold's face when he screamed for her to run. Somehow, he'd been able to momentarily fight off the consciousness invading him. The poison must have had at least a momentary impact. Perhaps with more time at her disposal, Casey might be able to create a more permanent antidote. But not now. Time was one of the many things she didn't have. The enemy would be coming. Soon.

Glancing over her shoulder at the emergency door, she scanned it for a lock. No such luck. That left only one option.

Kneeling beside the pipe, she felt along its belly, searching for heat but finding none. "No power."

"Lord knows it hasn't been for a lack of trying," Max replied.

Casey huffed, then stood and began flipping every switch she could find. Still nothing. The pipe was a giant vacuum of sorts, using low levels of radiation to suck up organic particles in gaseous form. It only worked half the time, and it had never been tested on a seeker, but in theory it should be able to stop them—or so she hoped. Then she discovered another problem. "There's not enough juice coming from the backup generator."

Ruthie pointed toward frost emanating from overhead vents. "At least the fridge is still running," she said through chattering teeth. "The cold should slow them down."

"Slow them, maybe," Max conceded, "but it won't stop them."

"How far along were the tech guys on those grav guns?" Casey asked.

Max glanced out the window at the cement-lined laboratory, the one the engineers called the Well. His eyes brightened, then narrowed. Casey could see the wheels turning. After a pregnant pause, his head sagged. "The bullets need the emitters embedded throughout the walls to travel," he said. "The weapons won't work in here."

Casey stood, approaching the glass. "They don't need to," she replied. A plan formed in her mind. A crazy, dangerous, just plain *stupid* plan, but it was all she had.

"We'll lure them in here, the cold will slow them down . . ."

"And then," Max continued, "we'll lead them into the Well and hit them with the grav guns?"

Casey nodded. "Once the bullets hit the bodies, the seekers should return to vapor, pouring out. We'll need to come back in here to trap the red mist."

"Could that work?" Ruthie asked, glancing from her husband to Casey.

"It's a long shot." Max said, then his face soured. "Even if it did, it means shooting, *killing*, anyone who walks in here, including Harold and probably some soldiers."

Casey had already taken that into account. "I'm open to other suggestions."

When no one answered, she opened the door, feeling warm air wrap around her like a blanket as she headed into the Well. Max and Ruthie followed close behind. Casey couldn't help wondering if Max had already had the same idea but didn't want to be the first to suggest such a grotesque solution. That was the problem with being the leader; she had to make all the shitty calls. Like, potentially, mass murder.

Rummaging through stacks of rifles, she found two that seemed complete, silver shells laced over a standard bolt-action Smith & Wesson. She handed one to Max, and they loaded the weapons and placed extra bullets in their parkas. Max gave her a sideways glance. "You ever shoot anyone before?"

"No," Casey answered without meeting his gaze.

"I did," Max said. "Back in the war. I was just a kid. Hadn't planned on ever having to do it again."

Casey turned to Ruthie, warming herself by jumping up and down, seemingly thrilled to be out of the cold. Casey, however, didn't feel any warmer. She doubted Max did either. Ruthie seemed lost in her own thoughts, rubbing her stomach. She hummed a tune to her unborn child while the others loaded weapons. Slipping a bullet into the chamber, Casey snapped the bolt shut and felt the weight of the rifle in her hands.

"It's heavier than I'd imagined."

"That's the metal coil wrapped around it," Max replied as he positioned himself across from the door. "We should hide here, behind the third row of cement blocks. It'll give us some cover for when they come in."

Casey shuffled over beside him, propping her rifle on one of the blocks, a box of bullets beside it. Staring at the metallic weapon that the engineers had created based on the ship's antigravity hull, a familiar question came to mind, the same question that had troubled her for years now. Why weren't these technologies available in the future? In 1985, at least in the version she remembered, no one had weapons where bullets could zip around obstacles. The idea of anti-gravity seemed more akin to something out of an Asimov science-fiction story. In fact, no industry or government in 1985 had *any* of the advanced theories or technologies she'd seen or helped develop decades prior. In 1958, Area 51 held wonders undreamed of in the future that she knew, which meant that either her coming back to the past had altered the future or . . .

Ruthie's soft voice broke into her thoughts. "What are our chances?"

Max and Casey exchanged a doubtful glance before Max turned to his wife, offering her a soft smile. "Depends how much the frost slows them down."

"And how many there are," Casey added.

Max nodded in solemn agreement. "We might be

good for three or four. More than that, we won't be able to stop them in time."

The group grew quiet, letting Max's warning sink in. Ruthie stood and began pacing.

Casey turned toward the wall to her right, finding a series of switches attached to chains and gears. Her eyes followed the chains up to the ceiling and then down in a spiderweb of links connected to various cement blocks. "This moves the obstacles around the course?"

"Yeah," Max said, nodding, "but they don't move fast enough to knock anyone's skull in, if that's what you're thinking."

Casey didn't reply; she had a different idea. Noting her interest, Max pointed to the three switches. "The obstacle course is divided into three quadrants," he said. He swept his hand over the levers without moving them, careful not to make any noise. "Up is move, down is stop."

Casey scanned the towering cement blocks. "Maybe we could—"

Ruthie's gasp snapped their attention to the window at the far end of the Well. Beyond it, the elevator descended into view.

Max pulled Ruthie toward the door, heading back to the Fridge. Casey hesitated, trying to see how many figures were inside the elevator. She counted five or maybe six dressed in military attire. Blanketed in thick shadow, their eyes blazed red.

Casey ran.

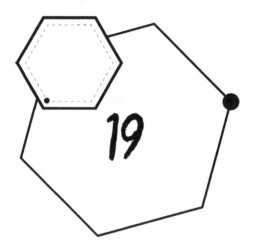

19

The soldiers surged out of the elevator, smashing through glass walls in a wave of fumbling limbs. As soon as they broke through, however, Casey noted their hesitation. The cold air must have hit them like a blow. Their movements slowed as they crunched over broken glass, silently crossing the Fridge. Though their movements languished, they still approached faster than expected in that environment. Casey noted the cold air escaping through the broken window behind them. She hadn't counted on them smashing their way in.

What was I thinking? That they'd politely use the goddamn door?

"They're not slowing down," Ruthie whispered. Max wrapped his arm around her, eyeing the exit to the Well. His shoulders leaned toward it, ready to bolt.

"Wait," Casey said, shuddering. "The closer they come, the colder it will get for them."

"And us," Ruthie said through chattering teeth.

As the soldiers continued forward, their footsteps began to slacken, their backs bent over while tiny wisps of red vapor escaped their lips. Lumbering toward Casey and the others, the soldiers plunged deeper and deeper into the freezing refrigerator. Dressed only in desert-lite uniforms, the seekers and their human hosts appeared weaker with each labored step, the red glow of their eyes growing dim.

"Holy shit," Max muttered, "this might just fucking work."

The three of them watched as the soldiers continued to slow, crimson mist drifting out of them like sickly frosted breath. Casey's heart leapt at the small victory. Even without her abilities, she may have found a way to stop the seekers, or at least slow them enough to escape. She blew out a heavy breath, the pressure in her chest having built up since the soldiers first appeared. Turning toward the door, she began to wonder how long they should wait.

Suddenly, the door behind them burst open, and a disgusting red-and-black form with pale white eyes lunged forward, grabbing Ruthie. She screamed as the Prime's talons tore at her heavy garments. Its long, needle-like teeth appeared behind strands of black saliva, dripping over her neck.

Writhing in its clutches, Ruthie hunched over, protecting her stomach.

Harold sensed a change in the seeker inhabiting his body as soon as they stepped through the doorway. Though unable to feel his frozen flesh or the extreme cold around him, he knew instantly where they were: the Fridge. Sub-zero temperatures turned the red emergency lights a purplish hue, adding to the horrific nature of the scene playing out before him. Taking in the nightmarish view in piecemeal chunks, Harold saw the soldiers in the center of the room, their eyes burning with red light. Their bodies seemed languid and slow while crimson vapor sputtered out of their mouths and noses. With each step they took, the light in their eyes dimmed. Still, they approached, arms stretched out toward Casey.

The Prime held Ruthie in its grip. She kicked and thrashed, to no avail, its arms wrapped around her like a lover's embrace. When the Prime opened its mouth, Harold glimpsed sharp teeth descending, as if to rip out her throat. Then Max barreled into the creature, knocking his wife free. The three figures tumbled to the floor in a mass of flailing limbs.

Harold charged.

He snatched Max off the floor, wrapping thin fingers around his neck, choking him. Harold saw Max's eyes bulge in recognition of his new assailant. As the life drained from his face, his flesh paled, turning from pink to white.

No! Let him go! Harold screamed in his mind. As Max's struggle intensified, Harold's pleas grew increasingly desperate. *I'm begging you. Stop!* But the thing in control of him either didn't hear or didn't care.

When Max's fist hammered across his nose and jaw, Harold saw his own blood splatter before him. Assuming it hurt the seeker, the damage came as a relief. His fingers loosened around Max's neck. He rolled backwards and kicked Harold aside. The world turned up and over until Harold found himself staring at the ceiling. A cloud of frost blanketed him, and then pain—sharp, warm, and welcome—flooded his senses.

Cradling his nose, which he assumed was broken, Harold wiped the blood from his face. The simple act felt glorious. Even better, the freezing air bit into his skin, and he felt himself convulsing from the extreme temperature while red vapor spurted from his mouth.

Seeing the mist up close, he noted that it wasn't quite as gaseous as he'd originally believed. Tiny sparkles glittered throughout the substance, like stars shining through a distant nebula. Under any other circumstances, the sight would have been quite beautiful. As abruptly as the vapor escaped his lips, though, it quickly returned, filling his lungs with a taste akin to battery acid. As the mist filled him, his limbs went numb. Once again, Harold lost control.

As he watched, silent and impotent, his body struggled to find its footing. He stood there, his red eyes scanning his surroundings. Ahead, Casey and Max dragged Ruthie out of the frozen room. The Prime was right on their heels, smashing through a glass door and vanishing with them into an adjacent laboratory. The Well.

Harold shifted his focus toward the other poor souls, like himself. The six soldiers were in various poses of distress. Some were still on their feet, struggling to escape the Fridge, while others had fallen to the floor, wisps of red vapor billowing from their lungs. Freeing their consciousness, Harold hoped, though he doubted their freedom would last for long. They'd go into hypothermia and then die. He wished he could help, but he couldn't even help himself.

His body lumbered on unsure legs toward the shattered exit. Each step he took brought the seeker closer to warm air and, ultimately, to regaining its full strength over him.

Desperate, Harold tried regaining control before they escaped the frigid room. He concentrated on his hands first, as they were the only things he could see through his limited vision. The problem was, he'd never considered how to move his hands before. He'd simply done it. As if sensing his attempt, an inner voice rose up in the back of his mind.

Do not interfere, it rasped.

It seemed that Harold had finally gained the creature's attention, though how or why eluded him. Perhaps it had something to do with their weakened condition inside the lab.

The exit grew closer. Harold knew he had mere seconds in which to attempt communication. Once they escaped into the warmth of the hall and the connecting labs, he doubted the creature would worry too much about what he had to say. Harold wanted to scream and shout, to plead and beg for his release, but as a scientist, he knew he must approach the moment using logic rather than base emotions.

You are endangering your own future, Harold said, struggling to calm himself. His body hesitated less than ten feet from the shattered doorway, as if momentarily distracted from the cold. Then the creature's voice returned.

You are too primitive to comprehend the need for our actions.

I understand that you believe you must return Casey to the future, Harold replied, *and that by doing so, you may correct some sort of damage she's caused.*

She was meant to be our savior, but instead she became our destroyer, the creature said, a note of sadness in its voice that caught Harold off guard. ***She must be returned.***

Before Harold could offer a reply, gunshots rang out. The noise reverberated in Harold's eardrums, interrupting their brief conversation. Without further hesitation, the seeker propelled them out of the icy, fog-drenched chamber.

Warmed by the outer hallway, Harold felt his consciousness shrink in the dark like a child locked in a vast closet while the being in control regained its full strength. A second round of gunshots shattered a pane of glass to Harold's left before they raced forward into the line of fire. As he entered the cement-lined laboratory, Harold found himself staring down the barrel of a rifle.

A second later, Casey pulled the trigger.

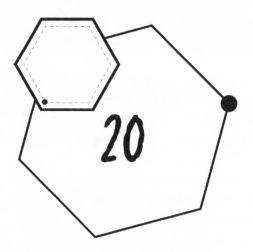

20

In the fall of 1927, two days after his mother's soul went to heaven, Thomas McKellen signed up to go to hell. Basic training had been a grueling affair, made even worse because of all that was expected from his father's son. This was before WWII, and McKellen figured if he could just get through training in one piece, his career afterwards would be relatively smooth sailing. Flash forward a few years, and a world-class jackass named Adolf Hitler popped up and turned that hope to shit. Still, McKellen always knew he was born to be a soldier, just like his old man. His dad had fought in the Great War. McKellen, it seemed, was going in for the sequel. Before heading off to Europe, his father offered two pieces of advice: "Always bring an extra pair of socks; dry feet will save your life" and "Don't pull the trigger until you're damn sure it's your enemy in your sights."

Colonel McKellen was reminded of the latter rule as he was led at gunpoint by his own men to a jeep, placed directly behind Prewitt's seat. McKellen couldn't help wondering who his dad would consider the real enemy at that moment. After all, the little gray guys weren't the ones betraying their own kind.

Prewitt turned, smiling with a smugness that McKellen desperately wanted to knock off his face. *Yeah, Pop would be just fine with me shooting this fucking weasel of a man. Just fine, indeed.* That notion kept him warm inside as they drove across the tarmac, heading toward the rising sun and the smoke-drenched hillside.

The last vestiges of fire from the explosion had died out by the time the group of trucks and jeeps returned, encircling the hangar's shattered entrance. The tanks appeared empty and abandoned, with no immediate attack or obstructions opposing their approach.

Where'd everyone go? McKellen wondered, his thoughts turning over and over. Surely, the seekers would have maintained some sort of protective perimeter.

Prewitt, on the other hand, didn't seem surprised in the least. If anything, the little shit appeared more distressed by the swirling dust dancing around his finely pressed suit than the quickly approaching giant black gash in the earth.

The hole with monsters waiting inside, McKellen's imagination whispered.

As the jeep pulled to a stop, McKellen discovered the answer to one question at least: the fate of the perimeter guards. Bodies, at least ten by his count, lay strewn across the dirt. Some hung off the sides of tanks, and more lingered beside the crash site and the hangar's entrance.

Following Prewitt and Sgt. Davis out of the jeep, Mc-
Kellen rushed to the closest body, dangling off a Sher-
man tank. The man's face was missing, blood and bone
ripped asunder, unlike the wound from any gunshot or
explosive he'd ever seen.

McKellen recognized the name badge on the body's
left breast. He turned to Davis. "This one's Mitchell. You
were friends, weren't you?"

Davis avoided his gaze.

Blood rushing to his head, McKellen rushed over,
grabbed Davis by the neck, and shoved him toward
the tangle of flesh, blood, and bone that had once been
Mitchell's face.

"Look at him," McKellen demanded. "If you hadn't
been performing in an episode of Mutiny on the Bounty,
we might have saved him!"

Tears formed in Davis's eyes, and his shoulders
slumped, but he remained silent, either too afraid or too
ashamed to reply. Probably both. McKellen tossed the
pathetic man to the ground in a swirl of dust.

Behind him, soldiers raised their weapons and
pointed them at McKellen's back, but he ignored them.
If they were going to kill him, they'd have done it by now.
No, he decided, Prewitt still needed him for something.

The beady-eyed little man sauntered forward, brushing dirt from his pant leg. As he passed various prone
figures strewn about, each one missing its face, Prewitt
offered a sad sigh. McKellen figured it was only for show,
and not a particularly convincing show at that.

"The tragedy surrounding us, Colonel," Prewitt said,
"is not lost on anyone."

"A tragedy that could have been prevented."

"By whom?" Prewitt gazed at the crashed plane. "You rushed back to the base to order reinforcements, did you not?" When McKellen didn't answer, Prewitt continued. "You know the protocols as well as I do. The Army would have cleansed this entire area." He paused as if for dramatic impact. "Your solution would have brought about everyone's death, yours included, while mine cut those losses in half." He looked at the soldiers with their weapons still pointed at McKellen. "These men will see tomorrow, no thanks to you."

McKellen wasn't moved by his words. Pacing toward the bodies, he studied the similar facial wounds that each of them had suffered. "What caused this? The seekers?"

"I'm afraid not," Prewitt admitted, a hint of nervousness permeating his words.

Stunned, McKellen's back straightened, and his head swam. "*Your* team did this?"

"Just like you, we've dabbled in our own form of research and development," Prewitt admitted, folding his arms defensively across his chest, "but where you failed to find a way to destroy the 'seekers,' as you call them, we succeeded."

"How?"

"Everyone and everything is food for something else," Prewitt said, leading them into the black, smoke-filled hangar. "Even the seekers."

"Dear God, man," McKellen said as he stepped over more bodies, "what have you done?"

"I've ensured our victory," Prewitt replied, turning to face him, "by finding a stronger predator."

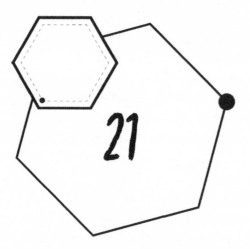

21

Fear turned to madness.

A twisted mishmash of flailing limbs crumpled to the floor as Max slammed into the Prime to save his wife. Stunned by the sudden turn of events, it took Casey several heartbeats to process the whirlwind around her. Behind her the soldiers continued their shuffling approach, slowed by the frigid cold. In front, Harold paused, his glowing red eyes blinking rapidly, seemingly as stunned by Max's attack as she had been. Shaking off her hesitation, Casey bolted forward, yanking Ruthie and Max to their feet before the Prime or Harold could renew their attack. Racing for the door, Casey pulled the couple behind her. When she finally flung the door open, the outer hall's warmth encircled her in a comforting embrace. Still, she didn't need to look over her shoulder to know that they were far from safe.

Slamming the Fridge door behind them, she spun toward the Well's entrance, twisting the doorknob. Shoving Ruthie inside, Max followed on unsteady legs. Casey's hands shook with adrenaline as she closed the door and maneuvered around various cement blocks to the waiting gravity guns.

Ruthie slumped down beside her, cradling her stomach. Max ran to her side. "You alright?"

Ruthie nodded, mute with fear as she looked up at him with wide, teary eyes. Before Max could press further, a crash of broken glass announced the Prime's entrance.

Casey grabbed her rifle. As she flicked open the optical sight, an infrared heat signature revealed the approaching creature behind two hanging slabs of granite. Her bullets, she knew, could only maneuver around one obstacle per shot. She needed the thing to get closer. Her palms sweaty on the heavy weapon, she placed the weight of the rifle against her shoulder, careful not to drop it through her slick fingers. The thing passed the first block, its heat signature now glowing orange and red.

Casey fired.

Her hands had remained steady enough, but the recoil was more than she'd expected. The bullet flew about, ping-ponging around the first block, then slammed into an adjacent wall. She'd missed. Behind the cement block, the Prime's pounding footsteps grew louder, closer. Casey fumbled for another bullet.

A second shot rang out, this time from Max's gun. The projectile zipped around the cement block, and a scream like that of a gutted animal broke the silence.

He'd hit his target. Without excitement or exclamation, Max reloaded. Casey did the same. Slapping her next round into the chamber, she shoved the bolt forward and down, locking it into place. Bringing the sight up to her eye, she saw the orange-and-red outline of the creature reeling behind the cement wall, injured but still moving. Then another figure entered the laboratory to her left. Harold. Swinging her weapon around, she leveled it at him.

Her finger twitching on the trigger, she saw his placid face and blazing eyes. He paused in the doorway as if expecting the shot, perhaps even welcoming it. Casey knew what she had to do. She had no choice, she told herself. Still, acid burned the back of her throat as she aimed dead center at Harold's chest and pulled the trigger.

If there was any fear or recognition behind Harold's red eyes, it didn't show. He just stood there, hovering at the lab's entrance with a blank stare.

The bullet spun in midair, attracted to the magnetic blocks. Careening to the right, the projectile zipped wide of Harold before slamming into a hanging cement block a few feet away.

Casey's breath caught in her throat. Shoving another bullet into her rifle, she spun, trying to get a bead on the Prime. Peering through the scope, she found the clone still approaching, highlighted in swirling colors behind an obstacle. Casey fired. The bullet spun around the cement, twisting in midair, and struck with a thick, meaty *thunk* somewhere in his chest area. Bullseye. This time she'd hit her target. But the thing kept coming.

Infuriated by the cement obstacle, it shoved the dangling obstruction aside. The cement block rocked, dangling from steel chains, before crashing down and spewing chunks of stone.

Casey and Max scrambled aside. Guns and bullets clattered across the floor as a dark figure loomed above them. Ruthie screamed over Casey's shoulder, a deafening cry that punctuated the thing's closeness.

Her weapon empty, Casey spun it around and stood, prepared to batter the Prime with the rifle like a club. As the monster came into fractured view, she noted the oil-like blood pouring from its shoulder and stomach, injuries that should have taken the cloned body down, but it still approached. As it raised its taloned fingers, she wondered if perhaps all the experiments and variant infections she'd pumped into its body really had made it stronger. Standing her ground, she knew there was no escape. At least not for her.

"Max, get Ruthie out of here!" she yelled over her shoulder.

The Prime lunged, and Casey swung.

The metal-wrapped rifle shattered over its head, knocking it back. Broken, the weapon dangled limply from Casey's hand. Tossing it away, she ran over to the control switches, flicking all three levers. Above, the sound of gears turning announced the cement blocks repositioning across the room. However, Casey didn't lower the levers, instead keeping them up so that the obstacles continued moving around the room, coming down with a loud chunk, then repositioning and moving to the next spot. Dozens of cement blocks moved about, clunking loudly up and down, creating an ever-changing maze. Timing her run to avoid them, Casey bolted past the first columns, maneuvering through the thick, heavy blocks as they rose and fell around her. Up ahead,

Ruthie and Max blinked in and out of view, seemingly headed toward the elevator. Fearing what else might lie that way, Casey wanted to shout a warning for them to turn back and head for the staircase, but her voice escaped her as she struggled to catch her breath while ducking and dodging through the cement maze.

An explosion of shattering glass announced the seekers' arrival. The soldiers had found them. Though concealed by wedges of shadow and thick concrete on either side, Casey doubted that Max and Ruthie would make it to the elevator in time. Even if they did, what horrors might be waiting above?

The rasping, wheezing breath and thundering footsteps behind told of the Prime's closeness. *Nowhere left to run,* she thought as her chest blazed, and her legs shook.

As Casey raced around the corner, Ruthie's scream announced the worst: the seekers had cut off their escape. Casey was just in time to see a swarm of red-eyed soldiers swarm Max. He went down under a cascade of thrashing figures.

Casey snatched Ruthie by the shoulders, shoving her past the chaos. Doubtful that the top level would be any safer than down there, Casey still felt like she had no choice. There was nowhere left to go but up.

Ruthie cried out in fear, struggling against Casey's grip to go back and save Max, but Casey held strong, dragging Ruthie along. The closed elevator was less than twenty feet away. Cursing herself for having brought these horrors down on them in the first place, Casey doubted there would be any escape for her, but perhaps there might be for Ruthie and her unborn child.

Before they were even within reach of the call button, the elevator descended into view. Half hoping it was a sign from God to save Ruthie, and half dreading that more red-eyed demons were waiting inside, Casey continued her approach. This was it, one way or another. Life or death.

When the elevator's grated door opened, Casey's heart stopped. Flailing black tentacles burst forth, and spidery legs click-clacked into view. In the center, pincers spasmed open and shut, spewing crimson drool from a sinkhole mouth as the stuff of nightmares leapt out of the elevator.

For the first time throughout the ordeal, Casey screamed.

Harold watched as his body, cut and bleeding, shambled through the twisted maze of concrete blocks. The Prime had already raced ahead; even injured it was much faster than him. Noting his body's slow pace, Harold wondered how severe his wounds were. If the cuts in his wrist had severed an artery, he was done for no matter how long the seeker was able to drag out the inevitable. On the other hand, he was glad that his slow pace meant he was no longer as much of a danger to Casey. Moments earlier, he'd seen her line up a shot to finish him off. She'd fired, seemingly dead center, but missed. The bullet had exploded inches away from him. Still, she hadn't even hesitated. Only the gravity well had saved him. The glazed, watery look in her eyes right before she fired was seared into his memory. Pragmatically, of course, he understood. Either way, though, his sudden fear of death overrode any hypothetical pragmatism. Casey had tried to kill him, plain and simple. Watching his body thunder through the twisting, moving maze, he wondered what would happen the next time he faced her. Who should he cheer for? Himself or the woman he'd grown to care for, desire, perhaps even love?

A scream up ahead tore him from his internal conflict. Turning his attention outward, he struggled to find the source of the scream. It hadn't been Ruthie this time; it was Casey, and the tone of her cry was bloodcurdling. Had the Prime caught up to her already?

Focusing on the darkness ahead, his body continued between moving columns and blinking darkness. A commotion in the distance finally gave him the answer. It wasn't the Prime; it was something else. Something worse.

So distraught within his own predicament and the flurry of events around him, it took Harold a moment to piece together what he was seeing. First, there was the undulating darkness slithering above, covering the red klaxon lights. Then there was the dark shape pounding forward on a series of legs. He couldn't tell how many or what type, but there was nothing human about it. A swarm of tentacles jutted outward, knocking the Prime aside and wading into the cluster of figures that were covering Max. Harold's body stopped, and he felt the seeker inside him tremble with fear. No, he realized, it was more than fear. Recognition. The seeker knew what the moving shadow was, and it terrified him. Backing away, sliding behind the shifting cement blocks, a single word came to mind, thundering through Harold's skull: *Abomination!*

Without warning, the seeker spun Harold's body around and fled. As he raced back through the shifting room, Harold could hardly believe what he was witnessing. This seemingly invulnerable foe, which could possess a person's body and thoughts, was suddenly turning tail and running.

The seekers are afraid of something. A warmth spread through Harold like a growing fire. The harder and faster his bloody body ran, the more desperately Harold wanted to turn and catch another glimpse of the tentacled creature, to know what could possibly cause so much fear in a being that, until then, had shown none.

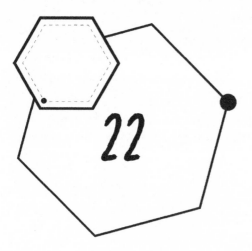

22

The black mass of undulating limbs and click-clacking spidery legs dove past Casey and Ruthie, seemingly unconcerned with them as it headed toward the swarm of seekers. Casey didn't stop to see what it was doing. Instead, she used the momentary respite to shove Ruthie inside the elevator. Hitting the button for the first floor, Casey remained outside as the door closed on her petrified friend. Ruthie continued sobbing and shouting for Max as the elevator began to ascend, vanishing from view.

Casey didn't know what was waiting above, but she assumed it had to be safer than down there. At least she hoped it was.

Screams erupted behind her. Hesitant to look over her shoulder, she heard men's voices turn to shrill cries. It wasn't until a sloppy crunch broke through the wails that Casey's eyes swiveled in their sockets, daring a peek. What she saw made her wish she hadn't looked.

The thing, whatever it was, stood approximately nine feet tall. Six tentacle-like appendages sprouted from its back, and another two thicker tentacles extended from its shoulders like twisted arms. Its head was domed, pointed toward its mouth, which had four pincers. From its belly to its pelvis, a series of thin, spidery legs propelled it forward with incredible speed. Despite everything she'd seen, this was the most "alien" creature she'd ever laid eyes on. And yet, its movements still reminded her of something terrestrial. A primate, perhaps, though with distinct arachnid and octopi characteristics. Worse than its appearance was what it was doing. Grabbing several soldiers at once, each of them flailing madly within the creature's various appendages, its pincers bore down on their faces, one at a time. Each attack took mere seconds, though all sense of time had abandoned Casey, along with her nerves. The men's screams died beneath the pincers, their gesticulating bodies going limp. Dropping each body to the floor, the creature moved on to the next. And the next.

Sliding one foot reluctantly in front of the other, Casey tried to find Max somewhere within the mass of discombobulated figures. Instead, her gaze fell on one of the fallen bodies. Its face was gone, a bloody stump of jagged bone and torn flesh in its place. Casey clamped her fingers over her mouth, attempting to stifle a scream, but it poured into her palm anyway. If the creature or the seekers heard her, they were beyond caring.

As another soldier's scream died beneath the thing's pincers, Casey decided that if she was going to find

Max, it was now or never. Still, her feet refused to move. Hunched down, her face against the floor, she gazed through the onslaught, past frantic limbs and flapping tentacles. Amidst the chaos, she spotted a sliver of white: Max's lab coat.

Sucking in hot air through clenched teeth, Casey forced her legs forward, ducking beneath the twisting tentacles. One of them slapped her back, wet and oily. "Sickly" was the word that came to her mind. Shivering at its touch, she ducked lower, continuing toward the spot of white sprawled several feet away. Sliding down, she knelt over Max's body, struggling to turn him over. His dead weight protested as she tried to get a grip under his chest. With an exhausted grunt, Casey flopped him onto his back. Her first thought was relief, as she couldn't see any blood or serious wounds.

"Max," she whispered. "Max!"

His lips parted, and a puff of red mist escaped. Casey flung herself backwards, away from the curling vapor. Max's eyes opened, blazing red. His meaty hands reached out, snatching her shirt and drawing her toward his waiting mouth and its swirling, putrid fog.

"N-no," Casey stammered, elbowing his jaw. She followed up with a right hook that caused him to loosen his grip.

Scrambling to her feet, she tried to run, only to be stopped by the enormous, undulating black shape looming behind her. Wetness from its limbs dripped over her face, hair, and shoulders. Its domed skull tilted downwards, as if studying her. No, she decided, not studying, *smelling*. The thing leaned in, rubbing disgustingly against her neck, sniffing for traces of the red mist. Tentacles slid up her legs and spine, drawing her closer. Shivering, with tears welling in her eyes, she felt helpless within its embrace. Her mouth opened and closed, but no sound escaped. Pressed against her, the thing smelled like a mixture of oil and acid. The stink of it seared her nostrils. Holding her breath, Casey stood, trembling within its clutches as it decided her fate. No light pierced its slithering form. For a long, drawn-out moment, nothing existed beyond the acidic smells and undulating limbs.

Then it released her.

Bolting behind Casey, the abhorrent thing grabbed Max. This time she couldn't bear to look. Eyes clamped shut, Casey remained planted in place, quivering as she heard Max's dying screams inches from her ears.

When the noise finally died, Casey focused on her jagged breath, trying to stop her body from trembling and to calm her pounding heart. She thought her chest might explode from the violence of its thumping. The thing click-clacked behind her, searching for more red mist to consume. Apparently not finding any, Casey couldn't help but wonder what had happened to the Prime and Harold. Had the thing eaten them as well?

Counting to twenty, she let out a slow, controlled breath and then opened her eyes. The black thing was lurking beside her, half hidden in chunks of shadow and crimson light. Casey slid her left foot backwards, then her right. When the beast didn't respond, she took two more steps. Turning slowly, she glanced around in the darkness, noting that the cement blocks were no longer moving. Someone had turned the obstacle course off. Then she heard breathing coming from the laboratory's shadow. Figures approached, covered in black from head to toe, armed men wearing face masks. The lead figure had a flamethrower strapped to his back, its pilot flame dancing from left to right as they approached. Beside it, two more flames glowed.

Casey blew out a long, relieved sigh. It seemed the cavalry had finally arrived. As she stepped toward them, she heard the creature's click-clacking legs thunder behind her, racing toward the soldier's flames.

"Get down!" one of the men shouted.

Casey hit the floor as a burst of red-and-orange fire engulfed the thing behind her. Wailing in agony, the creature's pained cry sounded distinctly human, which made it even more horrendous. Continuing forward, the burning thing waded past Casey, toward the soldiers. Two more streams of fire from its left and right consumed it in a raging blaze. As Casey shielded her eyes, a pungent odor of burning flesh mixed with an earthy oil reached her nose. Swallowing, she forced herself not to retch.

Finally, with a heavy flop, the tentacled thing collapsed in a heap of smoldering black tentacles and spidery legs. The weight of it caused the tiled floor to ripple beneath Casey, punctuating the size of the dead thing as it fell beneath a curtain of billowing smoke. Staggering to her knees, she pushed herself away, backing into a corner. Wiping tears from her eyes, she tried to put some distance between herself and the lingering stench and smoke.

Their flamethrowers extinguished, the soldiers approached.

"It's alright, Doctor Stevens," the masked leader said. "We're here to get you out."

The tone and texture of his voice seemed familiar, though she couldn't place it through his gas mask.

Without her abilities to sense emotions and motivations, Casey had to take his words on faith. She had possessed her abilities for a decade, and the emptiness she felt without them was akin to blindness. Grabbing his outstretched gloved hand, Casey pulled herself up.

As she scanned the pile of bodies strewn about, she didn't need to ask the soldiers if it was over. She knew it wasn't. Turning to the leader, her throat tightened as she struggled to speak. "There's two missing," she whispered. "A clone, called the Prime, and a researcher, Harold Stone."

"Don't worry," the leader said, kicking the dead beast, "the others will get them."

"Others?" she repeated, her eyes falling on the monster. "You mean, there are more of these things?"

"It's OK, Doc," the leader said with a shrug. "They're on our side."

His words didn't bring her any relief. As she stared down at the smoldering black beast, her stomach lurched to her chest.

Nightmares fighting nightmares, and me in the middle.

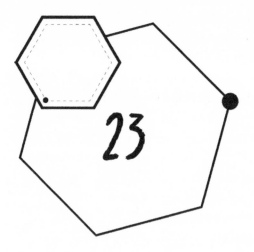

23

Barreling through the cloud-frosted fridge, Harold felt the first tingles of cold and pain crawl up his legs and arms, like a million invisible needles stabbing him all at once. The agony was momentarily glorious, but alas, it was all too brief. Propelled through an emergency door, he slammed it open with bloody hands and then stepped into a warm staircase. With the frigid cold gone, his bodily sensations left as quickly as they'd appeared. Shuffling down steps, his body staggered, his breathing labored. He doubted he would survive much longer without medical attention. Once done with him, Harold assumed the seeker would shed him like one might toss out soiled clothing, which led to another question: why keep him at all? Surely, the seeker could escape much faster in its gaseous form. Although his studies had proven that they couldn't remain in their gaseous form over prolonged periods without solidifying, Harold surmised it could quite easily find a new, healthier host with which to make its escape. Was there some reason why the seeker was keeping him alive?

Another missed step heading down the staircase sent him reeling. The seeker fumbled to maintain his balance. There were a lot of stairs, and Harold's blood loss made the traversal slow and clumsy. Watching through eyes that no longer seemed to belong to him, Harold worried about how hard the invasive creature was pushing his failing form. *Not much longer before I take one tumble too many, and the lights go out. Forever.*

From several flights above, an abstract noise, wet and meaty, caused the seeker to hesitate and turn. Its pace quickening, it pushed forward, descending the steps two at a time on shaky legs. The noise grew louder, closer. A faint hissing sound echoed through the narrow staircase. As their haphazard descent continued, the hissing persisted. It wasn't until they reached the bottom door that Harold glimpsed the black shadow above.

The thing lunged just as the seeker gripped the doorknob, yanking it open. Falling backward into the lower labs, the seeker scrambled to pull the door closed. Tentacles pushed through the opening, flailing about. As one of them slithered over his arm, Harold sensed the seeker's horror throbbing inside his mind like a chugging, sputtering engine. With a yank, the seeker slammed the heavy door shut, slicing one of the tentacles in half. It flopped around on the floor.

Harold's view changed as they struggled down the hall, passing Casey's office and laboratories on either side. The creature's incessant pounding on the heavy door behind them quickened the seeker's pace, pushing Harold's injured body to its final limits. Heading along the corridor, he raced toward the hangar.

We're headed for the ship, he realized. *But then what?* Even if the ship was somehow able to repair itself enough to fly, how could it take off when buried underground?

Unfortunately, those questions were muted as quickly as they came. Noting his slowing pace, sliding against the glass walls for support, he assumed the pause was due to blood loss. Then his ears picked up what the seeker must have already sensed: hissing sounds from all around. He didn't have to wait long to discover their source. Shadows descended in front of them, crawling along the walls like insects. Tentacles flapped, cutting off their escape. There was nowhere left to run.

Monsters in front, monsters behind, and monsters within, Harold thought. As the shapes approached, he knew his body was too slow and weak to escape. This was it.

The oily creatures dropped, their appendages coiling around him as a mouth of sharp pincers and needle-thin teeth lurched into view. Harold assumed this would be the last thing he ever saw.

At least there won't be any pain.

A shriek assaulted his eardrums, only it wasn't his own scream he heard. The grotesque thing was wrenched backwards, flopping to the side, revealing a red-and-black figure that was fighting two of the monsters at once.

The Prime.

In all the confusion upstairs, Harold had forgotten about the mutated clone, having assumed it must have met its end already. Yet, if anything, the clone seemed stronger and angrier than he'd ever seen it. While the seeker within Harold's body was clearly terrified of these creatures, the Prime wanted to tear them to shreds with its taloned hands. However, wanting to do something and being able to accomplish it were two separate things. After a momentary surprise, the Prime soon lost its ground, knocked back in a swirl of flagellating tentacles.

Harold decided that instead of being prevented, his death had simply been paused.

His eyes fluttered shut. Still conscious, he saw glimpses of his surroundings in fractured crimson light as his body tumbled to the floor. The seeker had used him up. Splashes of blood on his wrists revealed how bad the damage was.

As the seeker rolled him onto his back, he heard more than he saw. The creatures howled. Wet, slimy limbs fell beside him. He sensed more movement beyond, though he could barely make out anything within the blinking dark. His head swimming, Harold knew his death was finally at hand.

Unencumbered by pain or any other physical sensations, his thoughts drifted away from himself and toward Casey. Had she escaped? Was she still alive?

Facing his own end, Harold found it oddly comforting to consider someone else's fate. Consumed in heavy rumination, it took him a moment to notice the blurred red-and-black hands reaching down and grasping his body. As the clone tossed Harold's body over its shoulder and darted down the hall, the world went topsy-turvy. Peering at the floor, Harold's eyes followed a trail of blood. Within the pool, a familiar object glimmered. His mother's cross, drenched in crimson.

A moment later his vision dimmed, and light blinked out of existence.

Pain shot through Harold's body like a blazing fire, waking him with a start. At last, sensation had returned. His eyes fluttering, he used his arms to block out the blinding light above. His movement wasn't a conscious decision; it was a reflex, but it was *his* reflex. Noting the control of his hands, he sat up, bending his legs. He was so overwhelmed with emotion to be both alive *and* in control of his body once again that it took a moment before Harold stopped to survey his surroundings. When he did, much of his joy left him.

He was sitting on a metallic table in a large domed room with gray walls. Harold tried to focus on how he'd gotten there, but his mind drew a blank. One moment he'd been dying on the floor in the labs, and the next he was wholly revitalized and sitting in a room so unlike anything else he'd ever seen that his location left little doubt.

I'm inside the ship, his mind whispered.

The room shuddered in silent reply, urging him to action. Leaping off the table, he was relieved to discover strong, sturdy legs beneath him. Glancing at his wrists, he saw that the deep cuts were also gone, with only minute scars in their place. Harold sucked in a long, slow breath as he realized how strong he felt. He was alive. Someone or something had saved him.

The room lurched again. Bracing himself against the table, Harold spun, searching for an exit, but the curved walls around him held no doors. It seemed that he had simply traded one prison for another. Still, he wasn't dead. Those tentacled creatures hadn't eaten his face. The seekers had saved him.

They must need me for some reason. The realization offered him no comfort. Stifling a shiver, Harold dreaded what was to come.

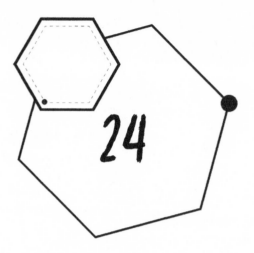

24

Moving from the warm morning sunlight into cool shadows, McKellen trudged angrily behind Prewitt. Thankfully, no more faceless corpses obstructed their path. Soldiers flanked them on either side. Sgt. Davis swept the darkness with his rifle as if expecting a bogeyman to jump out at any moment. McKellen half hoped one did. If ever there was a soldier who deserved to have his face eaten off into a bloody pulp, Davis topped the list. As smarmy and conceited as Prewitt was, he was still a government bureaucrat, following someone else's orders. To McKellen's knowledge, Prewitt hadn't betrayed anyone. The same couldn't be said for Davis and his men.

McKellen's thoughts returned to his dad's advice: *Don't pull the trigger until you're damn sure it's your enemy in your sights.* Glaring at Davis, McKellen's certainty wavered slightly. After all, Prewitt was pulling all the strings, and for the moment at least, that included Mc-Kellen's as well. He assumed the little weasel was merely a figurehead for some larger group hidden within the government, which only made matters worse. Questions about who they were and, more importantly, who they answered to, bounced around his skull. The very idea that a man in McKellen's position could be brought low by someone like Prewitt ate at his gut something fierce.

There it was, McKellen realized. His worst enemy right then wasn't Davis or Prewitt; it was his own wounded pride. Careful not to let stubbornness be his undoing, McKellen unclenched his teeth, along with his fists. Once again heeding his father's words, he decided to wait and see who his real enemy was before acting. There'd be time enough to deal with this insurrection later. For the moment his focus needed to remain on whatever dangers lay ahead. That meant he needed to be calm and clear headed. He chuckled inwardly. Easier said than done.

As they made their way into the hangar, McKellen concluded that the surrounding shadows didn't seem to contain any monsters. Upon observing Prewitt's casual stride, however, McKellen silently corrected himself. No *inhuman* monsters at least.

With the power out, the emergency backup generator had kicked in, turning the tunnel blood red. The color reminded McKellen of those poor men lying outside in the dirt. *Like discarded meat.* He released a long, steady breath, trying to slow his heart rate to something below its current thundering kill-or-be-killed mode.

Up ahead, clanging metal yanked his attention toward the elevator. Beside him, servicemen snapped their weapons to the ready position while the elevator slowly rose into view, stopping with a lurch. As the men took up positions around the elevator, a figure could be seen moving inside. Prewitt, however, slipped his hands in his pockets and shrugged, seemingly unconcerned. Again, McKellen wondered what the hell was going on and how much of it was that little weasel's fault. Before the day was over, McKellen was determined to get his answer— and, God willing, a little revenge to go along with it.

Their rifles raised, the soldiers around him tensed as the elevator door slid open. However, no face-eating monster or red-eyed demon was waiting inside. Instead, it was a scientist from the Out of Town labs. Ruth something or other. Even after the door opened, she remained cowering in the corner, her body trembling, her hands cupped over her round stomach.

The soldiers advanced toward the trembling woman. Worried that things were about to go sideways fast, McKellen bolted forward, pushing Davis aside as he entered the elevator. Though he found it impossible to offer a smile, McKellen managed to keep his voice soft. "It's alright, Doctor."

He offered her his hand, which she studied before taking. As he pulled her up, he felt her fingers tremble in his. Clutching her tightly, McKellen met her wide-eyed gaze. He wanted to ask her what was happening in the lower levels, but one look at her pale expression told him he'd get little information from her.

"Come on out," he said as soothingly as he could. "You're safe now."

As Ruthie stepped out of the elevator, her legs nearly gave out, and she leaned all her weight against McKellen. The soldiers' rifles remained leveled at them both.

McKellen sucked in his gut and stuck out his chest like a shield in front of her. "Our job is to *protect* civilians," he snapped, "not terrify them." He glared at the men, his eyes stopping on Davis. "Or have you abandoned that duty as well?"

Davis kept his weapon raised. "She could be contaminated, sir."

Veins popping along his neck, McKellen shoved Davis's rifle aside and stood nose to nose with him. "Look at her, Sergeant." When Davis hesitated, McKellen's voice rose several decibels, and his fists trembled. "Look! White eyes, *not* red!"

Despite McKellen's words, neither Davis nor his men backed down.

The world has gone mad, McKellen thought.

It was Prewitt, of all people, who finally broke the tension. His long fingers spread like a spider's legs around Davis's shoulder. "Lower your weapons," he said. "This poor woman is obviously not infected."

McKellen released a pent-up breath in the form of a low growl as the soldiers finally lowered their rifles. Yet, Prewitt's interference didn't relieve any of the tightness in McKellen's chest. If anything, the little shit's involvement only heightened his concern.

Prewitt took Ruthie's hand in his, guiding her away from the elevator and into the red light. "Can you tell me your name, Miss?"

"Ruth . . . Ruthie Burke," she said, her voice just above a whisper. "My husband, Max, is still down there." Her eyes grew wider, her lips quivering. "He . . . He's . . . please, you have to help him!"

"Of course we will," Prewitt assured her, his voice as

oily as his demeanor. "Is Doctor Stevens with him, by any chance?" When Ruthie nodded, Prewitt smiled.

McKellen felt his skin flush. All those monsters on the loose, and yet this tiny man in a suit concerned him most of all. McKellen knew why Prewitt wanted Casey, or at least he knew the reasons he'd been given, but something told him that the last thing he should be doing was helping Prewitt find her. As bad as communism was, at least it didn't eat people's faces or break the chain of command. What Prewitt said next set off even more alarm bells.

"Can you take us to them?" Prewitt asked as he offered Ruthie a handkerchief to wipe her eyes.

As if Ruthie had heard the same alarm as McKellen, she immediately withdrew her hand. Stepping away from Prewitt, she shook her head. "No! No way. I can't."

"Think of your husband, dear," Prewitt said, hovering in close proximity to her.

McKellen had heard enough. He shouldered his way between them and turned to face Ruthie. "What floor are they on?"

"Sublevel ten," she replied. "The Fridge."

"R and D. I know where it is," he said, spinning toward Prewitt. "We don't need her."

Prewitt hesitated as if unable to think of a reason to keep Ruthie there.

"I'll have one of my men take her back to base, sir," Davis offered.

McKellen could tell by Prewitt's beady, narrow eyes that he didn't like the idea of anyone leaving the hangar without his supervision. Seemingly unable to come up with a reason for Ruthie to remain, however, he relented with a sharp nod. "Do that, Sergeant," he said, his voice having lost all semblance of kindness. He pushed past the soldiers, stepping into the elevator. "Let's get on with it."

McKellen gestured for Ruthie to follow one of the men out as he went with Davis onto the lift. As she did, Ruthie turned and mouthed a silent thank-you.

The elevator door clanged shut, and Prewitt hit the button for sublevel two.

"The Fridge is on sublevel ten," McKellen said.

"My team is already down there," Prewitt said. "We'll meet them on sublevel two." Still feeling chafed from having lost a potential witness, Prewitt didn't say another word. McKellen smiled. It was a small victory but a victory nonetheless.

In the distance he watched Ruthie stumble into the sunshine before the elevator descended, blocking his view. As darkness swallowed them, a chill ran up his spine.

McKellen wondered if he'd ever see sunlight again.

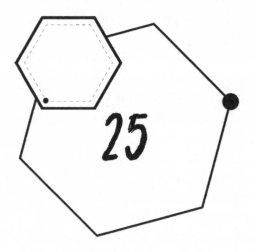

25

From the constant stench of moldy earth to the flickering red lights punctuating the darkness, the narrow stairwell seemed to be closing in around Casey. *Like a tomb,* her mind whispered. Climbing from sublevel ten to the top was not a simple matter of going up ten flights of stairs. The hillside's rocky walls, which had originally been carved out for diamond mining, formed huge gaps between each floor. Even traversing from one level to the next proved to be an exhausting distance. And they were going far more than a simple level or two. Following the armed men up the narrow, winding staircase, Casey struggled to keep her ragged breathing under control. Not wanting to show weakness, she pushed through the pain to keep pace with the squad leader. Thankfully, he didn't seem to be in much better shape than she was. The higher they climbed, the more she believed the soldiers could be going faster, but they were slowing down for him—and, she assumed, for her.

Still, the nagging suspicion that she'd recognized the leader's voice through his mask remained at the top of her mind. Casey wanted to ask him something, anything to hear his voice again in hopes of matching it to a face, but just breathing was difficult enough, and casual conversation seemed a faint hope at that point. *Best to keep moving,* she told herself.

A nightmarish hiss accompanied by the sound of something wet slithering in the dark pit below punctuated her decision. *One foot in front of the other,* she thought. *Slow and steady wins the race.*

Or they get eaten alive, her mind spat back.

By the time the team stopped, Casey's back and scalp were blanketed in sweat. Her drooping wet hair covered her eyes, obscuring her vision in a blonde blur. Blinking past her bangs, she noted a faded white label on the door: "Sublevel 2."

"Through here," the leader said.

"We need to go up another floor," Casey replied, panting.

"We used the back door to get in," the leader snapped, "and that's how we're getting out."

Her nose crinkled at that. There wasn't any back door that she was aware of. Lagging behind, she followed them into the sublevel's cavernous storehouse. Boxes piled over ten feet high on either side created a narrow trail for them to follow. When they came around the corner, Casey finally understood what he had meant by a back door. Not a door, a train.

Stretching like a black serpent along the tracks, the long cargo train vanished into an old tunnel. Not having used the tracks since they first brought the ship there in 1954, she'd forgotten all about it. Steam poured from beneath the train while an unseen engine chugged and coughed in the distance. How long had it been down there without her knowing it? Had McKellen expected something to go wrong and kept it at the ready?

The leader broke away from the squad, approaching several other darkly clad armed men. They were doing something high up on some scaffolding. Curious, she trailed the leader, noticing something blinking along the wall. A series of wires crisscrossed from one blinking box to another. The men climbed down and handed a small object to the leader.

"All set, sir," the first man said. Eyeing Casey, he stepped closer and continued in a whisper. "But we've got another problem." Gazing past rows of crates, he pointed toward an enormous black hole in the floor: the hangar's lift. Though it hadn't been used in years, Casey could tell by the way they shuffled their feet and dropped their masked eyes to the floor that it made the men nervous. Abruptly, the faint sound of gears turning gave her the answer.

"Jesus," Casey exclaimed, "someone's activated the platform."

"Yeah, that ship of yours is coming up," the leader said, far more relaxed than she would have expected. "Don't worry; we planned ahead." He showed her the little box in his hand. It had a red button with green lights blinking above it.

Casey paled. A remote detonator. Her eyes flew back to the ceiling as she realized what the boxes with intersecting wires were: explosives. Her mouth became a desert as she tried to push the words out. "You . . . you can't be serious."

"The experiments are loose in the lab, doctor," he snapped, "what else do you expect us to do?"

She tried to snatch the remote away, but two soldiers grabbed her arms. "You can't!" She screamed. "McKellen would never allow this!"

"I didn't," a gruff, defeated voice said from the shadows. Turning, Casey found McKellen approaching from the elevator, flanked by soldiers in standard green uniforms. In front of them, a familiar face emerged, the little man who'd first interviewed her after the Roswell crash. Prewitt. He grinned at her. There was no warmth in his smile.

"Ah, the *waitress*," he said, his white teeth glistening in the shadows. "I see you've been keeping busy."

Ignoring him, she met McKellen's sullen expression, noting one of his own men, Sergeant Davis, pointing a rifle at his back. Bile rose in her stomach. "Colonel?"

Before McKellen could answer, Prewitt stepped in front of him. "He's no longer in charge." He eyed the empty hole where the lift would soon arrive. "How long will it take to resurface?"

"Fuck you, shorty," Casey said.

The masked leader slammed his rifle butt into her spine. Casey crumpled, seeing stars.

"I asked you a question," Prewitt said, leaning over her.

Her head swimming and her back throbbing, she choked on her words. McKellen pushed through the men to help her. "Fifteen, twenty minutes tops," he snapped.

"Bring her," Prewitt said to the black-clad leader. "The rest remain here."

"Wait," Davis protested. "What about me and my men?"

No one replied.

Up ahead, Casey struggled and thrashed as several masked soldiers pulled her toward the train. McKellen lunged forward, trying to follow, but the masked leader stopped him, shoving his rifle's muzzle into McKellen's chest.

"I-I don't understand," Davis stammered. "What's happening?"

"You're being betrayed, son," McKellen said. "How does it feel?"

As the gravity of the situation took hold, Davis and his men raised their weapons in unison, only to be cut down in a hail of gunfire.

The green-clad soldiers tumbled to the ground, their bodies riddled with bullets. Casey screamed, fighting desperately against the men holding her. Struggling to keep hold of her thrashing limbs, they hauled her onto the train.

In the distance, standing erect over his dead soldiers, McKellen didn't budge, as if daring Prewitt's men to shoot him.

While the door to the train car closed in front of her, Casey curled into a pretzel, wrapping the soldiers' arms around themselves until she broke free. Scrambling toward the closing door, she tried to squeeze through.

McKellen met her gaze, shaking his head for her to stop. A slight grin crossed his lips. After all they'd been through, Casey couldn't believe this was how it would end. Prewitt raised a handgun, leveling it at the colonel. It was a familiar weapon: McKellen's own 9mm. She'd seen him carry it on his hip from time to time like a badge of honor, a keepsake from the war. Now it would be the instrument of his doom.

A burst of fire erupted from the pistol before the sound of the gunshot reached Casey's ears. Time seemed to slow as McKellen wavered on his feet. For a moment it looked as if he hadn't been hit. Then he staggered and tilted out of view. Casey tried to scream, but her voice died in her throat. Trembling in the doorway, she didn't notice a soldier's fist crashing down behind her until it was too late. Her vision swam as she tumbled backward into the train car.

The door slammed shut, pitching her world into darkness.

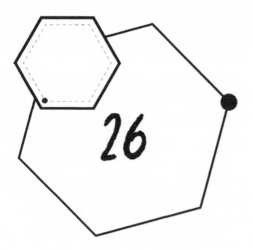

26

McKellen didn't feel the bullet enter his chest. He saw the muzzle flash just before the smoke exhaled from the pistol's muzzle, coiling around the barrel like a serpent. McKellen's body went numb, and his legs collapsed beneath him, sending him crashing into a crate. It shattered into splinters beneath his weight.

A shadow crossed over him as Prewitt leaned into view. His smile gone, he tilted his head, saddened. McKellen spit a wad of blood at him but missed.

"Your record will show that you died bravely, Colonel," Prewitt said. McKellen wanted to tell the little shit to go fuck himself, but his tongue had stopped working. "This was the only way this could end, you know," Prewitt continued. "Too many eyes on Area 51. Too many reports and documents. Too many officials keeping tabs." He huffed. "While Washington worries about future monsters and flying saucers, I'm going to save them from themselves."

Prewitt stepped away from McKellen and climbed onto the train, his figure reduced to a shadow as McKellen's vision dimmed. "Like I told you before, Colonel, contingencies."

The train snaked through the tunnel, vanishing in a billow of steam. Reverberations from the thundering movement rippled across the floor while McKellen lay there, bleeding.

So this is how it ends, he thought. *Done in by a bureaucrat.* Laughter turned to coughing. Blood dribbled over his lips and mustache. Twisting his head, he found Davis's dead eyes staring back, wide and full of surprise. *At least I'm not alone,* McKellen thought.

When the noise of the train melted away in the darkness, a new sound revealed itself. Chains turning, gears grinding. Behind him, the ship's platform was rising.

As he struggled to roll onto his belly, fire burst through his chest, igniting further with every inch of movement. After what seemed like an eternity of pain, he flopped over just in time to see the dark shape emerge into view.

The ship's once broken and fractured hull was now smooth. Its split ends and jagged lines were now curved and gleaming. It was so immense that McKellen could only see a sliver of the top of the thing, and yet he knew immediately that it could never be allowed to leave. Prewitt had been right about that much at least.

McKellen's eyes traced the edge of the emerging ship until it was obscured behind Davis's body—and his rifle. The ship was rising too fast, McKellen realized. Prewitt's detonators wouldn't ignite in time to stop it. It seemed that the little turd hadn't planned for every contingency after all. It was up to McKellen now.

Summoning the last of his strength, he ground his teeth, reaching for Davis's rifle. The ship's hull rose higher as the platform lifted toward the ceiling, heading for the top floor and the world beyond. His fingers slipped over the rifle's muzzle again and again, the weapon just out of reach. Preparing himself for the shot of pain that would follow, McKellen clenched his jaw, and his complexion reddened as he pushed himself forward. The pain was excruciating, but he only needed a few more inches. That's what he kept telling himself. With a final push, his shaking fingers grasped the rifle's muzzle. Pulling it to him, he wrenched himself onto his back and tried to find the explosives above through his blurry vision.

Blinking red and green lights shone in the dark.

Like Christmas, he thought, a chuckle drowning in blood. Then something moved in his peripheral vision. Red eyes in the dark. Shambling footsteps echoed before a familiar figure lurched into view. It was Cafferty. Noting the pulsing veins crisscrossing his face and arms, McKellen was reminded of the man's sacrifice.

Good soldier, McKellen thought. *We'll go together.*

Behind them the ship continued its ascent, rising on a massive platform as McKellen lined up his shot. Struggling to keep his aim steady, his arms shook, and his lungs filled with fluid. The scope's reticle danced around the distant red and green lights, refusing to stay still. From the corner of his eye, he clocked Cafferty's disfigured form lunging forward. His red eyes blazed, promising a fate worse than death. Still, McKellen kept calm. He knew what had to be done, and that sense of clarity gave him purpose. *Don't pull the trigger until you're damn sure it's your enemy in your sights,* his father had told him. The ship's icy black shadow crawled across his body as he sucked in one last breath. His weapon's sight found the explosives, steadying itself into focus. Cafferty's fingers grabbed McKellen's neck, clawing and tearing. Ignoring the assault, McKellen hummed a song in his mind: *The very model of a modern major-general . . .*

Then he pulled the trigger.

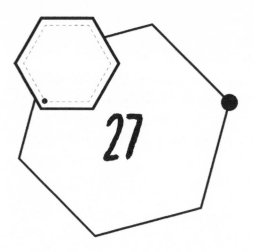

27

Harold paced around and around, taking in the seemingly alien room.

Not alien, he reminded himself, though nothing about the place appeared to make any logical sense that he could determine. Circular, with a single bench seemingly grown from its center, the room contained no instruments and no machines. As he kneeled to look below the bench for crease marks or rivets that might connect it to the floor, a thought popped into his mind: *Perhaps the ship reforms itself to suit its specific needs.*

Suddenly, the bench dripped through his fingers, mercurial, melting at his feet until nothing remained but a flat, silvery surface. The bench was gone. A sudden puff of air drew Harold's attention. His eyes grew wide, more expectant than surprised.

A giant curved door stood open, inviting, though Harold didn't approach it. After staring at it for a moment, awaiting any possible threat, the hairs on the back of his neck rose, and his flesh prickled. Feminine hands slithered over his chest, reaching around from behind, and hot, humid breath engulfed his left ear. His eyes swiveling in their sockets, Harold's body clenched as a woman curled into view. Tanned and naked, she had long black hair and crystal-blue eyes. He recognized her distinct features almost immediately. It was one of the slave girls from his sexual fantasies. Was this a dream? As she slithered around, her ample breasts pressed against his shirt. The heat of her body sent a shiver up his spine. Harold tried to speak, but the words wouldn't come. Her delicate fingers traced his jawline, slipping down his neck. Beneath those crystal-blue eyes, a wicked smile widened.

"So many desires," she whispered. "So many thoughts, wishes, and dreams."

Clearing his throat, Harold tried to gain control of himself and ignore his throbbing penis. Struggling to think past the pressure in his trousers, his voice flattened. "F-fear . . . p-passion," he stammered, "d-do you r-r-require strong emotional responses to f-facilitate c-communication?"

"That's it, Harold," she urged, her moist lips lingering inches from his. "Rationalize and compartmentalize the sensations, so you can study them objectively."

His back straightened. "This isn't real."

"Define 'real,'" she said, her bronzed fingers dancing over his chest. "Math, for instance. A made-up language in which you repeatedly rearrange numbers and equations until they provide an answer." Her tongue darted out, licking her lips. "But is it *really* an answer?"

"Y-you're trying to confuse me," he said, his body trembling.

"The universe isn't so easily quantified," she replied, grabbing his crotch. "And neither am *I*."

"You're the ship," he said. Shutting his eyes, Harold pushed her aside. As he backed away from her warmth, he felt an aching loss at the absence of her touch. Stumbling, he struggled to regain control of himself as he eyed the arched doorway, but the farther he backed away, the more of her body his eyes saw. Harold wanted to look away, to swivel his gaze back toward the exit, but he didn't. He had never seen a naked woman before. Not in the flesh, at least. The curves of her body were impossible to ignore, which, he assumed, was why the ship had chosen that form in the first place. The slave girl watched him, her head tilted to the side, which gave her the appearance of a cat studying a mouse.

"What do you want from me?" he shouted, panicked.

The room shook violently. Harold tumbled to the floor. Spittle dripped from his mouth as his knuckles whitened from the strain of trying to stay flat. Counting silently to himself, he hoped to ride the turbulence out. Instead, the violent upheaval only worsened. The room lurching end over end, he slid toward the open doorway. Grabbing hold of the doorframe, he clung to the wall while the ship tossed about. He glanced up at the round room swaying above him. It was empty. The woman had vanished.

His first thought was that he'd angered the ship, but the more the world shook, the more he doubted he'd had anything to do with the violence occurring around him.

The walls crinkled like an aluminum can squashed underfoot with Harold trapped inside.

Pushing himself off the wall, he ran down the quaking corridor. No longer the bending maze it had appeared to be the first time he entered the ship, this time the corridor was a long, straight shot, though to where he couldn't imagine. Struggling to remain upright, he ran, bouncing back and forth against the damp, pulsing walls.

Up ahead, a pale, sickly green light pulsed rhythmically, like a heartbeat, outlining a door. Glancing back over his shoulder, he realized the room he'd escaped had seemingly vanished, replaced by a hall that stretched into pitch blackness. Harold had nowhere else to go now but forward. A fleeting image of a lab rat locked in a maze came to mind. His feet scrambling along the slick floor, he continued toward the pulsing emerald glow. Coupled with the violent turbulence, Harold's stomach tossed about in his belly while vomit burned the back of his throat. As the doorway drew closer, the light grew brighter. With a final, desperate lunge, Harold stumbled through the door.

Whatever he might have expected to find on the other side bore no resemblance to what actually awaited him. Harold found himself staring at what appeared to be a swimming pool. Light reflecting off the water danced across his face as he braced himself against the door's archway. Sniffing the air, he didn't smell chlorine or any other familiar scent that one might equate with a man-made pool. Instead, the tank stank of mildew or aged cheese. Coupled with the violent quakes, the effect was overwhelming. Plugging his nose, he struggled to stop himself from retching his tumbling stomach's contents onto the shifting floor. The water, or whatever the liquid was, was contained within a tank at least twenty yards square. The enormity of it made it look more like a river than a pool, its size only adding to the strangeness of the room. At the pool's center floated a familiar form.

The Prime.

Its eyes were closed as it drifted. The sight of it might have been comical to Harold if not for the world tossing him around like a rag doll. To his left were three large chairs. Whether they had already been there or the ship had created them for him, he didn't know. And right then he didn't care. Lurching forward, he stumbled past the pool's edge and fell into the closest seat. *This must be the bridge*, he thought, though it was unlike any bridge he'd ever seen in the sci-fi serials or books he'd read. The oddity of the reflecting pool and the giant domed roof above it reflecting light across dancing shadows only punctuated the ship's otherness. The idea that it had been created a million years in the future by his race's own descendants seemed so fantastic that he doubted what he was seeing. Nothing about the bridge—or the entire ship, for that matter—appeared remotely human.

As Harold braced himself in the chair, water sloshed around his feet.

"What . . . what's happening?"

In reply, a vision appeared in his mind, as clear as if the image were directly in front of him. Boulders cascaded, crashing against the ship's gray hull, burying it in an avalanche of rock and dirt. Despite the ship's enormous size, it struggled to rise against the disintegrating earth. Harold understood the vision immediately. Somehow, the underground base was collapsing on top of them. Had the military sealed off the structure? Would they have been willing to blow it up with all of their secrets, and people, inside? If the situation were dire enough, perhaps they would. The ship was trying to escape; that much was clear.

In his mind's eye, the hull spun rapidly, slicing through giant slabs of rock like a chainsaw, forging a path through the crushing debris. But even with all its size and power, the ship couldn't stop an entire hillside from crashing down upon it. Still, the ship spun faster and faster, smashing boulders and tossing stone and dirt about in the darkness.

Harold sucked air through his chattering teeth as the bridge around him became transparent. Rocks and boulders passed through the ship and *through him* like ghostly apparitions.

His thoughts wandered back to his college studies as he wondered if, perhaps, he was witnessing some variation of the Einstein-Bosin Bridge. But that paper, published in 1916, had been mere theory. The reality he was facing was beyond description. Harold was both inside the mountainous blackness and outside beneath a cloudless blue sky. Above, birds flew in the distance, their white wings stretched out as they soared. Below, Area 51 lay barren and seemingly abandoned. Where had everyone gone?

Turning his gaze farther upwards, Harold noted that the sun had grown brighter, its light engulfing him, but its radiance was no longer warm. Like icy fingers wrapping around his skin, the light was numbing. His senses whirled as the ship spun faster and faster until it appeared that the hull was no longer moving. Finally, the world shifted, flipping over itself.

Like an origami sculpture, space and time creased end over end, folding around Harold.

Booming thunder announced the underground hanger's collapse through piles of smoky debris and rocky ruins. Yet, he noted, the military base, less than a mile away, stood untouched. Inside the bridge the wind howled, pressing Harold into the chair.

As his body was crushed by an invisible force, his consciousness perceived much more beyond the ship's hull. Below, a puff of smoke erupted from the hillside, offering the only hint that anything was amiss. Endless desert stretched out before him. Serene. Peaceful. Morning sunlight spread over him like a warm blanket. It was both terrifying and awe inspiring. He'd never felt so small or so alive.

Then, in a blink, the ship and Harold vanished.

28

Rickety thumping and a chugging engine snapped Casey awake.

She was lying face down on the floor, inhaling sawdust. Yellow sunlight poured through slats, revealing a cramped train car with stacks of wooden crates swaying overhead. The wind blew in flecks of sand, giving the shadows a roaring chill. Casey welcomed the frigid breeze as it jostled her further into consciousness. In the distance she heard voices, muffled and indistinct, like soft whispers drifting on biting air.

Sitting up, she scanned the small train car, not seeing anyone else. The voices jumbled on top of each other, growing with intensity, louder and closer. Covering her ears from the sound, she tried to block out the steadily building noise but couldn't. Then she realized the voices were not from outside. They were in her head.

Yes, she thought. The nanites were no longer dormant. She felt them filtering through her bloodstream. With a long, slow intake of breath through chattering teeth, Casey centered herself, reaching further inward and tapping the microscopic machines with her consciousness. She'd done it a thousand times, but never having lost her abilities before, she probed lightly, careful not to fully activate them. Doing so would alter more than simply her biochemistry; it would also change her appearance. *Into a monster*, she thought. But that hadn't happened in a decade. She'd learned how to control the nanites since then, only using them for simple tasks, usually to try to discover whatever secrets Colonel McKellen was hiding from her. The thought of his stoic expression when the gunshot tore through his chest burned her from the inside. Whatever their differences throughout the years, she knew he'd protected her from the government's constant watchful gaze. He'd helped her when no one else would, and now he was dead. Once again, Casey was alone.

Pushing the final image of McKellen aside, she crossed her legs and arched her back. Long, deep breaths slowed her heart and quieted the internal voices. As she calmed her senses, her arms vibrated at her sides for a moment before the nanites settled back inside her.

Opening her eyes, Casey stood, feeling her muscles tingle. The train car lurched, jostling under her feet and shaking the crates stacked around her. Casey's gaze followed them upwards, stopping at a square hatch in the roof. An emergency exit, she hoped. Taking stock of the size and possible weight of the mysterious crates, Casey put one foot on top of the bottom box and lifted herself up to the next. Pausing, she closed her eyes and reached out with her mind to determine how close her captors might be. A burst of laughter and cocky arrogance wafted in the distance, like a sour aroma drifting through a windowsill. They were close, maybe one or two cars to her left, toward the front of the train. She needed to be quiet. Opening her eyes again, Casey focused on the third box up. Above it, perhaps within arm's reach, lay the emergency hatch.

Wood groaned beneath her as she reached for the next crate, struggling to lift herself up. A nail scraped her thigh, drawing a thin bloody line along her leg. She didn't bother to look. Exhaling through clenched teeth, she moved up to the third crate. Like a stack of dominos, they swayed uneasily as the train jostled. Perched on top of the crates, her left hand reached up, wavering in midair, before her fingers snatched the hatch's handle. Raising her other arm, she attempted to gain enough leverage to turn the lock.

With a loud crack, the world fell out from beneath her.

Casey's foot broke through the top crate, a thousand splinters slicing her shin. The crates tumbled over, crashing in a pile below. Casey hung from the ceiling, holding onto the hatch for dear life. It wasn't the five-foot fall that terrified her; it was that she knew this might be her only chance to escape. Plus, the crash had been loud. She didn't need heightened senses to know that her captors had probably heard it.

Her legs flailing, she focused on the lock above her. Tightening her fingers in a death grip, she tried to force herself to turn the lock, but her hands refused to budge.

It was as if her reflexes were as aware of the imminent fall as her mind. Outside, she heard the clang of a metal bolt being released. They were coming.

Her eyelashes fluttering, she reached inward, activating the nanites to give her a boost of strength. Not too much, just enough to nudge her along. She twisted her wrist, and the lock snapped in her fingers. Only too late did she realize she'd pulled too hard. Casey fell, crashing into the crates below.

As Casey regained her senses, she saw round shapes with a blue tinge gleaming in the darkness, one of them inches from her face. *Rocks?* she wondered. Then a line sliced down the object's center, cracking it open. An appendage reached out. The "rock" cracked further, and the gap widened, spilling its contents onto the floor. A black shape, no larger than the palm of her hand, scurried across the floor. At its center, a single eye popped open. Behind it, tentacles reached out from its back, crawling toward her face.

Casey screamed and rolled over. The thing scuttled onto her back. She felt its tiny legs scramble up her spine while the tentacles reached around her neck, flapping into her open mouth. Biting down, she sliced the slimy wet things, hearing a shriek of pain in response. Seemingly undeterred, the thing moved away from her lips and crawled over her face, obstructing her vision.

Casey wanted to call for help, but her jaw remained closed. Tripping backwards, she spilled onto the floor as the thing positioned itself over her. The blackness of its tiny, hairy body blocked her vision. Casey was about to trigger the nanites again when a hand swatted the thing off her, followed quickly by a series of rapid gunshots blasting inches from her face. The noise echoed through the train car, shattering her eardrums.

Casey collapsed. The thing lay dead, its spidery legs curled upon itself and its long tentacles sprawled limply about. Lowering his pistol, the black-clad leader offered Casey his hand. It wasn't until she was standing that she saw his face. His mask gone, his features were immediately recognizable.

"I think it liked you," he said, grinning.

Casey's jaw slackened as her chest tightened, her legs trembling.

"Donovan?"

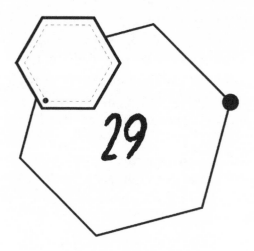

29

Ten years earlier, Donovan Daley's fingers had been wrapped around Casey's neck, tightening until her veins popped. *She's not human*, he decided as she thrashed about and gasped for breath in the liquid pool beneath him. Her face was normal now, sure, but he'd seen her for what she truly was. The oval black eyes, the scaly gray flesh. This cute little blonde *thing* was only a disguise. A pretty shell.

The thing that used to be Casey flailed as he pushed her below the surface or the water, or whatever the hell the liquid shit was. Donovan didn't care anymore. He wasn't going to let her infect him the way those things had infected her. The bitch was dangerous, no two ways about it.

The ship lurched in protest. Donovan figured it didn't much like him damaging its precious little experiment. *Yeah, well, you can go fuck yourself too.*

That was how it should have ended: Casey drowning, choking out her last breaths beneath him. But it didn't play out that way. The bitch had powers. Like, real, honest-to-God, *powers*. In the end, she'd won, and he'd been left alone on the bridge to die when the ship crashed.

Except, Donovan didn't die.

Lying in a fetal position, he rode out the violent crash, tossed about in a haphazard mess that left both of his legs broken and his right arm bent in ways that it wasn't meant to bend. But when the quaking reached its peak, and the roof tore to pieces above him, lashing him with sandy wind, he kept hold of the pool's edge and didn't let go. The noise was the worst of it, the wind screaming as pieces of metal tore away around him. Casey and Arthur were long gone, of course. They'd abandoned him to his fate. Maybe they were alive, or maybe they were dead. Either way, Donovan planned to stay amongst the breathing. He just had to hold on until the tumbling stopped.

When it did, the ship settled with a sigh of creaking metal, and then darkness swallowed him.

The next few weeks were a blur. Metal frames bent outward, revealing sunlight. Someone lifted him onto a stretcher. His body jostled on an airplane while a female nurse with large breasts leaned over him, strapping him in. He enjoyed the view, though he couldn't recall anything above her neck. After that he saw palm trees swaying in a clear blue sky without a cloud in sight. The scent of ocean air filled his lungs, making his head swim. It was a beautiful dream, but he knew it couldn't last.

Only, it hadn't been a dream. Not all of it, at least. The nurse might have been, Donovan thought, as he sat up in his hotel bed, still picturing the way her breasts had swung above him.

Snapping his attention back to the open windows, he watched as his fluffy white drapes parted in the breeze, revealing the Miami coastline beyond. He recognized the area from shows he'd seen on TV. As he glanced around his room, that thought brought up another realization: there was no television. Stuck in a room with his legs in braces and his right arm in a cast, he figured the least someone could do was give him something to watch—or bring back the nurse from the plane. Instead, his attendants were all burly guys who never smiled and whose vocabulary seemed to consist only of grunts, "Hmpf" and "Huff" being their two favorites.

Once the drugs had run out and his mind grew lucid, Prewitt came to see him. He was a government man who seemed to be running the show, with Donovan as the prize pony. Unfortunately, the first words out of Prewitt's mouth shattered the nice dream that Donovan had been having over the last few weeks.

"It's 1947," Prewitt said, handing him a newspaper as proof. "August eleventh, to be precise."

"You've gotta be shitting me," Donovan replied.

The meeting went downhill from there. Eventually, though, the situation improved, once Donovan learned what the game was and how best to play it. *Truth or dare.* Truth about history, politics, science, and whatever he could remember from high school got him treats: a bigger hotel room, plenty of women, and lots of cash. Donovan was amazed at how far a couple thousand bucks could get him in that time period—not to mention how much pussy. As for the dare, Donovan never saw a reason to try that route. He expected it would be something along the lines of being held in a tightly confined room somewhere with no money and no girls, so he just told Prewitt everything he could remember. It started with the ship, of course, then moved onto politics. Kennedy's rise and eventual assassination were of particular interest to Prewitt. From there Donovan continued to play all the hits: the fall of the Berlin Wall, Neil Armstrong on the moon, America's crushing defeat in Vietnam. Name the historical tune between 1950 and 1995, and Donovan played it. The more he sang, the more money, women, and comfort he received. At last, Donovan was living his own version of the American dream. Unfortunately, that dream ended too.

Five years later, after Donovan owned several houses and a dozen cars, with accompanying blondes and brunettes for each, Prewitt finally dragged him out of his cushy life and back into the world of monsters and bogeymen.

In 1953 the US government found something much larger than the ship and much more dangerous. Its discovery changed everything, including Donovan.

Now as he stared at the woman he'd tried so hard to kill all those years ago, his hatred was gone, and instead he felt pangs of sympathy. Donovan knew what was in store for her, and he couldn't help thinking that if she'd died before, it might have been a mercy. But it was too late for that now.

Then her fist smashed into his jaw, knocking him back over a jumble of crates, and his sympathy vanished.

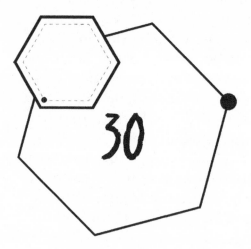

30

All these years later, Casey could still feel Donovan's fingers tightening around her throat. She tasted the water filling her mouth while her lungs screamed in protest. Donovan's crazed eyes bore down on her with glee as he plunged her deeper into the ship's pool.

And now there he was, a little older but still offering that crooked, smarmy grin. Her fist slammed into his jaw before she was even conscious of her actions. Her knuckles throbbing, she watched Donovan tumble over a crate as his gun fell to the floor. If she'd been thinking clearly, Casey would have picked it up faster, but her head was swimming, her reflexes slow. Her throat tightening, she struggled to push words out.

"They told me you died in the crash," Casey said through clenched teeth. Tears stung her cheeks as she thought of the others who hadn't survived, especially her fiancé, Arthur. He was gone, yet this piece of shit was still breathing.

As Donovan rose on unstable legs, Casey clenched her fists. Then Prewitt's voice slithered behind her, accompanied by the click of several rifles cocking.

"McKellen had you for a pet," Prewitt said, "so I needed one of my own."

She spun around, finding his beady eyes staring back at her. Casey trembled with anger. "You murdered the colonel!" she screamed. "Why? What the hell do you want?"

"To save humanity from communism," he replied, shrugging.

Casey's jaw fell open. "Wait, what?"

"You heard me," he said, his voice even.

Casey hesitated, unsure how to process the sincerity in his voice. He was serious. Suddenly, the absurdity of it all crashed over her like a wave. Casey burst out laughing. Her face wet with tears and her muscles aching, barely able to stand, she laughed harder than she had in years. It wasn't funny, but it was a release. Prewitt and Donovan exchanged a worried glance before she finally righted herself.

"After all these years," she said, "you've finally found a sense of humor."

"You think I'm being funny?" he asked, "While you've been hoping to stop something that *might* happen centuries from now, I've been trying to stop a very real, present-day threat."

"No, you're not funny, Prewitt," she said, wiping her eyes. "Just an idiot."

"I suppose," he said, withdrawing a syringe from his

coat pocket, "that it would be too much for a glorified waitress to understand."

Casey's laughter faded, and her eyes narrowed at the needle. "What's that?"

"Just something to dull your infection," Prewitt replied. "We wouldn't want your so-called seekers to come find you before we're ready."

She backed away, bumping into Donovan. Grabbing her shoulders, he locked Casey in place. Cornered, Casey's eyes fluttered as she reached inward and accessed her nanites, waking them.

"I wouldn't do that," Prewitt warned. She opened her eyes, noticing several eggs rattling around. "These creatures feed on seekers. Careful they don't mistake you for one."

"What are they?" she asked, hesitating. Within her, the raging nanites quieted, simmering just beneath the surface of her skin.

"When the seekers' red gaseous form is exposed to oxygen for prolonged periods, years even, they eventually harden, becoming something else." He picked up an egg, which was harmless to his touch. "They eat their own."

Casey thought of McKellen bleeding from a gunshot wound. "They're not the only ones."

"Sarcasm," Prewitt replied, nodding. He dropped the egg and raised the syringe.

It was now or never, Casey decided. Like a spark of fire igniting her system, Casey activated the nanites. Abruptly, time stopped. The needle dangled inches from her face. Donovan's tight grip loosened. The surrounding soldiers stared blankly, frozen in time.

Not frozen, she reminded herself, *only slowed*. She needed to move. Fast.

Slipping out of Donovan's grip, she grabbed his fallen pistol and raced for the door, weaving between soldiers and shoving her way outside. Less than a second passed. Pausing between train cars, she saw more soldiers in the next one. Tilting her gaze, she chose the only other route available.

Up.

Casey clambered onto the train's roof. Reaching for the ledge, she noted gray patches growing along her right arm. The dreaded transformation had begun. More a reflex than a decision, she deactivated the nanites. As she slowed her body, time returned to normal. Flopping over the ledge and onto the roof, she felt the wind slap her face. Below, Prewitt peeked out of the train car as Casey ran along the jostling roof, toward the rear. The sun hung low overhead, casting the desert in orange and ochre. Maybe if she could get some distance, she might find a place to jump. Rocky ridges lined the landscape. It would be a hard fall, but it was better than the alternative.

Then a chill ran up her spine, and a gasp escaped her.

An enormous shadow blocked the sun, drenching the train in darkness. She didn't need to look up to know what it was. She could sense the ship's presence, reaching out, like an itch in the back of her skull. It was trying to communicate. Whatever the ship had to say, though, she didn't want to hear it.

Casey ignored the incessant itching sensation as best as she could, concentrating instead on making her way along the train's rooftop without falling. Behind her, soldiers scrambled over the ledge, following. Donovan was in the lead, his face flushed with anger. She knew that look; he wanted to kill her. But at the moment, the ship was a larger concern. How could she escape something a mile wide, blanketing the sky?

Casey ran, stumbling along the jolting, jostling train.

Suddenly, her feet stumbled, and time slowed once again, only this time she wasn't doing it. She fought against the force as if trying to lift her legs out of quicksand. A sickly emerald light engulfed her while an invisible hand snaked around her belly, yanking her off the roof.

Like a fish dangling on a hook, she writhed, her limbs flailing in the air.

Casey grabbed an iron bar that ran along the edge of the train car's roof. Nanites surged in her arms, turning them ashen gray while offering her enhanced strength. The metal bar bent under her grasp. Behind her, soldiers lifted a crate of eggs into the green beam that had engulfed her. With a *whoosh*, the crate shot upwards, rocketing through the sky before it vanished inside the ship.

The railing broke, and Casey flew into the emerald light, floating end over end toward the giant ship.

It had her.

And then, it didn't.

The green light blinked, sputtering. Casey was sent tumbling. Missing the train, she fell into a cloud of dust and rocky debris. Rolling over sharp edges and jutting rocks, her body was cut and bruised in a dozen places. She struggled to curl into a ball, but her reflexes had slowed from the impact. She saw the ship vanish above, replaced by sunlight. With a silent snap, time resumed, and the train hurtled away in a cloud of dust.

Lying there bleeding on a pile of rocks, Casey watched through blinking eyes as the train vanished from view. She imagined she heard Prewitt's furious screams echo across the valley. It probably wasn't real, but she smiled anyway. Chuckling to herself, she coughed, splattering blood across her dust-covered face. Her body grew heavy, and her mind drifted as she lost consciousness.

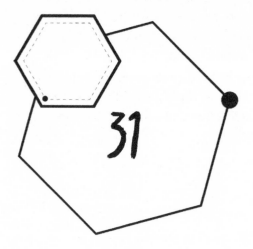

31

The ship lurched beneath Harold's feet, sending him crashing to the wet floor. Lights flickered, and the pool's glow dimmed. Something was wrong, but he couldn't comprehend what. He'd watched through the ship's projected thoughts as it snatched Casey from the train and then waited, impotent, as the ship dragged her upwards, locked within its emerald clutches, until a crate of rocks was sucked up within the beam. Almost immediately, he felt a pang of anger erupt around him. Furious and perhaps frightened, the ship released Casey, flinging her to the ground below.

Sparks shot across the bridge, snapping Harold back to the present. Unsure if he should be elated or terrified, Harold struggled to his feet. Gasping for breath, he stumbled along the pool's edge, searching for an exit. Propped beside the arched doorway, however, stood what appeared to be a rifle. That hadn't been there before.

His pace slowed as he approached it. It was unlike any rifle he'd ever seen. There appeared to be a jar of fluid near the trigger, where ammo should be. As the stench of propane wafted through his nostrils, he realized what it was: a flamethrower.

Turning back toward the bridge, he saw the Prime's red-and-black figure emerging from the liquid, dripping onto the floor. As it approached, Harold's first instinct was to rush to the flamethrower and burn the damn thing right where it stood. Though he doubted he'd survive such an attempt, he couldn't help thinking it might be worth the trade.

This vessel is damaged, the Prime whispered in the back of Harold's mind, its voice flat and rough. ***You must destroy the abominations.***

"I'm not helping you," Harold said. "Let me go. Let me out of here!"

They will consume the ship, the Prime replied. ***We are too weak to stop them all.***

His back straightening, Harold forced himself to sound braver than he felt. "If I go, you go."

Again, the bridge lurched. Harold steadied himself against the curved doorframe. The Prime remained planted at the water's edge, staring at him with blank white eyes. Sparks flew from above, cascading around it, but the creature remained locked in place, seemingly oblivious to anything but Harold. After a pregnant pause, its chest heaved, as if sighing, and it turned away. As it squatted at the pool's edge, its back to Harold, the creature's voice returned. ***Then we die.***

Harold hesitated in the arched doorway. His eyes fell on the flamethrower, which had clattered to the floor during the last quake. His gaze drifting from the weapon to the creature and then back to the weapon, Harold didn't know what to do. Blooms of blue sparks rained about. Dim chunks of light and shadow flickered. Inhaling humid, dank air through gritted teeth, he wanted to sit and die as bravely as the creature. But he couldn't. Exhaling, he grunted in defeat, his shoulders slumped. "What do you need me to do?"

The creature didn't reply. Harold rolled his eyes, suddenly more frustrated than frightened. Snatching the weapon, he wanted to scream and curse at the damnable thing, but instead he shrank into the hall.

The once-straight tunnel curved and bent before him, offering a twisted route. As he turned left, the opening behind him closed, revealing a new wall, as if the ship were constantly rearranging itself. Harold wondered if that was by design or due to whatever was happening to it. After being blocked again by another wall, he assumed the latter.

His stomach twisting, he felt the ship wobble beneath him, dropping with a lurch, then straightening. The more violent the turbulence, the clearer it became that time was running out, only he had no idea where he was going or what he was supposed to do.

Shadows moved overhead. Harold stopped fidgeting with the flamethrower. He thought of the creature from the base, giant blackness surrounded by flailing tentacles. Was he supposed to fight one of those things alone? His feet faltering, his steps slowed, and his hands sweated profusely, causing the weapon to slide around in his palms. He'd never used a flamethrower before. He hoped it was like in the movies: point and fire.

As he raised the muzzle over his head so he could

use the pilot flame to help him see what was hanging above, his foot hit something hard.

Reeling, he landed amongst several large rocks. Blue phosphorescent light emanated through the tiny cracks along their jagged surfaces. Peering into the closest one, he found the side of it open but nothing inside. It was hollow.

Not rocks, he realized. *Eggs.*

The realization was accompanied by cracking noises echoing around him. His heart thundering in his chest and his ears, he scanned the floor. More empty eggs filled the room. At least a dozen lay within view, and he wondered how many more there were. Taking a step back, he wanted to run to the bridge, but he knew nothing was waiting for him there except certain death.

Another quake sent him tumbling into one of the empty shells. Scrambling to his feet, he swallowed and then held his breath as he made his way farther into the egg-covered corridor. With each step he took, the temperature seemed to drop. His breath escaped in haggard, frosty gasps. Through the corner of his eye, he saw chunky shadows in the next corridor moving about with a life of their own. Harold followed, crossing the tunnel as he swung the flamethrower around, expecting to find enormous creatures ready to lunge at any moment.

But no giant, hulking monsters lurked around the corner. Instead, tiny shadows flitted about. The ceiling crawled in a black mass. Below, dozens of tiny spidery bodies chewed at the walls, tearing apart gray sheets like skin being torn from a body. The ship wasn't made of metal, Harold realized; it was some sort of tissue, perhaps living tissue. Mercurial, the surface tore apart in strips under their tiny pincers. Beneath the ship's skin lay an exposed mess of wiring. Red mist billowed from the ruptured tubing like gaseous blood. As the creatures consumed the vapor, their black flesh glowed, pulsing crimson before reverting to black.

Wounded, the ship lurched.

Bracing himself, Harold raised his weapon and assumed a wide stance to remain upright. His heart was pounding so hard in his chest that he worried the spidery creatures might hear it. But if they did, the sound went ignored. Wiping his hands against his thighs, he got a firmer grip on the flamethrower. Then, offering up a silent prayer, Harold squeezed the trigger.

A burst of fire erupted from the weapon, much larger than he'd expected. Eyes wide in astonishment, he watched the tiny black bodies scurry about, trying to escape the flames. The thickest group of them burned, screaming before they died, their skin hardening into something akin to dried lava. Those on the outside, however, quickly vanished back into shadows and out of view.

Harold took a step closer. Emboldened by his success, he sent another stream of fire along the wall, but this time nothing moved or screamed. He'd missed some, he knew, peering around. *Come out, come out, wherever you are . . .*

From above, tentacles shot out, clambering over his eyes, nose, and cheeks.

Tripping over his own feet, Harold stumbled backwards and lit the ceiling on fire.

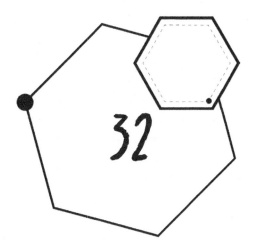

32

An endless array of shimmering stars welcomed Casey back to the land of the living.

As she rolled onto her back, jagged rocks and dry sticks poked her from various angles. Something slithered behind thick bushes. Steading herself, she remained still for a moment as she searched inward to assess her body's condition. If she'd been injured, the nanites must have done their work. She didn't sense any pain, only a throbbing headache, which often accompanied her use of the tiny machines that had infected her bloodstream. After trying to find a way to "cure" herself from them, she couldn't help but recognize that without them, she probably would have died from the perilous fall.

Lifting herself up, Casey searched the surrounding desert. A billion stars shone overhead, though their light cast a limited glow. This wouldn't be an easy walk.

Keeping a slow, steady pace, she stumbled over craggy earth and dry ridges. Casey tried to calculate how far from Groom Lake she might be, but since she hadn't been conscious for much of the trip, she didn't know if it was dozens of miles or hundreds. She hoped for hundreds. Groom Lake Base had been situated in the middle of nowhere on purpose. If the train hadn't taken her out of the surrounding drylands, Casey doubted she'd survive long on foot. Prewitt's men would be back, looking for her, so she had no time to linger.

She heard a rattling sound close by, breaking the silence.

Perfect, she thought. *Girl abducted by flying saucer travels back in time, only to die from a snake bite in the desert. News at eleven.*

She chuckled. The rattling followed. Casey kept walking.

Somewhere along the way, her slithering companion finally gave up the chase, leaving her with nothing but the sound of her footfalls for company. At first, Casey welcomed the silence, until it became just as deafening. She'd never been completely alone before. At the base she could always sense someone's presence, even if she couldn't see them. Before that she'd been trapped on the ship. And before that . . .

An image of Arthur studying in the kitchen flashed across her mind. Casey stumbled, her feet catching in the tracks. *No, don't go there*, she thought. *Think about something else. Anything else.* Those memories needed to stay buried.

Before she could stop them, however, more images flashed. Working at the diner, balancing plates of pancakes and orange juice while her polyester uniform chafed her neck. Back then, living in Blackwood, Oregon, her biggest concern had been waiting to get out of town, waiting for her life to truly begin. And then, waiting to marry Arthur. A life of waiting. That's how she'd spent her early years. Still, she decided, waiting had been a hell of a lot better than this. Like most kids, she didn't know what she had until it was gone. Once the waiting had stopped, and her new life began, it had been nothing but one nightmare after another. As she trudged along the seemingly never-ending tracks in the darkness, Casey decided she'd give anything to be able to hit a reset button.

A life free of spaceships and monsters. Wouldn't that be nice.

Without a watch, she had no idea how much time had passed until she saw the first hint of civilization. She doubted it'd been more than a couple of hours when she heard a noise ahead. At first, Casey thought it was her imagination, but the closer she drew to it, the louder the familiar sounds became.

You must be joking, she thought with a groan.

It was the sound of a flying saucer. *Ooooowww— wheee-ooooww—wheeeeee-ooooowww.*

Not a real one and certainly not the type that only hours ago had attempted to wrench her from the train. No, this was something altogether different. The familiar sounds conjured images of rickety silver shapes hanging from strings and accompanied by high-pitched musical notes, the kind found in movies.

Over the cliff's edge, dozens of cars were spread out below, lined up in rows in front of a giant screen. On the screen, a silvery flying saucer was flying over Washington, DC.

It was a drive-in movie theater.

If she'd had the strength, Casey might have laughed. Instead, she ground her teeth and shifted her gaze down the rocky slope, trying to find a path. Though jagged and steep, she decided it was not impossible to traverse. At least she hoped not as she descended toward the movie screen displaying the black-and-white flying saucer.

Half stumbling and half sliding, she made her way down the rocky ridge, kicking up dust along the way. By the time she made it to the bottom, lurching to a stop behind the giant screen, the last of her strength was gone.

Casey staggered past the rows of cars toward the concession stand. Ahead, blinking lights advertised Coca-Cola and popcorn. All she wanted was water. The closer she drew to the stand, the more aware she became of the cracks in her lips and the dryness of her throat. Unable to recall the last time she'd had anything to eat or drink, Casey dug in her pockets, finding only lint and a rolled-up tissue. No money.

Behind the counter, a young man's eyes widened at Casey's approach. With her rumpled clothes covered in blood and dirt, she could only imagine how awful she looked. *Like roadkill,* Casey assumed.

"Oh my gosh," he stammered. "Are you alright, ma'am?"

Clearing her throat, she found it difficult to speak. "I was in an accident," she said. "Could I get some water?"

The young man quickly poured her a cup and handed it to her. As she downed the entire cup in one gulp, the coolness of the water sent a shock through her system. Awakening her senses, the sudden jolt caused the sounds around her and the voices in her head to grow exponentially louder. It was as if an invisible door had opened in her mind, opening the floodgates. The effect was over-whelming. Her legs gave out, and Casey sat in the dirt. Taking a series of deep breaths, she tried to quiet the noises reverberating through her skull. She heard kids laughing in cars. Heard the boy behind the concession talking to his boss about calling the police. Heard two lovers moaning in the backseat of a blue Buick. The boy was excited; the girl was faking it. And then, within the cacophony, she felt red-hot rage burning through the crowd of cars, drawing closer.

Donovan.

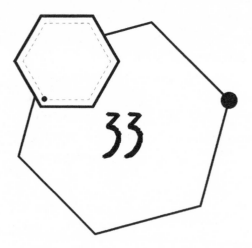

33

Bolting upright so fast it made her head swim, Casey glanced left and right, scanning the rows of cars. Behind her, she distantly heard the young man ask her again if she was alright. Casey ignored him. Focusing on Donovan's anger, she saw blooms of red and orange scattered amongst the vehicles. He'd brought soldiers. How many, she couldn't ascertain, but it was more than enough to stop her.

The kaleidoscope blooms continued their approach, scattered about the drive-in. They hadn't found her, not yet anyway, but they were looking, fanning out between the parked vehicles. As this was the first and only sign of civilization along the train track's route, it made sense they'd come there. Still, she doubted Donovan would have been clever enough to figure it out. *Prewitt,* she thought. *That little weasel must be here too.*

Casey ducked behind the concession stand, hiding from the approaching red and orange lights. Behind her the rocky ridge jutted upwards, back toward the tracks she'd come from. Glancing at the blooming figures through the concession stand's wooden walls, she doubted she could go back up the hillside without being spotted. That left only one other option. She needed a car.

The closest vehicle was the Buick with the young lovers humping in the backseat.

Casey bolted toward it, hunched over as she ran to the driver's door. Through the open window, she saw the young boy's buttocks rising and falling in the backseat. Keeping rhythm, the girl's sock feet bobbed in the air. The boy's moans grew shrill, as did the girl's.

Casey reached for the door handle.

"Stop!" a familiar voice shouted. Spinning around, she saw Donovan stepping into view. Wearing a heavy coat that bulged along one side, she assumed he was carrying a rifle.

Casey stood up. Flanking the rocking car, several more men in heavy coats appeared.

Donovan smirked. "Keep calm, Casey," he whispered, showing his empty hands. "No need for a scene."

The men drew closer. Between them, the car rattled and shook as the young boy, oblivious to what was happening outside, reached his climax. Donovan grabbed Casey's arm, pulling her away from the driver's door and any chance of escape. As she glanced around at the rows of cars, no one seemed to notice as Donovan and his men shoved concealed weapons into her back. Nudging her forward, they led her down an aisle of cars toward the exit.

Ahead, Prewitt stood by a black sedan, holding a syringe and grinning from ear to ear.

Exhausted, Casey felt the blood drain from her face. Trying to pull herself free, she struggled weakly against the soldiers' grasp. With each step closer to the sedan, her spent body quivered, growing warmer, hotter, as if a raging fire were blazing inside. Sweat dribbled down her face and across her back, the heat turning into an inferno. Her feet faltered, stumbling. Casey blinked rapidly, and her vision dimmed. Her blood boiling, her legs wobbled beneath her. She'd never felt such a sensation before. The fire in her belly grew.

Donovan wrapped an arm around her waist, dragging her toward the sedan. "Don't make this harder than it has to be, sweetheart," he grunted.

Casey's eyes rolled back in their sockets, and her back arched. Her arms outstretched, the nanites in her body activated with a burst of energy, seeming to be working of their own accord. An invisible wave of red-hot energy burst from her body, rippling outward. Casey screamed from the intensity of it. She imagined her skin blackening from some unseen fire, consuming every inch of her. Instead, the burst knocked Donovan and his men to the ground. Along the aisle, cars roared to life, horns blared, and headlights blazed. Inside the vehicles, stunned passengers screamed in fear, not understanding what was happening.

Casey's feet left the ground, lifting several inches into the air. She felt as if she were being torn apart from the inside. Her muscles ached, and her nerve endings screamed. Whatever was happening was beyond her control. She couldn't have stopped it even if she'd wanted to. And she didn't.

As the soldiers scrambled to their feet, drawing weapons from under their heavy coats, the cars around them shifted into gear. Tires spun, kicking up dirt and rocks. Several vehicles lurched forward, while others spun backwards, slamming into the soldiers.

Donovan yanked out a weapon. Casey recognized it. It was McKellen's gun, his 9mm. The sight of it enraged her further. Still floating, her eyes went black, and her flesh turned pale, riddled with red, pulsing veins. Donovan leveled the pistol at her. His finger twitching on the trigger, his eyes narrowed.

Suddenly, the blue Buick with the lovers inside, their faces pale with shock, careened backwards, slamming into Donovan.

Casey fell to the ground, rocks digging into her knees. The sharp pain snapped her out of the daze. As cars spun around, knocking into soldiers on either side, Casey stood and made her way toward Prewitt. He wasn't smiling anymore.

Casey's pitch-black eyes glared at the syringe in his long, delicate fingers. She swiped it aside with one hand and grabbed his neck with the other. Picking him up by the throat, she tightened her grip, squeezing the life out of him. The little man thrashed about, struggling to breathe.

Do it, a voice hissed in the back of her skull. ***Tear his throat out.*** Unsure if it was her imagination or the tiny machines infecting her body, Casey hesitated. Prewitt's face turned pale above her. His fingers released her arm as the life drained out of him.

Casey smiled. She wanted to see Prewitt's last gasp before he died, just like McKellen.

Out of the corner of her eye, she noticed her reflection in the sedan's side mirror: eyes black, skin pale with red veins. She was a monster.

Gasping, Casey opened her fingers and released Prewitt. He tumbled to the ground, coughing.

The inner voice returned, infuriated. **Kill him. Now. While you still can.**

She'd heard that voice once before, an inner beckoning, back on the ship when she'd held Donovan's life in her hands, just like she had held Prewitt's. She'd chosen not to kill then, and she wouldn't allow herself to do it now either. Casey shook her head, silencing the voice.

Turning, she witnessed the chaos she'd unleashed. Cars spiraled in circles, kicking up dirt and sand in billowing clouds, preventing Donovan and his men from reaching her.

Backing away from the surreal scene, Casey decided she'd done enough. Clambering into the sedan's driver's seat, she ignited the engine with a touch. The car spun out of the drive-in theater, heading down an open desert road.

Her fingers trembling on the steering wheel, she tried to calm the thundering in her chest. Slowing her breathing, she tilted the rearview mirror down, finding her own pitch-black eyes staring back. They reminded her of the dream she'd had the night before about the gray monster hiding in the car, only this time *she* was the monster.

As the nanites slowly deactivated, her eyes regained their color, and the veins along her arms withdrew. By the time her body had returned to normal, hunger pains were stabbing at her stomach, and her vision was blurred. Exhaustion was taking over, but she couldn't stop.

Casey needed to find somewhere safe to hide. Safe from Prewitt. Safe from the ship.

Safe from herself.

PART III

RETROCAUSALITY

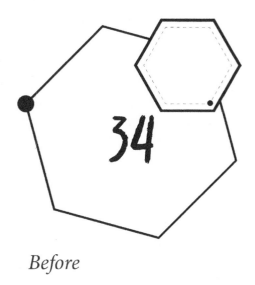

34

Before

Growing up, everyone had called him Donny. He hated that name. It made him sound like a child, someone who sucked his thumb and wet his bed. Eventually, people began calling him Donovan. Others called him Mr. Daley. He was open to either. If they said his name with a slight tremor, so much the better.

Donovan had worked his way up the corporate ladder; he'd paid his dues. When they made him general manager at the Crisco plant, they gave him an office overlooking the factory floor and a shiny new badge with his name in bold print. Donovan figured that what the badge really said was, *Don't fuck with me cos I'm the boss.* Sometimes he'd glimpse the workers peering up at him as he stood by his window, watching with his morning cup of Joe. They'd scamper and whisper to themselves like frightened sheep. Donovan enjoyed imagining what those little sheep might be going on about. He assumed it wasn't nice. That was OK as long as they respected him. As long as they were afraid.

Now it was Donovan's turn to be afraid. His mouth tasted of cotton balls, and his legs vibrated beneath him with a life of their own. He stumbled through the ship's twisting halls, each one the same as the last. None offered an exit. This new tunnel compressed into a trench, tightening around him. *Maybe I shouldn't have left the others,* he thought. *Never too late to go back.* He shook his head. *What would that get me? A crazy red sphere that might turn me into a ghost. No sir, not me. Next!*

That's right, Donny, you don't need them. It wasn't a voice so much as an itch in the back of his mind, whispered words tickling his skull.

Turning another corner, he found himself in a well-lit hallway with tall gray lockers. A yellow tiled wall to his left had a banner on it that read, "GO TIGERS!"

Donovan knew that hall, and it frightened him worse than any spaceship. Spinning back the way he had come, he realized the lockers stretched as far as he could see. Sunlight blazed through distant double doors marked "EXIT." Donovan made his way toward them, his feet stumbling over each other as he glanced into full classrooms. On his left was a math class, Mrs. King standing front and center. She glared at him as he rushed by. On his right, Mr. Dunhill's English class was in session. He looked at Donovan with a furrowed brow. "You're late, Donny! Late!"

Donovan picked up his pace, trying to get to the exit at the end of the hall, but it continued to stretch out of reach, as did the lockers and yellow tiles. He ran faster. At each classroom he passed, children turned, laughing. They pointed their stubby little fingers and stuck out their pink tongues as he passed. Sweat slopped down his face and chest, staining his white shirt. The sunlight shining through the exit door's window blazed brighter and brighter, turning from yellow to red. A coppery red. Blood red.

Donovan was almost at the exit when a figure appeared in front of it. Principal Adams. An old crone of a lady, she hated Donovan worse than anyone. Her eyes were flaming, her mouth filled with razor-like teeth. "You're late, Donny! Laaaate!"

Too close to the exit to stop, Donovan barreled through her. She evaporated into black smoke as he burst through the door, drenched with blood-red light.

The airplane bounced along the tarmac, waking Donovan from his nightmare. Even after all these years, the ship still haunted him. He'd never forgotten what he'd seen and experienced inside of it, and he doubted he ever would. Wiping drool away from his mouth, he sat up straight.

Prewitt was sitting beside him reading an issue of *Life* magazine. Peering over his reading glasses, he glanced at his sweat-covered companion. "Bad dreams?"

Donovan ignored the question, instead looking out the window at the flat midwestern landscape. "Where are we?"

"The middle of nowhere, or the next best thing." Prewitt put down his magazine and set his reading glasses aside as the plane taxied to a stop. "Welcome to Indianapolis."

"If you were looking to get away from it all," Donovan quipped, "I'd have picked Vegas."

"Don't you read any of the material I give you?" Prewitt asked. When Donovan didn't reply, he sighed in frustration. "This is where her mother lives."

"You think Casey would be stupid enough to come here?"

"That's just it, Donovan," Prewitt said, standing up and straightening his suit. "*I* think, *you* do."

Donovan bit his lip, quivering. Without another word, he followed Prewitt off the plane. At least Prewitt hadn't called him "Dipshit Donnie." Not yet at least.

As it turned out, fortune had at last favored Donovan. He'd been right. Casey wasn't there.

Neither was her mother. After two days of canvasing the city, Prewitt had come up short. The little weasel fumed as he paced in their hotel room. This time it was Donovan's turn to gloat. Not out loud, of course, but his growing smile was hard to contain. *Maybe this means I can finally go back to Florida*, he thought. Images of his numerous homes and accompanying girlfriends danced along his thoughts until Prewitt's voice snapped him out of it.

"Why are you just sitting there?"

Sprawled on the bed, his shoes off, Donovan offered up his best "Who, me?" expression.

"If we don't find her soon," Prewitt continued, "the ship will."

Good riddance, Donovan thought. He liked Prewitt better this way. Desperate. Afraid. *Where's all that self-righteous confidence now, you little turd?* Huffing, he sat up. "Maybe we should call Washington. Get some help. Expand our search."

"And let someone else take over?" Prewitt asked, his voice shrill.

Yep, Donovan thought, *pipsqueak is definitely afraid.*

"Over my dead body," Prewitt continued.

Uh-huh. Donovan had to work overtime to suppress a grin. *That's the idea.*

"With the details I've given you about the future, you still hold all the cards, Boss."

Prewitt sank onto the bed, deflated. "But without Casey, I don't have any leverage over the ship."

Donovan shrugged. "Then just let the damn thing have her."

As soon as he said the words, he wanted to take them back. Squirming on the edge of the bed, Prewitt's expression contorted into something akin to a Jack o' lantern. When he spoke, however, his voice was thin, barely above a whisper. "We can't. I can't."

"I told you," Donovan replied, "communism falls all by itself. We don't need the seekers."

Bracing himself for an outburst, Donovan was surprised when Prewitt instead took out his wallet, handing over a black-and-white photograph. It showed a strong man in his mid-thirties cradling a young boy—Prewitt, he assumed. Donovan studied the older man's face. "Your dad?"

Prewitt nodded. "He served his country faithfully in the war. When it was over, like everyone else, he came home, settled down, and started a family." Prewitt took the picture back. Stunned into silence, Donovan watched him blink back tears. In all these years, he'd never seen Prewitt project anything but arrogant confidence.

One tiny setback, and the little weasel's about to sob on my shoulder. Go figure.

Prewitt put the photo away, wiping his eyes. "My father worked for the government. Strictly mid-level stuff. Paper pushing, sending communications from Washington to various branches overseas. Nothing, as far as I can tell, of any great importance."

Prewitt stood, turning away. Not wishing to let the moment of weakness go, Donovan prodded further. "What happened to him?"

"A woman," Prewitt replied, his voice turning frigid. "A Russian operative. She seduced him, blackmailed him . . . destroyed him."

"And you think that if you stop communism, you can stop her?"

"She's already dead," Prewitt said. "Committed suicide in jail." He spun back to face Donovan, his body rigid. "But the damage was done." He leaned toward Donovan, gaining momentum as he spoke. "I intend to make sure no one else suffers that same damage."

"But we have no idea where Casey's gone, Boss," Donovan protested, frustrated at seeing Prewitt regain his confidence

Prewitt approached the window, his hands crossed behind his back. It took all the effort in the world for Donovan not to roll his eyes. *God help me, the little prick thinks he's Patton.*

"She can't run forever," Prewitt said. "It's just a matter of time."

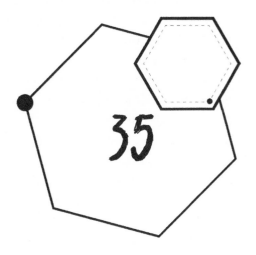

35

The isolated fishing village of Quinn's Peak lay at the head of Orca Inlet on the eastern side of Prince William Sound, near the mouth of the Copper River. As a lead supplier of one of the most sought-after fish, the Copper River salmon, everyone in town, whether directly or indirectly, survived and thrived off its export. With a population of only 1,200 people, to outsiders the small town seemed as if it had been frozen in time. But not to Casey. If anything, the people there reminded her of her hometown back in Oregon, except for the constant smell of the sea and the permanent odor of fish, which seemed to permeate everyone and everything within a ten-mile radius of the town. Yet, it wasn't the stink of fish or the town's isolation that had further dampened her spirit once she arrived. It was the constant rainfall. The innkeeper had told Casey that, on average, it rained about 157 days per year and that during the spring months, one had about a one-in-three shot of getting soaked every time they stepped outside. Casey had been in Quinn's Peak for three days, and so far she was three for three.

On the second day she'd invested the last of her meager resources in a pair of galoshes and a raincoat. Thankfully, her trek across the desert had eventually landed her in a small city with one of her bank's branches. Withdrawing all the money she'd earned over the years and never had much reason to spend, she'd gotten enough to take a series of buses and trains all the way up to Alaska. It hadn't been the easiest journey, but it was easy enough to cover her tracks. No one inquired much about the now-brunette girl with a seemingly permanent stoic expression covered behind sunglasses, even in the pouring rain. Granted, hair dye and sunglasses weren't the most original disguise, but she worked with what she had. And so far, no one had found her. Not Prewitt, not Donovan, and best of all, not the ship.

Still, paranoia never left her, and she was constantly glancing over her shoulder. Casey had to be careful because it wasn't just herself she needed to protect. Quinn's Peak wasn't a town she had chosen randomly in which to hide. She knew this place; she'd seen it in photos as a child. This was the town her mother had moved to after her grandmother died in 1955. It was also the place where her mother and father would meet two years from now. That is, if Casey didn't stop it.

On the long way up there, she'd had a lot of time to think about her situation. All that reflection had made one thing crystal clear: if she wanted to stop the ship and whatever plans Prewitt had, she needed to change the only thing she could. Casey hadn't come to Quinn's Peak to meet her mother; she'd come to warn her. If Casey had never been conceived, then perhaps the ship would not have killed all those people trapped inside either. Arthur, Major Reese, Earl, and so many others would all be alive. Max and Colonel McKellen too. So many people dead because she'd fought back against the seekers. Knowing the consequences to humanity if she hadn't, she had always assumed she'd made the right choice. Now Casey believed that she wasn't simply at the center of everyone's deaths; she had inadvertently been the cause. It was time to put an end to it. One life in exchange for the lives of many more. Major Reese's daughter would not lose her father. Arthur's sons wouldn't lose theirs. Max's baby would have his. On and on the faces of those who had died so that she might live moved past her closed eyelids like a silent picture show without an end. It needed to end, though. Someone else would have to fight the future. Anyone else. Just not her.

Casey crossed the street, stomping through puddles in her heavy galoshes. It was a little after 4:00 p.m., time for her mother's shift to end at the local grocery store, after which she would head home to her aunt's house. Time for Casey to follow her. Maybe this time she'd have the courage to stop her mother in the street, pull her aside, and warn her about the man she would meet and fall in love with two years from then. It would have to be a convincing story, a real whopper. Yet, after a week of trailing her mother, she still didn't know what that totally convincing, non-crazy-sounding story might be. But time was running out. Eventually, Prewitt or the ship would find her, and then it would be too late.

Casey quickened her pace, catching up to the young girl blinking in and out of view. Her mother stopped at a crosswalk, waiting for the light to change, even though there wasn't a car in sight. Casey assumed it came from having grown up in a big city instead of a small town where rules were more guidelines than laws. Casey caught up to her, stopping inches behind her back. Long blonde hair, just like Casey's natural roots, peeked out from beneath a hat and scarf. Her mind whirling, Casey knew she had to say something. Anything. A week of stalking, and she'd chickened out every time. But not today. Recalling how her mother had died giving birth to her, she added one more name to the list of deaths that she was determined to prevent.

Casey reached out and touched her mother's shoulder.

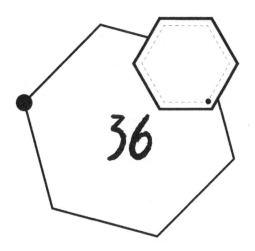

36

L ying against a coral reef, the ship hid at the bottom of the Atlantic Ocean.

An odd place to hide, Harold admitted, though he couldn't imagine where else a mile-wide craft might escape to for repairs. Fortunately, water hadn't leaked inside.

Not yet, he added, sighing.

Having been trapped down there for so long, Harold would have lost all sense of time if not for his food supplements, which were seemingly provided on a regular schedule. Consisting of vitamins and proteins, the injections made his arms numb and his vision blur, but they kept him alive. More importantly, they offered a possible calendar for him to follow. Keeping a running count in his head, he knew he'd received forty-six injections at approximately two doses per day. If his calculations were correct, he'd been trapped in the ship for twenty-three days, though it felt much longer. Making the injections even worse, the Prime, on the few occasions when it spoke, mocked him by announcing, "Mealtime." Harold would have thought the creature was gaining a sense of humor if not for the complete lack of emotion that the phrase carried in his mind. "Mealtime" was an order, not a joke. They needed him alive and unharmed. Harold assumed he was meant to be a host body again. *Like a fresh pair of underwear. They want me all clean and dry.*

After what seemed like days, the abominations had finally all been destroyed. Burnt and then ejected from the ship's hull, Harold had been forced to do it alone. Still, once he realized that the creatures were no harm to him, he began to admire how quickly the pesky spiders had insinuated themselves within the ship's machinery. *Or body*, he corrected inwardly. Nothing about the place reminded him of a spaceship. If anything, it was a living organism that seemed just as eager to finish repairs and leave as the Prime was, perhaps even more so. The ship, Harold felt through their seemingly permanent tethered connection, appeared desperate to leave and find Casey. At least the alluring slave girl hadn't returned. Harold assumed the ship was too busy repairing itself to toy with him, though what the point of the naked woman had been still eluded him. Harold doubted the ship did anything without purpose. Trapped at the bottom of the ocean with only the Prime for company, Harold had spent a lot of time trying to decipher the ship's motivations. From what little information he'd gathered, the seekers were dying. Casey, it seemed, was somehow both the cause of their future destruction as well as their potential cure. The precise details escaped him, but from what he'd pieced together, Casey carried a virus that was dangerous to humans but necessary for the seekers' survival. One thing had become abundantly clear, though: she'd lied to everyone. The government, the military, even her own scientists. Whatever else Casey Stevens was, only part of her remained human. Perhaps, Harold considered, Casey had also been lying to herself.

Lights flickered brighter overhead. Chugging noises reverberated along the hall that Harold had snuck down in a vain attempt to be alone. He was never alone, he reminded himself as he clambered to his feet. The floor beneath him hummed, and the walls glowed blindingly. It seemed that the ship's repairs were almost complete. And then what?

Harold strolled through the ship's lower levels, checking to see what had changed since the last time he'd passed that way. New corridors and rooms awaited him at every turn. Only, they were never truly new. The layout, while always changing, had begun to create a pattern over the seemingly endless days and weeks. The more he wandered, the plainer the pattern became. The tunnels were less like a maze and more like a series of interconnecting circles, leading farther and farther inward. Every time he wandered through the gray, dimly lit corridors, he hoped to discover some answer or potential enlightenment regarding the seekers. So far, he'd found nothing. No art, no information logs, no books, not a single machine or data point. Nothing that might explain who they were as a species. He'd tried discussing it with the Prime a couple of times, but it had been a one-way conversation, with Harold asking questions and the Prime ignoring them. After a while, Harold gave up and instead focused his attention on trying to find answers hidden somewhere within the massive ship. So far, his ventures had proven fruitless. Disheartening, even. If a race had no art and no personality, at least as far as humans understood it, how could he possibly reason with them? The drabber the gray walls, the less his chances of finding a way to communicate on equal terms. He needed something to understand them better. Perhaps if armed with more knowledge, he might be able to convince them to let him go, although he admitted it was a long shot. Still, it was better than sitting around waiting for his "mealtime" injections.

He turned down another corridor, then another and another. Most days he alternated between left and right, but this time he stayed right the entire way. After a dozen or more right turns, he hit a dead end.

Harold slid to the floor, defeated.

"When the righteous cry out for help," a familiar voice said, "the Lord hears and delivers them from their troubles."

Harold glanced up, finding his mother standing at the end of the hall. Her dark dress made her appear like a black spot amidst the hall's pulsing light. Instead of feeling surprised or concerned, Harold simply shrugged. Such visions had become commonplace. He realized it wasn't the ship communicating directly with him. The visions were more like echoes of their ever-present mental connection. Sometimes the visions were of Casey and sometimes his mother. All things considered, it was only a matter of time until he saw a burning bush around there too. Usually, he ignored the voices and accompanying images, but at the moment, seeing his mother, even if only a phantom version of her, made him feel a little less alone.

Struggling to smile, he cited the verse she had offered, Psalm 34:17.

The vision approached, black heels clacking along the gray floor. His mother glared down at him. There was no love in those eyes. While his mother was a hard woman, she wasn't without affection. The echo that had created this vision didn't understand her, not really. It was a surface view, nothing more. Still, her wrinkled face attempted to smile. No warmth, just a hollow grin. "The Lord is with you, Harold, even down here," she said. "In the dark."

Harold chuckled as he glanced at the lights overhead. "Actually, it's not that dark, Mom."

"Isn't it?" she asked. "Look at where your fancy books and too-smart-for-your-own-good theories have brought you. At the bottom of the sea, in a ship where even angels fear to tread."

Harold rose, meeting her lifeless black eyes. "That's not what she would say," he replied. "Oh, you've got the basic gist, I'll give you that, but no, she wouldn't use those words."

His not-mother smiled, this time with more warmth. "Then what would she say?"

Harold considered the question. Without anywhere else to go or anything else to do, he decided to use the moment as a simple brain exercise. What would his mother say to all of this? The ship? The seekers? Months earlier, he would have assumed she'd have called it all the devil's work. Now, trapped in a time-traveling spaceship at the bottom of the ocean, he reevaluated his original theory. Wheels spun in his mind as he thought back to the various Bible verses she might quote at a time like this. Sifting through them like scattered seashells lying along the shore, he turned each verse over in his mind, searching for potential answers. Then his eyes lit up. He'd found it!

"Though they climb up to the heavens above, from there I will bring them down," Harold said. "Though they hide from my eyes at the bottom of the sea, there I will command the serpent to bite them."

His not-mother nodded with approval. Having seemingly won the silly game, Harold slunk back to the floor and waited for the vision to vanish. When it did, he continued to imagine how his mother—his real mother—might react to seeing where her little boy had ended up. Alone, trapped, with zero hope for survival. Harold hoped that she'd simply tell him that she loved him. No verses, no lectures, just her kneeling beside him, saying how much she loved him and how proud she was of him. That would be the only comfort he'd need.

As he chuckled softly, tears stung his eyes. She wouldn't say any of that.

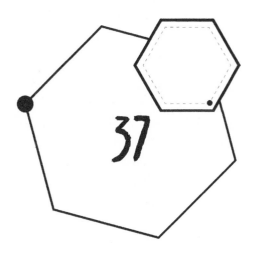

37

Blinking expectantly, Casey's own green eyes stared back at her.

Now that the moment was finally there, Casey didn't know what to say. Her mouth opened, closed, and opened again, but no sound escaped her lips. Seeing her mother, young and alive, staring right at her, inches away, gave Casey a jolt, like an electric shock through her nerve endings. She wavered, stunned and mute.

Her mother's smile faltered. "Yes?"

"S-sorry," Casey stammered. *Come on, Case, say something.* "I-I-I'm l-looking for Maple Street," she said, finally finding her voice.

Her smile returning, her mother's face brightened. "Oh, it's just a few blocks down, on the left." She looked Casey up and down. "Actually, I'm heading that way now if you wanna follow."

Casey smiled back. "That'd be great, thanks."

"Sure thing." Her mother held out her hand. "I'm Sarah."

"Casey."

Casey slowly raised her hand and clasped Sarah's. Even through gloves she felt her warmth.

"Neat name," Sarah said. "It works for both—"

"A boy and a girl," Casey finished. "Yeah, I was told my mom said the same thing."

Blinking past tears, acid crept up Casey's throat, stinging the back of her tongue. This was no time for sentimentality, she reminded herself. She already had a script laid out in her mind, along with a plan A and a plan B, just in case. Too many lives were at stake for her to get emotional now. What she said and did over the next few moments could mean the difference between life and death for everyone she'd lost over the years, including the young woman standing right in front of her.

Once the traffic light changed, they crossed the street.

"A bit of a fish out of water, huh?" Sarah asked.

Pushing down the thunderstorm raging in her stomach, Casey blinked. "I'm sorry?"

"I just mean you don't look much like a local."

"That obvious?" Casey asked, trying to regain her smile.

Sarah leaned over, sniffing her coat. "No sea stink."

Casey laughed, and just like that, the storm inside her quieted. For the moment.

As they walked, the conversation flowed effortlessly, though Sarah did most of the talking. It helped that they had a similar sense of humor. Casey could tell where she'd gotten her sarcasm from. There were other traits as well, mannerisms that only Casey would have noticed. The way Sarah tilted her head when she smiled or rolled her eyes when she wanted to avoid a particular subject. Even her hand gestures were similar. It was like looking at a distorted mirror, eerily similar and yet different. Their conversation continued over coffee at a corner bistro, then over drinks at the bar across the street. Drinks turned to a fish-and-chips dinner. By the time they paid the bill and decided to finish their journey up to Maple Street, the sun had gone down. Casey was careful to keep the conversation focused on Sarah. She did so for two reasons: first, it helped her hide the swirling emotions that still threatened to spill out in a gush of tears. Second, she was waiting for an opening in which to execute her plan.

Unsure how best to warn her mother about the truck driver she would meet two years from now, Casey's father, for the moment Casey kept things light. However, she couldn't help noticing that Sarah seemed much more immature than Casey had been at that age. Then again, Casey's experiences had forced her to grow up much faster. Though in her late twenties, Sarah was still trying to decide what to do with her life. All she seemed to know for sure was that she didn't want to marry a fisherman. Casey frowned, attempting to nudge her away from that line of thinking. As they passed a handsome young fisherman on their way out of the bar, Casey nudged Sarah.

"He's cute," she said, pointing.

Giggling, Sarah pushed Casey's arm down. "Don't point, I know him. He's a drip." Ducking low, she led Casey out the door and into the rain. "Gimme someone who will get me far, far away from the smell of salmon."

Casey's stomach tightened as she began to understand how her father had lured Sarah to Oregon in
the first place. Sarah was young for her age, and naïve.
Casey had been like that once, before the ship came.
She couldn't go back to being like that now, and she
doubted she would want to. Arthur, the cabin, Blackwood, all of it had been home to a different version
of herself. She'd loved Arthur, but she also understood
how her insecurity had caused her to settle for him. She
hadn't seen the world and hadn't had many options,
just like Sarah.

Fingers snapped in front of her eyes, waking her
from a daze. "Earth to Casey."

"Sorry," Casey stammered. "I was thinking about my
. . . mother." Caught off guard, she regretted admitting
that as soon as the words left her lips.

"What was she like?"

"Don't know," Casey replied. Hesitant to go down
that route, but not seeing any other path toward her
goal, she reluctantly continued. "My mom died during
childbirth."

Sarah's eyes grew wide. "Geez, sorry. Must have been
rough growing up like that. I lost my mother as an adult,
and it nearly crushed me."

Casey's enhanced vision noted a fiery orange blaze
along her mother's form. She was lying, or at least not
telling the whole truth.

"How'd she die?"

Sarah paused, and the bloom brightened. "Car
accident."

"If you were an adult when it happened, why come
here to fish town?"

Sarah giggled. It wasn't out of humor, though. As if struggling with her own inner conflict, Sarah remained tight lipped. Hoping to discover a thread that might help lead her mother away from Alaska, Casey reached out and probed Sarah's bubbling thoughts. Flashes of yellow erupted in Casey's mind. Not memories but emotions. After having had her abilities for so long, Casey knew that yellow usually meant guilt. Sarah blamed herself for her mother's death, but why?

Casey offered Sarah a sympathetic smile. "I'm sure it wasn't your fault."

Sarah stopped dead in her tracks. "I didn't say it was." Casey stayed silent, waiting for Sarah to continue. The colors around her dimmed until, finally, Sarah huffed. "My mom . . . she . . . was coming to pick me up from work. It was snowing pretty heavily. I could have taken the bus . . ."

Sarah's pace quickened along the sidewalk. Casey struggled to keep up, then decided to change tack. "How's it living with your aunt?"

"OK, I guess," Sarah said as she led them onto Maple Street. Wood houses with weathered paint lined either side. "I came here right after Mom died because I didn't have anywhere else to go."

Another lie, Casey thought. *She came here to make amends.*

"I don't know," Sarah continued. "Maybe I should have stayed in Indiana,"

Casey saw an opening. If Sarah left this town now, before Casey's father arrived, Casey would never be born, and so many people wouldn't have to die. Could she change the future? Did time even work like that?

Stopping Sarah on the sidewalk, raindrops slapped their coats as Casey locked eyes with her. This was it, the moment Casey had been building up to. The moment she'd dreaded. Plan A.

"You should go," Casey said. "Right now. As soon as you can. Travel, see the world. Find a good man, not just the first one who offers you a way out of here. Stand on your own two feet."

Sarah giggled nervously beneath Casey's hardened gaze, then lowered her eyes. "It's not that simple."

"Your mom's death wasn't your fault. You don't need to stay here." Casey pulled out an envelope. "This is fifteen hundred dollars. Enough to start over."

Sarah's face flushed, and her eyes turned to saucers. Casey shoved the envelope into her hands. "Take it," she said. "Leave here and never come back."

"Is this a joke?" Sarah hesitated, feeling the weight of the envelope between her fingers. Peeling open the top, she found a stack of cash. Her fingers trembling, Sarah handed it back. "What the hell is this?"

"You don't understand," Casey pressed. "If you stay here, you'll meet someone. A bad man. A really, really bad man."

"I-I've got to go," Sarah stammered. Turning, she raced toward a blue house several doors down. Casey followed.

"Please, just go away," Sarah called back over her shoulder.

"Hold on!" Casey shouted, waving the envelope of cash. "I'm trying to help you."

When she reached the weather-worn picket gate in front of the house, Casey noticed a black sedan parked in front. Pausing, she leaned over and glanced inside. The car was empty.

Behind her, Sarah continued up the front steps. Her stomach lurching, Casey spun toward her.

"Mom, wait!"

The front door flung open, and two figures emerged, blocking Sarah's path.

Donovan and Prewitt.

"There you are," Prewitt said, looking past Sarah to Casey. "We've been looking everywhere for you."

Before Casey could reply, a woman in her early sixties, Casey's aunt, stepped out of the doorway, standing between the two men. "Sarah, come inside, dear," she urged.

"What's going on?" Sarah asked, her eyes darting about.

"This young lady is ill," her aunt said. "These men are here to help her get better."

Leering, Donovan stepped off the porch, hands shoved into his jacket. A bulge in the right pocket caught Casey's attention. A gun? If so, it was pointed at Sarah. Prewitt came down the steps, smiling. His glare froze Casey in place.

"I'm afraid your friend is quite sick, Sarah," Prewitt said. "We're here to take her back to the hospital."

"Casey?" Sarah asked. "What's wrong with her?"

"She has . . . episodes, sometimes," Prewitt replied. "Delusions, I'm afraid." He turned away from Sarah. "Isn't that right, Casey?"

Donovan flanked Sarah. No one except Casey seemed to notice the bulge in his jacket. She assumed that was the point. Her mind whirling, she imagined all the ways she could try to stop this. Could she move fast enough to evade the bullet? He was so close to her. Still, it might be worth the risk. If her mother died there, so would Casey, but perhaps everyone else she'd lost over the years would survive: Arthur, Earl, Max, McKellen, Reese, and countless others. It was a simple trade. Two lives for the lives of so many. Would they live if Donovan pulled the trigger and ended it all right there?

Of course, that would mean having to watch her own mother die in front of her. Worse, Casey would be the one who allowed it to happen. Sarah was still so young, with many more years ahead of her. Did Casey have the right to take those years away?

As if reading her thoughts, Prewitt drew closer.

"No one knows what will happen if Donovan pulls the trigger," he whispered. "Maybe time will somehow reset itself, and maybe it won't." His beady little eyes locked with hers. "Do you really want to find out?"

Shuddering, Casey exhaled and looked away. No, she decided, she didn't.

"That's a good girl," he said. Prewitt turned to Sarah and her aunt. "I apologize for this entire ordeal. I assure you, Casey will receive the very best care."

Donovan inched away from Sarah, approaching Casey. Prewitt waved her toward the car.

Her heart thundering in her chest, Casey knew this was her last chance to save her mother, and, potentially, all the others. *Time for plan B.* She ran over and gave Sarah a hug.

Pushing her thoughts out, Casey ignited the nanites within her. A rush of images leaped from her mind into Sarah's, downloading a multitude of memories in a flash.

Growing up in Blackwood, Oregon. An abusive father closing Casey's bedroom door as he entered each night. An image of her mother's photo on the bedside table. Moving forward in time, Casey said "yes" to Arthur's proposal in the woods. Again, the vision shifted as green light blazed overhead. Stumbling through darkened corridors, Casey was chased by a once-human beast. Beyond that was the future. A crimson spire loomed over an endless sea. The world at the end of time. The seekers. And then, finally, a violent crash. Casey lying in the dirt, stranded in the distant past.

A cacophony of images erupted, tumbling over each other, cascading from Casey's thoughts into Sarah. It took mere seconds, but the effect was immediate. When the din eventually quieted, Sarah stumbled backwards, meeting her daughter's gaze.

"You can be whatever you want," Casey whispered, shoving the money into Sarah's coat pocket. "Go anywhere. Do anything. Live your life."

Sarah paused, glancing at the envelope, then back at Casey, confused. Still processing everything she'd seen, Sarah simply nodded.

Hoping it had been enough, Casey did the same. Prewitt's grip tightened around her arm, pulling her to the sedan. As she climbed in, Sarah ran over.

"Your eyes, I never noticed," Sarah said. "They're just like mine."

Casey's lips curled into a Cheshire grin. "Yes, they are."

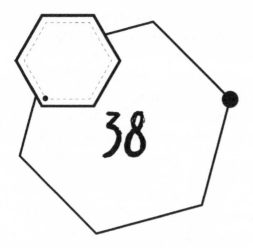

38

Mealtime, a voice hissed. Looking up from the floor, Harold found the Prime lingering in the distance. Wiping sleep from his eyes, Harold rose but didn't approach. He was still at the dead end, having slumped down, crying, until he fell asleep. He wondered how long he'd been gone before the Prime had noticed his absence. Again, Harold heard its voice at the back of his mind. *Mealtime.*

"What if I don't go?" Harold asked. "It's not like you can damage your human flesh suit."

The ship can repair any lacerations or broken bones I might inflict upon you.

The calmness of the voice slithering around Harold's skull only punctuated the seriousness of the creature's words. It was a statement, not a threat. His shoulders sagging, Harold lumbered over. The Prime turned and led him down another corridor. The silence grew deafening. Harold wanted to scream, to bash the red-and-black thing over its enlarged cranium until crimson smoke poured out. But even if he somehow succeeded, he knew there would still be no escape from that place. His search for answers, for any kind of glimpse at who the so-called seekers were, continued to elude him. With a suppressed huff, he decided to try again.

"Why does Casey call you the seekers?"

He hadn't really expected an answer from his mostly mute companion and was surprised when the creature spoke, not through telepathy but with spoken words.

"Huuuumans feeeeel the neeeeed to cateeee-goooorize and naaaame eveeeerything," the creature hissed through seemingly damaged vocal cords, an effect, Harold assumed, from all the secret experiments that Casey had performed on the clone's body. "It is dooone ouuuut of feeeear."

"I don't understand."

"Preeeecisely," it replied. "Yoooou feeeear what yooooou dooon't understaaand."

Harold shook his head. It was the same argument the ship had made earlier about mathematics. Still, neither of them had answered his question.

"But why 'seekers'?"

"Weee seeeeek a cuuure," the thing replied. The harshness of its serpentine voice made the hairs on Harold's neck stand on end. Still, this was progress. Not wanting to let the first chance at actual conversation slip past, he quickly followed up with another question.

"And Casey has this cure inside her?"

The Prime stopped, regarding him. Harold felt the creature's blank stare burrow into him. "Yoooou thiiiink us monsteeers."

Harold averted the thing's lingering gaze, struggling to smile. "What gave me away?"

The creature glared, not responding. Harold assumed it might not understand sarcasm, so he decided to clarify. "You're monsters because you take what you want without any regard for those whose lives you destroy."

As soon as the words escaped his lips, Harold withdrew a couple of steps backwards, outside the tall creature's immense shadow. Yet, the thing didn't move. Instead, it tilted its head, as if listening to a separate conversation, before nodding to itself. Then, with a wave of its hand, a door appeared within the gray wall behind Harold. It irised out as blinding light poured in from beyond. Harold raised his arm as his eyes adjusted to the sudden burst of luminescence.

"What's in there?"

Answers, the Prime replied as it entered.

His heart jackhammering against his rib cage, Harold took a step closer into the light. As he entered the room, his vision still adjusting to the brilliance, he didn't notice the door shutting behind him, sealing them inside.

Harold found himself within an angular room. At the center, an inverted pyramid pointed downward. It was roughly twenty feet above the floor with a beam of green light pouring from it. The light spread out like a spiderweb, connecting to threads around the room with holographic symbols, a dancing mishmash of odd designs and glyphs. Along with the images, a faint stench filled the oddly shaped chamber. "Burnt copper" seemed the most appropriate description, Harold thought, or perhaps "dried blood." Wiping his nose, he tried to ignore the stench, focusing instead on the swirling symbols.

He turned to the Prime. "Is this your written language?"

Before the Prime could answer, a sweet feminine voice whispered in Harold's ear. "It is how we express ourselves, yes."

Spinning toward the sudden breath on his ear, Harold was startled to find the female Roman slave peering up at him. Her closeness made him lurch, but his feet remained planted. Struggling to avoid her nakedness and keep his mind clear, his throat tightened. "You mean, art?"

Ironically, the warmth of her body made him shiver. Her breasts pressed against his arm as she took his fingers in hers, gliding them above the symbols. "Art, music, science, these are not separate things," she replied. "At least not to us."

Pressing his hand against the glyphs, Harold felt a rush of sensations burst through his fingertips and ripple up his spine. As his hand crossed from one symbol to the next, he experienced different sensations. Anger burned red with fire. Calmness was a cool blue. Passion pulsed orange. So many emotions locked within glowing symbols. He couldn't understand their precise meanings, but the emotions that each symbol poured into him were so overwhelming that he felt tears drip down his cheeks.

His lips quivering, he tore his hand away. "Wh-what is that?"

"Our culture," she said, her dark eyes meeting his, "all of which will be lost if Casey is not returned to the future."

"Why?" Harold asked, his face reddening. "What's so important about her?"

The woman's form shifted. Her hair grew lighter and her skin paler, her eyes blazing with emerald fire. Harold found himself staring at a naked version of Casey. A *not-Casey*. He wanted to turn away, but his eyes continued to roam.

"What are you doing?" he demanded, though his voice had no strength.

"I thought this form might be more . . . alluring." She glanced down, noting the bulge in his pants. "It seems I was correct."

Harold shook his head. "You planted those thoughts about her in my head."

Not-Casey giggled. "You know better, Harold." She snaked closer, her milky white breasts pressing against his chest. Suppressing another shiver, Harold couldn't summon the will to withdraw. "I simply *encouraged* what was already there," she added in a throaty whisper.

The words rang true. Still, Harold shook his head, frustrated. The ship was toying with him, though for what reason he couldn't begin to imagine. Her voice matched Casey's in tone, but the inflections were all wrong. For one thing, she had called him Harold. The real Casey, much to his chagrin, always called him Harry. Also, the illusion's voice held none of the cocksureness of the actual woman. Though beautiful and inviting, this carbon copy lacked the qualities that Harold had been drawn to most: Casey's strength and intelligence. Even, he forced himself to admit, her arrogance. This version lacked her Cheshire grin, the knowing glint in the eyes. To Harold, Casey's beauty had never been simply skin deep. This not-Casey was merely a vague imitation, much like the not-mother in the hallway. It seemed to him that despite the ship's immense intellect and abilities, it lacked a basic understanding of what made humans human. It could copy someone's words and appearance, but when it came to subtle inflections or the inner workings of their mind, the ship came up short. It didn't understand their . . . soul, for lack of a better word.

Harold pulled free from her grip. "Just tell me what you want," he said, his voice hardening.

"I must fulfill my purpose," she said, the flatness in her tone returning. "We tested over a million subjects. Casey Stevens was the only viable candidate able to contain the genetic code without it harming her."

"You speak as if she were a monkey in a lab."

She shrugged, nonplussed. "Casey will be returned to a time outside of the causality loop that she created by coming here. The future must be fixed."

Harold swallowed, unsure if he wanted an answer to his next question. "How does any of this involve me?"

"The first time I touched you, in the hangar, I tested your genetic makeup," she replied, her face lighting up with a broad smile. "No abnormalities. No disease. A perfect male specimen."

Harold trembled. "A specimen . . . for what?"

In silent reply, not-Casey's lips parted as red mist snaked out of her mouth. Harold tried to escape, only to be stopped by the Prime's steel grip. It loomed behind him, holding Harold in place. The slithering mist snaked through his nose, taking control of him from within.

Spectral fingers clutched Harold's consciousness, dragging him back into the void, screaming.

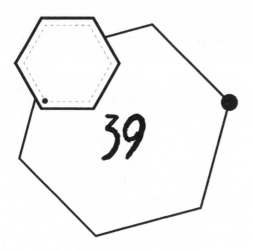

39

Black trees rolled by in an endless wave, blanketing Casey's view as far as the eye could see. Her head thundered, still reeling from the aftereffects of whatever Prewitt had injected her with. Some sort of nanite-dulling drug, she assumed. Even though she could still feel the microscopic things crawling beneath her skin, the sensation seemed distant and vague, much like a television's volume that had been lowered to a buzzing hum. Not muted, simply turned down to a barely audible whisper. Casey sat in the backseat of a tan Studebaker, keeping her eyes closed to mere slits, waiting to see where they were taking her. They'd switched vehicles while she was asleep, having traded in the sterile Ford sedan for a car that stank of greasy burgers and fries. With any luck, Donovan and Prewitt might both die of a coronary. She knew they wouldn't, but the idea made her smile, nonetheless.

Glancing down, Casey surveyed her body. She appeared unmolested, and she didn't feel any pain anywhere. More surprising, they hadn't handcuffed her or tied her arms. In fact, the car's doors weren't even locked. She considered jumping out and bolting for the tree line, but curiosity got the better of her. Besides, she was tired of running.

Returning her attention to the view outside, she stared at a familiar tree-lined road. Ahead, a sign read, "Umatilla River, 25 Miles."

Back in Oregon after all these years. Talk about taking the long way 'round.

The town she'd grown up in, Blackwood, wouldn't be built for several more years, and they didn't appear to be heading toward Carson Creek, the single road leading up that way. Instead, the vehicle snaked along the base of the mountain, heading to the northern edge. In the 1980s, a few industrial complexes had been spread out along the base of the mountains, but they were nothing of note. She couldn't imagine what Prewitt expected to find all the way out there. When she was young, she had hoped to leave Blackwood, run off with Arthur to the East Coast, and never look back. *Like Mom,* Casey thought suddenly. *Did she leave? Nothing's changed. I'm still alive.*

The ship had once told her that she'd created a time loop by venturing into the past, the idea being that nothing could be altered within the loop. Yet, the ship had also warned her against interfering with her mother's life. Casey didn't know what to believe anymore. For ten years the ship had been her companion. Now it was hunting her. She sensed the dormant nanites flowing through her bloodstream. *Like sleeping children,* she thought. *Nasty, dangerous children who want to spread disease.* Casey wouldn't allow that, no matter the cost. If the ship came for her, she would find a way to destroy it—or herself. One way or another, this had to end.

The Studebaker slowed. Pushing those macabre thoughts aside, Casey sat upright. Prewitt turned back in the front passenger seat. "Good," he said. "You're awake."

Casey didn't respond. Outside, the sun hung low, shining through a thicket of dark trees and revealing twin domes. They looked like a pair of breasts peeking over the horizon. As Donovan drove down the bumpy road, Casey saw that the domes were attached to a jumble of yellow pipes and concrete buildings. A water reclamation plant, Casey realized. For a moment she pictured herself drowning Donovan in there the same way he'd once tried to drown her. Her smile returned.

"Look familiar?" Prewitt asked, mistaking her expression for excitement. Again, she didn't answer. Casey didn't want to engage with the man who'd killed McKellen and all those poor soldiers. Unperturbed, Prewitt continued, "When Donovan told me that he'd been taken by the ship up in Oregon's mountains, near the same location you had been, my curiosity about this place grew." He leaned closer. "Your so-called seekers didn't pick this area at random." That got her attention, but she tried not to show it. Though her insides were churning, she kept her expression neutral. Prewitt gestured toward the domed structures ahead. "We call it Outpost 119."

A fancy name for a water reclamation plant, Casey thought. Despite her disgust at the little weasel and all the havoc he'd brought, she secretly wanted to hear more, if only to finally learn why Blackwood had been chosen in the first place. Or, more pointedly, why her life had been stolen. If Prewitt was right, and he really did hold the answers, then Casey was more than eager to hear them. Yet nothing could explain away everything she'd been through or everything she'd lost. No answer would ever take away the pain. Not now, not ever.

In her lap, Casey continuously clenched and un-clenched her fists while she released a long, heavy breath. Growing anxious, it took all her self-control not to bolt out of the moving vehicle and tear the place apart, piece by piece, until she found the damned answers for herself.

With a thunderstorm brewing in her belly, Casey's eyes left Prewitt, sweeping over the metal-and-cement structure as the car passed through an iron gate. Armed men dressed in black from head to toe guarded the entrance while snipers lingered on raised platforms. As they parked beneath one of the giant domes, Casey wondered if all this security was to keep someone out or to keep someone—or something—in. Her mind drifted back to Area 51 and all the security they'd had there—planes, tanks, soldiers. None of it had saved them. If the ship came to this place, she doubted these bastards would be any safer either. Not that she cared much anymore. She was there for answers, and she was determined to get them. All of them.

Prewitt opened her door, reaching in to grab her. Casey shrugged him off and climbed out on her own.

As she approached the structure, flanked by Prewitt and Donovan, she noted an overbearing silence emanating from the domes. No machines running or gears grinding. Not wishing to reveal her growing eagerness, she stifled the butterflies twirling in her stomach. After all she'd been through, Casey's curiosity was reaching a boiling point. Her pace quickened as she led the march toward the cement-and-steel structure.

"What is this place?" she asked.

"This," Prewitt said, opening the front door, "is why you and Donovan were abducted in the first place." Casey forced her face to remain placid, as if only mildly interested. Prewitt cocked his head as he continued. "Surely you must have wondered why so many of you were taken from the same location over a period of decades?"

Of course, I have, she thought, chewing the inside of her cheek until she tasted blood. Still, she had to admit that she'd never really looked into that particular connection before. Over the years her focus had been on the seekers and the ship, not on the location they'd chosen for their abductions. That, she now realized, had been an error, one that this little turd of a man hadn't made. What else had she missed?

Casey glanced back at the open doors and the utter darkness beyond. The entrance reminded her of an enormous vault. A mixture of growing apprehension and fascination caused the hairs along her arms to stand at attention.

Stepping through the first set of doors, they came upon a second. Each door was six inches thick, made of reinforced steel. With so many precautions in place, she doubted anything good was waiting on the other side.

"Walter's Water Company began construction of this plant a couple of years ago," Prewitt said, ushering her through. "However, six months before the plant was to go online, the builders hit what they thought was an underground power line."

Donovan unlocked the third and final set of doors. Casey lingered, unwilling to enter. "Another ship?"

"Better," Prewitt responded, flipping a light switch. "Much better."

Inside, dozens of hanging light fixtures illuminated the concrete dome, revealing a crisscrossing network of catwalks suspended several feet above ground. Donovan nudged her forward onto the walkway. Her feet shambled along metal grating. She braced herself against the railing as breath escaped her lungs. Eyes wide, she peered over the ledge at a broken concrete floor two levels down. The ground was covered in brown dirt and gray rocks, as if workers had stopped midway through construction. At the center a round platform shimmered with a crimson luminescence. Its eerie glow reflected along tall cranes and various pieces of abandoned equipment.

Noting Casey's slack-jawed gaze, Prewitt giggled. "Look familiar?"

She shook her head. Whatever it was, though, it wasn't another ship.

Heading down a narrow staircase, they passed a large stack of wooden crates. Peeking inside, Casey saw hundreds of the rock-shaped eggs covered in a phosphorescent blue tinge. It seemed the answers to her abduction were also somehow connected to the strange rock creatures she'd seen before, the ones that had tried to eat her. A knot tightened in her gut.

Before she could ask about the rocks' connection, Donovan shoved her forward. They continued, stopping on the bottom floor. Hovering along the dirt-covered edge, they lingered only a few feet away from the shimmering disc.

This is it, Casey realized as she stared at the shimmering saucer. *The end of the road.*

As soon as the thought occurred to her, Casey found herself wavering. Donovan was too. He stayed back, keeping one foot on the staircase, frightened by whatever the thing was. Prewitt, meanwhile, stepped onto the shiny surface without delay.

"It's safe, I assure you." he said, practically gleeful.

While his assurance meant little, Casey's boiling curiosity had reached such heights that she had no choice but to follow. She stepped onto the platform.

Donovan, however, didn't follow. It wasn't until Prewitt shot him a sharp glare and cleared his throat with a nonverbal command that Donovan finally obeyed. With a huff, he trudged over.

Casey grinned at him, baring her teeth. "What's the matter, big boy?"

"You'll see," Donovan muttered, lumbering onto the platform. The fear in his eyes caused Casey's smile to falter, along with her confidence.

Maybe this isn't a good—

The platform dropped, plunging them into the Earth.

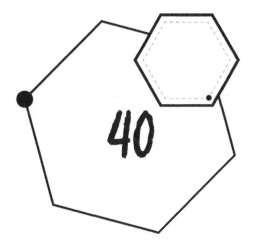

40

Casey knew the place; she'd been there before.

Shattered red beams surrounded them, bent and twisted within dirt and rocks. Her heart hammering in her chest, Casey couldn't believe her surroundings. It simply wasn't possible, she told herself over and over while the platform continued its unrelenting descent far into the earth. The crimson spire. There, *now*, a million years before it should even exist.

"It's an observatory," Prewitt said, his voice echoing as they rushed through the darkness.

"Observing *us*?" Casey asked, steadying herself on wobbly legs.

Prewitt nodded. "Like a telescope peering into time. Just imagine what one could do with such technology." He sighed dramatically. "We've been trying to make it operational for several years now, to no avail."

"Th-this place can't be here," Casey stammered. "I destroyed it in the distant *future*."

Prewitt chuckled, seemingly giddy at her confusion.

The platform's descent slowed as they approached the bottom. Light appeared at their feet, revealing machines and equipment. Large glass containers contained dozens, if not hundreds, of mummified gray cloned bodies. Long dead, their withered forms were mere fragments of bones and tissue.

"How could something from the future be buried in the past?" Casey asked, having lost any remnants of hesitation or restraint when speaking with Prewitt.

"Surely, someone with three doctorates can at least offer a guess," he chided. "Or is it too much for a mere waitress to comprehend?"

I can comprehend my fist smashing through your skull, Casey thought but decided against saying it, at least for the moment. Her fists clenched and trembling at her side, Casey swallowed her rage and stepped off the platform, approaching the mummified remains. Peering through the glass, she studied the clone's hollow ocular sockets. Her mind whirling, Casey tried to create a plausible answer, *any* answer, but the more she considered the problem, the more a vast numbness throbbed behind her unblinking eyelids.

Obviously enjoying himself, Prewitt bounced on the balls of his feet. Behind him, Donovan wasn't nearly as excited. His gaze darted around the cavernous room as if ghosts might jump out from the shadows at any moment. Casey couldn't blame him; a part of her felt the same. No matter how many extraordinary things they'd witnessed over the years, at least the past and the future had been presented in chronological order. But this, standing in a structure that shouldn't exist for thousands of millennia, made no sense.

"Causality," Prewitt finally said, as if offering a hint.

"Causality," Casey repeated, breaking free from her jumbling thoughts. "Cause and effect. Somehow, this place was destroyed in the future, and the effect was it being buried here in the past." She shook her head; it still made no sense.

Enjoying his perceived moment of intellectual superiority, Prewitt's smile grew. "*Retro-causality*, to be more precise," he said, "wherein an action in the future affects the past."

Casey's teeth clenched as a theory formed in her mind's eye. "The hyperspheres," she said, her voice barely above a whisper. "There were hundreds, perhaps thousands, of ships attached to this structure. When the tower fell, the hyperspheres inside them must have ruptured—"

"Turning time *and causality* on its head," Prewitt finished. His face drooped slightly, seemingly frustrated that she'd pieced it together so quickly. She doubted Prewitt's scientists had created their theory nearly as fast. But pride wasn't a concern to her now. Scientific curiosity had suddenly given way to the horrific implications piling on top of themselves, one by one, the more she considered the problem.

"If the spire's remains are here *now*," she said, gasping, "then they are also spread throughout the future."

Prewitt nodded. "With each passing year, the debris will grow until it finally breaks through the surface and reveals itself to the world."

"Which means," she said, following his train of thought, "I've altered the future."

"And if *you* can do it," he said, his smile returning, "so can others."

Casey walked down the line of glass containers, studying their contents more closely. Various amounts of black rock-like eggs stretched from case to case. Peering inside, another thought occurred to her. "The seekers, the ones who attacked the base, where did they come from?"

Prewitt nodded toward two empty containers at the end. "We'd hoped to revive the red mist specimens we had in order to strike a bargain of sorts," he admitted, then sighed. "Alas, it didn't work out as planned."

"It didn't work out?" Casey burst into laughter. Her reaction caught both men off guard. "You think you can make a *deal* with them?"

"Donovan," Prewitt said, gesturing to his stoic companion, "tells me that the USSR won't fall until the early 1990s. Decades from now. He's been kind enough to give me a roadmap to our future failures—an assassinated president, a war in Vietnam without victory, and, worst of all, an entire generation fighting communism. I intend to change all that."

Casey shook her head, not believing what she was hearing. "Look at it," she snapped, pointing to one of the horrific figures. "*That's* our future. *Not* communists and nationalities."

Prewitt shrugged. "Perhaps, but it's also not a *present* threat. The beings who built this place can and will help me secure our nation by bringing an end to communism." He paused, eyeing the dead creatures. "After that, let someone else fight the future."

Stunned, Casey peered past him. "And how about you, Donovan?" she asked. "You've seen these things in action. You really think pipsqueak here is going to bring the seekers to their knees?"

Donovan didn't answer, Prewitt turned toward him, as if also awaiting his response. When none was given, Prewitt shrugged. "Fine, then I'll just have to prove you both wrong."

He strolled farther into shadow, moving to the back of the chamber, toward a round doorway. Casey eyed Donovan, noting sweat dripping down his face.

"It's not too late to stop this," she whispered.

"It is for me," he said, exhaling a long sigh.

"Why?" Casey asked. "Since when are you such an obedient lap dog?"

"He's got me by the balls," Donovan replied, his eyes studying the floor. "And now he has you too."

Without another word, he nudged her forward with the butt of his rifle. Whatever was going on between the two of them, it was clear that Donovan was even more frightened of this tiny bureaucrat than he was of the seekers. Walking beside him, she felt a sudden urge to activate her nanites just enough to probe Donovan's thoughts, but the sight of the crates of phosphorescent eggs stopped her.

Stepping through the doorway, they entered another familiar site: the cloning chamber. Casey was reminded of the last time she had been there. This time, however, no ghostly vapors were swirling in the air, and the hanging sacks that once contained countless cloned bodies lay torn open and empty. With the sacks gone, crumpled in a withered heap along the floor, she saw the room clearly for the first time. Arched with curved beams erected hundreds of meters high, it was like a giant colosseum hundreds of meters below ground. Her footsteps echoed along the dusty path as she peered at the floor, wondering if the giant hypersphere still lay in the level below. Had Donovan and Prewitt discovered it yet? If something four-dimensional had indeed shattered, it might explain how and why this structure now lay in ruins a million years before its construction. During her studies of physics, she'd paid particular attention to the beliefs of the period regarding a fourth dimension and its probable properties. Though their research was limited to mathematical equations, she'd seen it in practice on the ship and had a basic understanding of how it worked. Past, present, and future were concepts born of a three-dimensional existence while a fourth dimension would potentially step beyond those barriers, observing time from the *outside*. That's how the ship had transported her across time and, possibly, how the tower's ruins were now spread around her in the distant past.

Sucking in her breath, she decided that she needed to know if the sphere was still below them. Her eyes fluttering, she gently activated the nanites throughout her body, stretching her consciousness outward, searching for the sphere's presence.

Instead, she found something dark and violent reaching out from the depths in response.

The eggs.

Though she didn't see any in the cloning chamber, she felt them beyond the walls. Countless angry, hungry pinpricks of darkness swirled in her mind, creating an image of tentacled beasts hungry for the disease within her. Not wishing to trigger the darkness further, Casey shut her nanites down, turning them dormant and blinding her senses. The abruptness of her withdrawal caused her to stumble. Casey reeled, gasping for breath. Prewitt reached over to steady her, but she swatted his grimy fingers away. Better to collapse right there on the floor than be helped by him. Finding her footing, she lifted her gaze, only to find the muzzle of a gun staring back at her.

Donovan's rifle was pointed dead center at her chest. His face was contorted in a wash of emotions, as if fighting within himself. It wasn't anger in his stoic eyes; it was more like resignation. She was about to ask him what he was doing when Prewitt stepped into view.

"We've taken all of the eggs out of this room," he said. "You're safe to activate those tiny insectile machines running through your bloodstream." Casey gasped, surprised by how much he seemed to know about her. "I assure you," Prewitt continued, "it's quite safe for you to use them in this room."

She glared. "Safe for whom?"

"Unless you're faster than a bullet," he answered, "it should be safe for all of us."

"You . . . you *want* me to use my abilities?"

"I'm counting on it," he said. "Unless I'm mistaken, the ship found us on the train because you activated that virus running through your body." He stepped closer to her, his face losing the last semblance of false kindness. "Now be a good girl, and call it again."

Suddenly, it all made sense. Casey understood why they'd brought her down there, to the bottom of the crimson spire's debris. The eggs were gone from the room, waiting outside. Once she activated her nanites, she'd be trapped, at least until the ship arrived.

Casey shook her head. "Fuck you."

"Fine, have it your way," Prewitt said, shrugging. He turned his back to her. "Donovan?"

Bang!

A gunshot echoed through the room, shattering her eardrums. The noise was so intense that it took a moment for her to notice the red smear seeping across her chest. Coughing up blood, Casey wavered, stumbled backwards, and fell.

More shocked than afraid, she couldn't believe what was happening. Donovan stood in the distance, his expression an unreadable mask.

Prewitt leaned over her, grinning. "That should do it."

As Casey gasped for air, it felt like her lungs had abandoned her. She couldn't breathe, choking on her own blood. Shadows pooled overhead. Her limbs heavy, she struggled to crawl along the floor, but she didn't make it far, feeling the life drain out of her.

Guess I was right, she thought. *End of the road.*

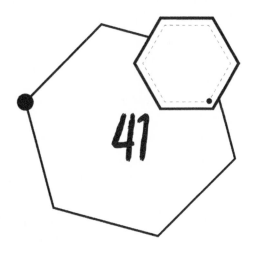

41

The dark was numbing. Dulled fire writhed across Casey's chest, a contrast to the cold floor at her back. It all seemed so far away, as if she were observing the faint pangs of pain in a dream rather than reality. The coppery stench of her own blood clung to her nostrils, tethering her to the physical world. Behind her closed eyelids, an all-consuming emerald light rose from within. Casey felt the light drape across her shattered body like a warm blanket. Slowly, the last vestiges of pain withdrew to a tiny pinprick, growing smaller and smaller until the fiery pangs vanished. In its place the light blazed brighter in her mind's eye, accompanied by a faint chorus of whispers. *No, not voices*, she decided as her thoughts became more coherent. The sounds rose to a gathering storm within her until she finally realized what they were: the nanites had fully activated, consuming her, likely attempting to heal the gunshot wound.

When her eyes eventually blinked open, though, she sensed something was wrong.

Raising her hands into view, Casey lost her breath. Where her pink fingers should have been, ashen fingers tipped with talons clawed into view. Peering down, she realized her entire body was covered with scaly, inhuman skin.

No! No, no, no . . .

The grotesque form that she'd hoped to suppress forever had, at long last, erupted fully back to the surface. Through newly formed oval black eyes, she perceived the world around her with heightened vision, revealing a fresh spectrum of light waves. The effect was so disorienting that she didn't have time to focus on the tumultuous storm raging in her belly. Light and shadow had reversed, causing the once-dark chamber surrounding her to blaze in a gamut of bright colors. Distant, muffled voices pulled her gaze away from the light and back toward the two men looming at her gray feet. Through the kaleidoscope of colors, she recognized Prewitt talking, though she had to concentrate to make out his words:

"You see?" he asked Donovan, his voice cheerful. "I told you she would survive."

Casey struggled to lift her head, which now felt heavier due to her newly enlarged cranium. As if providing further evidence of her transformation, clumps of hair lay across her boney shoulders. She wanted to cry but seemed to lack tear ducts. Blinking, she found Donovan's repulsed expression glaring back.

"If you call *that* surviving," he said, stepping back toward the exit, as if hoping to put as much distance as possible between himself and the thing lying on the floor. The thing that Casey had become. She didn't need a mirror to know what she looked like. Bulbous head, black eyes, ashen skin; the virus in Casey's bloodstream had transformed her as it had years ago, back on the ship. To save her, the virus had once again mutated Casey into the very thing she'd always dreaded: a human-seeker hybrid. A monster.

I'm no longer human. The words echoed from a waking dream she'd had the night after the crash. She'd tried for so long to prevent the change from occurring, and now that it had arrived, all Casey wanted to do was remain on the floor and beg Donovan to fire his weapon once more. But her lips, now a simple gash across her ghastly visage, didn't seem to work. Still numb from shock, Casey struggled to speak. No words came from her, though, as the men went back to the open doorway. Tilting to her side, Casey used all her strength to simply lift her left hand, trying to wave for them to stop. If they noticed, however, her pleas went ignored.

Prewitt grabbed the door and began to slide it closed, but it was seemingly too heavy for him to move by himself, so he gestured to Donovan. "Help me secure this before the eggs out here wake up."

Hunching over, Donovan leaned into the massive round door. "We're leaving her?" he asked, his voice trembling.

Casey struggled to crawl forward. Her taloned fingers dug into the ground, clawing inch by precious inch toward the men. Donovan, she assumed, saw her, but he kept his gaze averted.

"Miss Stevens should be safe enough from the creatures in there while we go topside," Prewitt assured him. "If I'm right, our visitor will be here shortly."

With a heavy clang the door finally closed, turning Casey's world to shadow.

No!

Her limbs burning, Casey collapsed onto her stomach. Gray, misshapen appendages twitched at her side. Opening her thin mouth, she gulped air, attempting to steady her thundering heartbeat. And yet, even encased in a dark chamber hundreds of meters below the planet's surface, Casey knew she wasn't alone.

A malicious consciousness blazed behind the closed door.

The eggs were hatching.

Donovan steadied himself on the ascending platform, eager to find sunlight. But so far, only darkness greeted him overhead. *Need to get out*, he thought, repeating the words over and over as if his mind were a laundry machine, tossing and turning. He hated it down there. Though the seekers were long dead, the walls whispered. Prewitt didn't seem to hear them. Or, if he did, he pretended like he didn't. Donovan tried to do the same. The place reminded him of the sights and sounds he'd been accosted by onboard the ship years prior. While no visions appeared this time, and no voices called out, Donovan thought he could still detect faint echoes bouncing around the vast red beams and angular corners.

Echoes of the dead, he thought. *Or, worse, the not yet born.*

When they'd first discovered the buried spire and Prewitt's scientists had rambled on about retrocausality, Donovan's brain physically ached from trying to figure out what the hell they were going on about. Pieces of the future flung back into the past. *Like me,* he thought. *Like Casey.* As soon as her name entered his mind, he tried to shove it aside. He didn't want to think about her or what he'd just witnessed. Blonde hair tumbling out of her scalp like loose straw, revealing a bulging, pulsing cranium. In the center, oval black eyes stared back, seemingly burrowing into his skull, peering right through him. If they did, he already knew what those black eyes had found—revulsion, disgust, and, most of all, fear. He'd been terrified of her the moment he'd seen what Casey had become all those years ago, back on the ship. What the ship had made her into. A thing.

Please, he begged, shivering, *anything but that. Better to die whole and human.*

As they continued to approach the surface, sunlight still hadn't appeared. Peering through a broken opening in the domed ceiling above, Donovan tried to make out a hint of sky or clouds, but he found nothing.

"Four-thirty," Prewitt mumbled beside him, checking his watch. "Too early for the sun to be down."

"It's not down," Donovan said through trembling lips. "It's blocked."

Once the platform stopped, they rushed outside. Standing in the courtyard, Prewitt lost his smile, and the color drained from his face as he realized they were standing beneath an enormous shadow. Under any other circumstance, Donovan would have mocked Prewitt for his ignorance, for his arrogance and his stupidity. But it was too late for that now. Instead, Donovan groaned, stifling back tears.

The ship had arrived.

A network of pipes and wires blanketed their view. As he peered up at the ship's underbelly, suspended only a few hundred yards above, the enormity of the thing dwarfed the reclamation plant.

A gasp escaped Prewitt's lips, and Donovan felt a sudden urge to berate the little man for inviting their doom, but Donovan couldn't tear his eyes off the giant structure. He'd never seen it from the outside before, and now, staring up at its dark gray shell with streams of green light emanating between the pipes, he wished he hadn't. Engulfed in a seemingly endless shadow, Donovan had never felt so small.

And I thought this thing looked creepy on the inside.

Through the corner of his eye, he noted soldiers putting on gas masks and raising their weapons in preparation. The image was almost comical, tiny dots scrambling around for something to make them feel safe beneath a ship large enough to block out the sun. Even so, Donovan pulled out his gas mask as well, secured it around his head, and then checked his rifle's chamber. His movements were languid, slowed by the knowledge that none of their pathetic weapons or safety equipment could possibly save them. If the damn thing wanted to, the ship could simply land, squashing them all like bugs. Donovan winced at the thought.

Bugs. That's all we are to it.

Once his mask was secure, he turned to find Prewitt had already donned his own. Somehow, the little man's shoulders remained square, his back rigid. It was as if Prewitt were a king awaiting his court. Despite himself, Donovan couldn't help but be impressed. Even in the face of absolute defeat, Prewitt stood ready, perhaps eager, to negotiate with the damn thing. For once, Donovan wished he had a bit of Prewitt's arrogance, if only so his rapid breathing wouldn't continue to cloud his mask.

He tried to thrust his shoulders back to match Prewitt's, but it was a hollow gesture. Peering up at the hulking monolith above, a single thought repeated itself in Donovan's mind:

Please don't let it take me back inside.

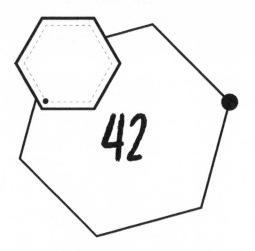

42

An emerald void pulled Harold through the air, descending toward the group of scrambling dots below. Soldiers, he imagined. Once again, he was a mere passenger trapped in his own body. Like a silent voyeur, Harold watched the rushing people below grow larger and larger. The seeker within him seemed anxious. The farther they drew away from the ship, the more its agitation boiled to the surface. As soon as Harold's feet touched the ground, the energy beam vanished. Above him, the ship hung motionless, blocking out the sky.

Along the structure's raised catwalks, snipers scurried, aiming their weapons. However, the seeker ignored them, instead turning its focus toward two men standing twenty yards away. One was tall, holding a rifle. The other was short. The second man stood with his hands on his hips, waiting, as if he owned the place. For all Harold knew, perhaps he did.

Harold's legs stepped forward, propelling him to-ward the waiting soldiers. When the seeker drew within five yards of the men, though, something caused it to stop. Harold felt his heart racing. Was the seeker fright-ened? Surely not by these men.

Behind them, an enormous metallic enclosure was wheeled into view. Soldiers flanked it, nervously eye-ing its contents. Small holes along the side offered hints of what waited within, but the way the box thrashed around, its steel walls clanging, Harold could easily guess its contents.

A full-grown abomination.

The seeker came to a stop, eyeing the rattling box. In front of it, the taller man turned, as if noticing the cage for the first time, while the little man never took his masked gaze off of Harold.

"Welcome," the little man said through his gas mask. "I've been expecting you." Even though his voice was distorted by the mask's air vent, Harold couldn't help noticing how seemingly unaffected he seemed by the ship or Harold's appearance. The little man acted as if he were inviting someone over for tea and crumpets. Per-haps it was the cage's contents that gave the small man so much confidence. The taller man, however, didn't seem to share his companion's enthusiasm. His rifle bobbed up and down, as if he were trying to keep it steady in his shaky arms.

Bile slithered up Harold's throat as the seeker kept his eyes fixed on the thing in the box. As if noticing, the small man turned, gesturing toward the enclosure.

"Nothing to be alarmed about," he assured the seeker. "Simply a precaution so that we might have a productive conversation."

A conversation, Harold repeated inwardly. The seeker wasn't amused. Harold felt acid burning his throat. The creature inside him was growing angrier by the moment.

"I have something you want," the little man continued. "Casey Stevens."

The seeker turned Harold's eyes down toward the little man. That seemed to have gotten its attention. Considering how Harold had imagined this might go, he couldn't help but be impressed that the little man was still breathing, let alone talking.

"I have her secured below, surrounded by hundreds of these . . ." He paused, nodding toward the cage. "These, well, whatever you call them."

"Abomination," Harold heard his own voice say in a low guttural tone.

"Yes," the little man replied, approaching the enclosure. He peered into one of the air holes to get a better look before quickly withdrawing. "Apropos name, I guess. Disgusting creature, to be sure. But you have no need for concern," he assured the seeker, throwing his arms wide. "I have something you *want,* and it just so happens that you have something I *need.*"

Dear lord, Harold thought. *Is this guy really trying to negotiate?* He couldn't believe what he was hearing. The seeker, however, seemed neither astonished nor impressed. Glowering, it simply watched and waited.

"In this time period, there is a government called the USSR," the little man said matter-of-factly. "Give me the knowledge and the technology to destroy them, and I'll give you Casey."

Wind kicked up dust around them as Harold noted his own breathing growing shallow in his chest. His eyes never left the little man, studying him. When the seeker didn't respond, however, the little man's voice hardened. "I should tell you," he said, "Casey has been shot in the chest and may die if you don't get to her shortly."

At that, Harold's body twitched, and the bile returned, burning his stomach and throat. The seeker seemed to tremble inwardly. Fear, Harold decided. The creature was afraid, not for itself but for Casey. It needed her alive. His feet took several steps closer. The taller of the two men retreated, but the little one held his ground. Behind him, the metal enclosure rattled more violently the closer Harold approached.

Seemingly unconcerned, the little man smiled confidently. "Do we have a deal?"

The seeker stopped. Harold felt his own muscles tense. He wanted to scream for the men to shut up and run, but his protests were muted. Boiling rage bubbled up within him, flushing his skin.

Faster than the eye could register, the seeker gave his answer. With a single swipe, Harold ripped out the little man's throat.

PART IV

HOME

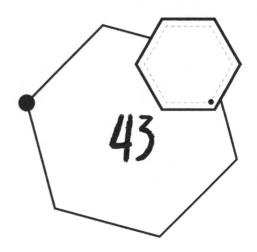

43

It began with a faint scratching, something clawing at the door.

Many somethings, Casey thought, judging by the sound of it. The incessant noise grew louder, ear piercing. Once the metal began to creak, buckling from a weight behind the door, Casey found enough strength to push herself off the floor. As she scrambled to her feet, something caught her eye. Below, drenched in a pool of blood, lay the dislodged bullet. The nanites must have pushed it out before sealing her wound. Still, her chest burned, and her legs felt like limp noodles, twisting beneath her. The doorframe buckled. She needed a way out. Quickly.

Casey hobbled away, inching farther into the darkness behind her. Yet, the blackness also revealed flickers of light, fiery blooms of orange and crimson. Her new eyesight made out heat signatures radiating from deep within the darkened room. Struggling toward the bloom's light, she hoped for an exit. As she stumbled past vacant, fleshy sacks, she wondered where all the cloned bodies had gone. By her count, thousands of corpses should have been blocking her escape, but the dusty floor lay barren. Up ahead the light bloom brightened. Behind her the metal door whined, cracking open as the spidery things clawed their way inside. Fire cranked up her ashen-gray body, propelling her faster and faster into the shadows.

The bloom in the dark came more clearly into view. It wasn't a door; it was a vent. Hot air seemed to be erupting from a lower level at the floor's base. As the rushing scamper of spidery legs edged closer, Casey didn't bother to worry about where the opening might lead. She needed an exit, and this would have to do.

With relative ease, her clawed arms tore the cover grate off, and then she flung herself feet first into the heated hole. Noting her distorted form, Casey prayed she'd be able to change herself back to her normal when this was over. She'd done it before, years ago, but even if she could, now wasn't the time. Casey needed an edge to keep herself strong and moving, even at the cost of her own humanity.

Dropping through the hole, she tumbled through a slender octagonal tube as the red-and-orange bloom burned brighter and brighter beneath her until, at last, Casey fell out of the tube and into an empty, musty atmosphere. With a heavy *thud*, she hit something that snapped and broke beneath her weight. Rolling over the rough surface, Casey reached out to slow her momentum. Her clawed fingers coiled around something brittle, which began to give way until her movement finally stopped.

Catching her breath, she peered back toward the vent, waiting to see if the spidery things had followed. If they had, they didn't seem to be close, at least not yet. It seemed she had bought herself a momentary reprieve.

Rolling onto her stomach, she rose to her knees, then stopped when she found herself staring at two large, empty eye sockets. She was lying on top of a gray clone, its body withered, mummified. Flinching backwards in disgust, Casey saw dozens of mummified remains on either side of her. She was lying on top of hundreds of broken corpses. She would have screamed if her lungs had allowed it, but the burning in her chest from the still-healing gunshot wound caused the scream to lodge in her throat.

Casey tried to scramble to her feet, but every action caused her to sink farther into the pile of deformed bodies. It was like some sort of multi-limbed quicksand. She dropped waist deep as limbs and appendages wrapped around her. It was as if the dead were trying to drag her to hell. All things considered, such a description wasn't too far off the mark. This *was* hell. With her body twisted and changed and spidery creatures quickly approaching, anger swelled in Casey's chest. Ignoring her fear, she clawed her way out of the dusty, mummified remains. At last she tumbled free, collapsing onto a hard floor. The pile of bodies towered over her like a monolith of the dead.

Finding purchase, she rose to her feet and hoped she wouldn't be the next addition to this buried graveyard. She needed to find a way out. Twisting her oversized cranium around, she found the source of the heat bloom. Through her new eyes, it appeared as a giant ball of red fire.

The tower's hypersphere.

As the four-dimensional sphere rotated in the darkness, it pulsed with flickering light.

Buried down here for a million years, and the damned thing is still functioning.

Casey approached it hesitantly. The last time she'd touched a hypersphere, it had taken her to her own future, though she hadn't understood that at the time. Could it now take her out of that tomb? If so, what would it reveal? Would she even want to see it? Stepping closer, she was so enthralled by the spinning shapes and moving light that it took a moment before she noted the sounds approaching from above and behind her.

Tiny legs scampering along metal. The creatures were in the air duct.

Stopping less than ten yards from the enormous sphere, Casey spun around, spotting a black mass pouring from the overhead opening. At first it looked like a pool of black water shimmering along the roof. Then the blight grew closer, and their distinct shapes scrambled into view. Countless creatures swarmed overhead while others crawled above the pile of bodies behind her. She scanned left and right for any possible escape but found none.

The creatures dropped from the ceiling, pouring over her. Countless tiny legs and pincers jabbed and cut through her scaly flesh. As she writhed beneath the onslaught, Casey's inflamed lungs finally allowed her to scream.

Legs crawled into her open mouth, pushing past her teeth and reaching for her tongue. Her engorged skull grew heavy from the mass of undulating bodies until, at last, she stumbled, crumpling to her knees. More creatures appeared in her peripheral vision. Pincers and legs thrust and sliced into her scaly skin like a thousand needles injecting her from a thousand angles. Casey collapsed under the weight of it. Flinching, prone on the floor, she struggled to activate her internal nanites in the hope of slowing time and creating an escape, but the effort merely caused red mist to pour from her mouth and nose as her body weakened under their attack. The creatures sucked up the mist from her mouth like starving children at her breast. She was helpless. Swarms of tiny bodies blotted her vision as the creatures covered her face.

The world became a crawling mass of darkness.

She felt biting pincers tear through flesh, ripping at her arms, chest, and legs. Buried beneath the mass of hungry mouths, she was no longer able to scream, move, or fight.

The creatures were eating her alive.

And then, as suddenly as they'd arrived, the spiders vanished from view. A wave of burning, blinding crimson light blazed, dissolving the creatures into clouds of black dust. Her vision returned as the bodies vanished from her deformed face. Gulping air, she felt the stale oxygen fill her lungs as she writhed on the floor. The blinding light pulsed brighter, causing her to throw her clawed hands up to shield herself from it. When she was finally able to see, she realized she was alone on the floor, covered in black dust.

Above, the enormous hypersphere spun unimpeded. It had saved her.

Sensing the nanites within her bloodstream scurrying to repair the hundreds of bite marks, Casey struggled to rise.

The sphere continued to spin, creating various shapes within its moving rings. Circles within circles within circles. Seemingly endless. As she hobbled over to it, Casey's breath grew shallow, and her appendages twitched from an abundance of adrenaline. The red light was warm and inviting. Trapped hundreds of meters below the ground with no other exit, Casey reached out with shaking fingers and touched the swirling sphere. As she had done a decade earlier, she spoke to the sphere not through words but rather through emotions. To communicate, she chose a single phrase: *Escape!*

In silent reply, the sphere spun faster. Red light engulfed her, swallowing the world. When the light subsided, darkness once again overtook the hollow chamber.

Casey was gone.

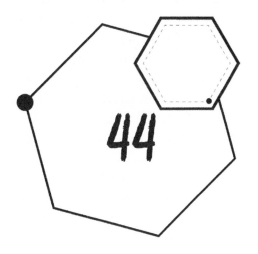

44

Pandemonium became a slow-moving picture show. Like images flickering before the eyes, one by one, a fractured piecemeal of various horrors assaulted the senses all at once. Warm blood splattered Donovan's shocked face, dripping into his open mouth. The taste of it made him retch. To his left, Prewitt gurgled, clutching his slashed throat before collapsing in a puff of dirt. His red-eyed murderer, drenched in gory spray, spun around, looking for its next victim. Donovan raised his rifle, his arms trembling. It seemed to take an eternity to line up a shot.

Beyond his target, a green light erupted once again from the ship as a silhouette descended. *Another one,* Donovan thought with a curse, inching his way back as he tried to steady his finger on the trigger. When the ship's beam vanished, a red-and-black figure emerged on the balcony overhead. Its movement was a blur, rushing from one sniper to the next. Donovan couldn't make out the thing's precise actions, but its intentions were all too clear. Along the balcony, soldiers and weapons flew over the side in a gory mess. Closer, the blood-drenched man rushed forward. Releasing a pent-up breath, Donovan fired, but a black mass of undulating appendages knocked him aside just as he pulled the trigger. The shot went wild.

Donovan fell to the ground, unsure who or what had caused him to miss. Then a thing beyond description emerged from the metal box, blinking past. Six tentacles flailed, extending from its back. Its head, arms, and body appeared more insect than man. A domed skull dripped into view. Its silhouette seemed to scan the area, first lingering on Donovan, then turning on the red-eyed man. The black, oily thing lunged at Prewitt's killer.

Thank Christ, Donovan thought, scrambling to his feet. *Let the monsters kill each other.*

On the platform above, the third creature with its red-and-black skin leaped down, jumping between Prewitt's killer and the tentacled beast. Lying in a cloud of dust, Donovan fumbled to reload his weapon. Overhead, the grotesque clone and the red-eyed killer faced off with the giant monstrosity. The oily thing spun this way and that, as if deciding which creature to devour first.

Sitting up, Donovan faced a similar question as his rifle's sight jumped from one target to the next. If he fired on any of them, he'd be helping the others. Grinding his teeth, Donovan tasted blood in his mouth and wondered if it was his own or Prewitt's. That thought broke him out of his internal debate. A squad of soldiers appeared, weapons raised but holding their fire. He assumed they weren't certain who to shoot either. Without a clear target, Donovan lowered his rifle, then turned and ran back inside the reclamation plant, deciding to let the others fight it out.

Inside the plant, Donovan paused above the open pit and round platform, glancing around for somewhere to hide. Not wishing to head back down into the spire's wreckage, he clanged up a series of steps, crossing the third-floor catwalk and rushing toward a series of small offices at the end. With no power to the upstairs levels, the rooms were cloaked in darkness. *Good*, he thought. He needed to be somewhere quiet and dark. Someplace safe.

If there even was such a place.

It wasn't until he flung open the office door and dove beneath a wooden desk that he remembered the giant ship overhead, which could land any second, crushing them all like bugs. *Should've run to a car*, Donovan thought, cursing.

Trying to remember how far across the open field he'd have to get before reaching a vehicle, he quickly tossed the idea aside. Shuddering beneath the desk, his body spasmed, and his head swam due to his hyperventilating. His nerves frazzled, Donovan was in no condition to try to make another run outside. It was better to stay there hidden and wait it out.

Maybe they'll all be too busy killing each other to come looking for me.

An itch at the back of his skull replied. **No, Donnie, no one's forgotten you.**

Donovan's head banged against the underside of the desk as he jumped up, letting out a strangled squeal. He knew that voice. He remembered it. The voice from the ship. After all these years, it had found him.

*Yes, **Donnie**,* the voice said in a mocking tone, ***run, hide***.

Donovan's eyes watered, and his lips trembled.

Ready or not, here we come!

His rifle rattled so violently in his hands that he nearly dropped it.

Outside, the sound of gunshots snapped Donovan's attention toward the door. The firing only continued for another moment before it died out, followed by silence. If the soldiers had all been killed, that meant the monsters would be coming. Half of him still wanted to make a run for a vehicle outside, hoping to get out from under the ship's mammoth shadow. The other half wanted to simply stay put and whimper in the dark. The latter half won.

An echoed reverberation of feet clanging up the metal staircase shattered the thick silence. Fidgeting with his rifle, Donovan made sure a bullet was locked and loaded before he leveled it at the closed office door. He heard footsteps stop outside, accompanied by a rasping breath. It sounded as tired as his own. Salty sweat dripped down from his hairline, stinging Donovan's eyes as he slid his finger over the trigger. As he waited for the door to open, every second felt like an eternity.

And yet, the door didn't open, and no one entered. Instead, a hoarse, inhuman voice hissed from beyond. "Yooou wanted aaa deeeal. Weee don't want yooou."

His chest thundering like a jackhammer, it took a solid twenty heartbeats before Donovan's mind caught up to his ears, and he understood what was on offer.

"If I take you to Casey," he asked through clattering teeth, "you'll let me go?"

"Yeeesss."

Keeping his weapon raised, Donovan used the back of his hand to wipe spittle from his mouth. Even in his panicked state, though, the offer seemed too good to be true. "How do I know you'll keep your end of the bargain?" he asked.

"Yooouuu doooon't."

Clenching his rifle in his dripping palms, Donovan pushed it against his shoulder, ready to fire. Still, the door remained shut. The thing had to be only inches away, but if Donovan fired through the door and missed his target, he wouldn't have time to reload before it was too late. Still, the thing outside offered no guarantees.

His mind racing, Donovan lowered his weapon and crawled out from under the desk, having decided that a possibly empty promise was better than no promise at all.

"Fine," he said, "But I keep the gun."

Lurching forward on wobbly legs, he struggled to remain upright as the doorknob slowly turned.

The door opened, revealing a shadowy silhouette. Then a red-and-black figure pooled inward. *Like liquid shadow*, Donovan thought. Its eyes were white with red lines along the edges. Bloodshot. The stuff of nightmares made flesh. Donovan swallowed.

"Deeeaaal," the creature hissed.

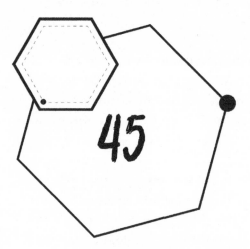

45

Another time, Another place

No mother should ever have to watch their child die. Casey Anderson, formally Casey Stevens, stood beside her daughter's bed, separated by a plastic sheet. The stink of disinfectant wafted into her nostrils while, overhead, the air conditioner droned on and on, assaulting Casey's eardrums with its constant whirl. Her vision blurred behind her teary eyes and the hanging plastic sheet. Even the doctors and nurses, floating in from time to time, wore plastic suits and masks. Her daughter, Sarah, had just turned seven, and unless something changed, Casey doubted she'd make it to eight. Casey's father had always said that doctors and scientists were no damn good. Now, having watched them poke and prod her little girl over the past couple of days with the same damn tests over and over again, she was starting to think the bastard might've been right. These doctors had no answers. All Casey could do was stand there, helpless.

Waiting. She couldn't even hold her daughter's hand. Another wave of tears blurred her vision. Casey didn't bother to wipe them away. *Let 'em come,* she thought. *Some things can't be stopped.*

Glancing through the open door, she noticed more doctors rush by. Like scurrying rats, she thought. *Why can't any of you people do anything?* A throbbing flame ran up the back of her calves. Plopping down, she sat in the lone chair beside the plastic-covered bed. Checking her watch, she wondered where her husband had gone. He had said he was out following leads, hoping to find the virus's origin, but that had been two days ago, and Casey needed him at her side. She wasn't strong enough to bear another day alone. The weight of it was too much for her. All these doctors and nurses and support staff, yet Casey had to sit alone beside her dying daughter. She wanted to scream and rage and smash something, but instead she simply sat there, waiting.

Have they tried a silicon-based protein injection? a feminine voice asked.

Casey looked up from her lap, expecting to find someone in the room with them, but there was no one. Before she could open her mouth to ask who it was, the voice returned.

It may slow the nanites' effect.

It wasn't a voice, Casey realized; it was her imagination.

You know what to do, the voice pressed. ***Why are you just sitting there?***

"What?" Casey muttered, her voice barely above a whisper. If this was her imagination, it seemed to have a life of its own. Perhaps she was more tired than she realized.

You passed the virus on to her, the voice snapped.
How could you be so stupid?

Casey stood, swaying back and forth. Blood rushed
to her head as she stumbled from her child's bed to
the private bathroom. On the walls and toilet were
more plastic coverings. Casey leaned over the sink and
splashed water over her face. She was just beating herself
up; that was it. Blaming herself for whatever was wrong
with Sarah. No one knew what had caused the strange
infection. It wasn't Casey's fault. Maybe it wasn't anyone's fault. It was a disease, as simple as that. And dis-
eases were caused by nature, not people, she reminded
herself.

Bullshit! the inner voice screamed so loudly that it
made her head throb. ***You did this!***

Again, Casey splashed water onto her face, hoping
the coldness of it would drown out the screams rattling
around in her skull. *I'm losing it,* she thought. Peering
into the mirror, she felt a sudden inner horror at how
much she'd aged. At forty-one, she was still a handsome
woman, but age lines had begun to leave their mark.
Something inside of her seemed as shocked by what she
saw as Casey was by what she heard. It was as if another
version of herself was staring through her eyes at the
foggy mirror and didn't like what it saw. Turning off the
water, she went back into the room, wiping her eyes and
stared down at her sleeping child.

Sarah's eyes were open but pitch black, like inky
pools, no irises or whites within them. Her skin had
turned ashen gray, and red veins crisscrossed over her
tiny, fragile body.

Why don't you remember? the voice asked, softer in
tone. ***The virus came from the ship.***

Casey's back straightened, more curious than frightened.

"What ship?"

Then, a jolt, like an electric shock, burst through her body, and the image shifted.

Abruptly, Casey found herself standing in a different hospital room. A mirror on the wall revealed her own, normal, thirty-three-year-old reflection. Another time, another place. *But when?* she wondered.

Nurses rushed around a bed while an unseen baby screamed. Hovering in the doorway, a familiar face loomed. Casey's father. Only he didn't appear as the decrepit, broken-down drunk she remembered. His face was free of jagged frown lines, and his hair was brown instead of ashen. He almost looked handsome, Casey thought. *The past*, she realized. *Which means . . .*

Rushing past nurses, Casey found her mother lying in a pool of blood, her legs spread, a crimson smear drenching her sheets and the bed. Clutching her baby daughter against her chest, an older version of Sarah struggled for air through shallow breaths.

"She's losing too much blood!" one of the nurses screamed. "Get the doctor!"

No! Casey screamed through ghostly lips. The world around her paid no notice to her pleas. Unable to bear the moment of her mother's death, Casey's eyes fell to the floor. Why hadn't Sarah listened? Why hadn't she taken the money and run off to a new life? A better life. A safer life. Casey turned and lurched away. She didn't want to see this.

Then, a thought entered her mind. It was Sarah's voice. *My daughter deserves to live.*

Spinning, Casey's jaw slackened as she met her

mother's weakened gaze. Sarah was staring directly at her, as if she somehow saw her ghostly daughter's visage. *You are my life now . . .*

". . . Casey," Sarah finished aloud.

Casey's father inched closer. "What did you say, hon?"

"Casey," she repeated weakly, handing the baby to him, its screams growing in volume.

The adult Casey bent down, embracing her dying mother.

A rush of red light returned Casey to the underground lair and the swirling hypersphere. Lying on the floor, she stared up at the twisting, turning shape, shocked by what it had revealed. The past and the future. Mothers and daughters, connected through time. Would Casey's own daughter die too? *That won't happen*, she vowed. *I won't let it, no matter what.* She would never allow the machine virus to spread, not to a potential offspring or anyone else. She would rather die.

And, hopefully, I'll take the ship down with me.

Shaking the vision away, Casey spun around, searching for an exit. The only one her still-black eyes could detect was the mild heat signature wafting back up through the vent she'd fallen through. Her gaze lowered to the bodies piled beneath. She'd have to climb over them to get back up. Suppressing a shiver, Casey trudged determinedly back the way she'd come.

Pausing at the base of the towering corpses, she again eyed the vent above. If the bodies didn't crumble beneath her, Casey could reach the vent. Still, her gray feet didn't move. It seemed that her alien body wasn't any more excited to make the climb than she was.

Reaching out with a clawed hand, she gripped the lowest appendage and began her ascent. Mummified remains snapped and broke under her weight, but enough of them held for her to continue. Keeping her attention on the vent above, Casey didn't bother to look down. She didn't have to. She could feel the torsos, skulls, and tangled limbs crumbling beneath her. Her gut twisting, she moved slowly, careful not to put too much weight on the delicate remains stacked to the ceiling. Overhead, the vent hung, waiting.

An escape, she thought, *but to what?*

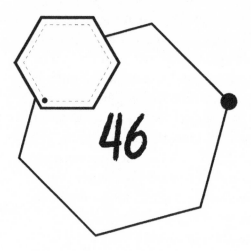

46

Donovan hovered between two daunting figures, clutching his weapon as if to remind himself that he wasn't entirely powerless. As they stood on the platform, the disc rushed them ever deeper into the earth. On his left was a blood-soaked man dressed in a once-white lab coat. To his right was the ghastly red-and-black creature. Every which way Donovan looked, horrors stared back at him. The farther they descended, the smaller his bolt-action rifle felt in his sweaty hands.

When the platform finally slowed to a stop, Donovan felt no relief. Before, he had been above ground, surrounded by monsters. Now he was buried hundreds of meters in the earth, standing right alongside them. If anything, his chances seemed even slimmer than they had been earlier. He just hoped these creatures kept their end of the bargain.

After, of course, they found Casey.

Casey. Jesus, how he hated the sound of her name. Ten years of being manipulated, used, and haunted by others, all so they could get their grubby little fingers on that woman. Donovan was a mere afterthought in the equation, a pawn used to capture the queen.

Queen bitch. Let them have her. I'll be glad to never think about or hear about her again. He chuckled to himself. *If I even survive this.*

Stepping off the platform, Donovan shone a flashlight across their barren surroundings. Broken red beams and jagged rock intermingled to create an eerie cave. Behind him, Donovan heard one of the creatures suck in a hard breath. Twitching the light around, he found the source of his captors' concern: countless rocky eggs lay strewn about at their feet. Newly opened, broken apart by violent hatching. Donovan spun his light this way and that in search of the spidery things that had crawled out of them, but nothing moved. The shadows remained dormant as they continued into darkness. A few more steps, and Donovan's light wavered; his heart leaped in his chest, and his eyes watered.

Shit! Not now!

He shook the light, and it regained some of its brilliance. Sighing with momentary relief, he continued.

Ahead, the light's beam caught the entrance to the cloning chamber. Curled metal opened into darkness, the shards like jagged bones. The door had been torn asunder. Gulping stale air, Donovan's relief vanished as quickly as it appeared. The spidery creatures had gotten inside, sealing Casey's, and possibly Donovan's, fate.

Reluctant to turn back toward his captors, and terrified to see their reaction, Donovan pushed shrapnel aside and entered, thinking it was better to keep moving forward. The sound of his captors' footfalls echoed closer, flanking him. With each step forward, Donovan's heart thumped faster in his chest. Sweat cascaded down his face, burning his eyes.

Only, the cloning chamber was empty. His heart leaping in his chest, Donovan whipped the flickering flashlight around, frantic. Where was her body? And where were all the spider creatures? Quickening his pace in the hopes of increasing the distance between himself and the two looming behind, Donovan searched every wall and crevice with his light's beam. Withered sacks lay clumped everywhere, but there were no spider things and no Casey to be found.

At last, the black-and-red monster behind him spoke. The sound of its hissing voice in the dark made Donovan's feet falter. "Sheee iisss noooot heeeere."

Sucking in cold breath, Donovan spun, leveling his weapon at his captors. "Stay back!"

The red-eyed man in the bloody lab coat knocked the rifle aside so fast that it took a moment for Donovan to realize he was no longer holding it. As Donovan backed away, his knees gave out and he stumbled to the floor. Tears and saliva were smeared across his quivering lips. "Please . . ."

The possessed man and the sickly clone loomed on either side of him. *This is it,* Donovan thought as the red-eyed man reached for his throat. *This is how I go out, blubbering on the floor.*

Behind them a loud *whoosh* grabbed their attention. Someone had activated the platform outside. Turning in unison, the two creatures bolted from the room toward the antechamber, leaving Donovan quivering on his knees. His face covered in tears and snot, he keeled over and clutched his pounding chest. Crying on the floor, he glanced around for his fallen weapon. As he scanned the darkness with his flashlight, the bulb flickered, and its illumination dulled to a pale yellow. At that moment Donovan realized what could be worse than being killed by those things: Being left down there alone, buried alive.

Snatching his rifle, he leaped up and ran out of the room, trailing the creatures.

It didn't take long to find them. Heads tilted upwards, they watched the platform shoot up the spire and out of view. Without the platform's glow, Donovan's flashlight became a pinprick in the dark.

"What happened?" Donovan asked, despite himself.

Angered, the creatures spun toward him.

"She is trying to escape," the red-eyed man said.

Donovan felt his throbbing legs twitch beneath him. If Casey was alive, then maybe there was still hope for him. It was a long shot, but Donovan decided to press his luck. "Th-then she's trapped," he stammered. "The ship is out there. We've got her!"

"Nooo." The ghastly clone glared at him with blood-shot eyes. "Something eeelse awaits heeeer."

Beside him, the red-eyed man nodded. "Something worse."

47

As the platform rocketed toward the surface, Casey concentrated on slowing her breathing.

Reaching inward, she calmed the firing nanites, slowly changing her body back to normal. Her hair regrew, her eyes morphed from black to green, and her scaly gray skin turned pink. Under her shirt, she saw breasts bulge, returning her to her natural, feminine form. As the platform's glow illuminated the change, relief washed over her like a cold, cleansing shower. Still, she knew the monstrous visage, with all its enhanced strength and rage, was simmering just beneath the surface, waiting for her to need it again. Only, next time, she decided, she'd be using her power against the ship. Casey should have destroyed it long ago and swore not to make the same mistake again. If given the chance, she'd tear that damnable thing to shreds. For the moment, though, she just needed to get the hell out of that place, to lick her wounds and live to fight another day. It was a nice thought, but she doubted it would be that easy. It never was.

Overhead, a dim light grew from a small pinprick into a large circle as the platform rose to the surface. She'd escaped. She sighed. Then, as the platform stopped, her heart did the same, until—

She spotted something moving out of the corner of her eye.

Lurking at the domed structure's entrance, a black tentacled shape blocked her way.

Yep, she thought, *never easy.*

The thing appeared to be the same type of creature she'd seen back at Area 51, except this time, she knew, it smelled the infection inside her. Casey backed off the platform, glancing left and right for a place to hide. She was too late. The hulking thing roared with a voice akin to a screaming child. The noise made Casey nauseous. Instead of escaping, she'd simply traded one nightmare for another. The creature lumbered forward, limping on its right leg, seemingly wounded, but its slower pace didn't stop its tentacles from lunging, reaching for her.

Casey ran, and the monster followed.

Its thundering footsteps pounded close behind as she raced up a metal staircase. The creature didn't attempt to climb the steps; it didn't have to. Instead, its tentacles snaked upwards. The first one knocked her against a concrete wall. The second one snatched Casey by the legs, yanked her into the air, and dangled her over its pincer-laced mouth. Its jagged teeth snapped hungrily. The stench of its breath made her stomach turn as she flailed madly in its grip. Over the thing's shoulder, she saw the platform several feet behind it. Struggling within its wet, sickly grasp, Casey had an idea. Executing it, however, would be easier said than done. Her eyes fluttering, she activated the nanites within her, careful not to overdo it. She just needed a small boost of speed and strength, enough to break her free from the thing's writhing clutches.

Fire burned through her chest and limbs as the nanites scurried in her bloodstream. Around her, dust particles in the air slowed, the creature's tentacles loosened, and its approaching pincers ceased their snapping. Time had slowed. Moving faster than the creature could comprehend, Casey twisted herself out from the coiling appendages, slid down to the ground, and kicked the beast square in the chest. With a snap, time resumed, and Casey's movements turned languid.

Reeling in shock, the thing stumbled back from her enhanced blow and then edged closer to the platform. Casey needed to drive the creature farther back. Leaping, she raced past it. The thing spun, flailing. A swarm of oily black limbs swirled around her as she navigated beneath them.

When she was inches from the platform, one of them coiled around her waist, squeezing the oxygen from her lungs. Casey saw stars. The dim light from outside and the shadows from within blurred. Another tentacle went for her throat. Delving into the last of her reserve strength, she threw her arms up, blocking the flailing appendage. Still, the thing pulled her closer. Below, the platform was mere inches away. However, Casey realized the creature was too big and too heavy for her to pull it toward it. She needed another element of surprise. Instead of pulling away, Casey spun in its grip and lunged forward, smashing her fist into the creature's snapping pincers. They cut through her knuckles and wrist, turning her hand bloody, but Casey continued her onslaught.

Surprised, the creature slackened its tentacles. Now was her chance.

Bending backwards, Casey used all her heightened strength to bring the thing forward. She dropped to the floor, pulling with her arms and legs to propel the thing above her head, flipping it up and over onto the platform.

The oily black thing landed with a violent *thud*.

Activated by movement, the platform lowered. Casey lay just outside of the round hole, catching her breath. Then two tentacles reached up, flailing madly, trying to find purchase and drag her down with it. One of them slapped her leg with wet ooze. It slithered around her calf, pulling her over the edge, into the pit. The thing's weight was too much for her to bear. Her fingers flailing, unable to grab onto anything, Casey slid over the side.

At the last second, her hand found the edge, holding onto it for dear life. However, as soon as she'd grabbed hold, her grasp loosened. Below, her leg was being crushed by the coiled tentacle. As if in automatic response, her left arm changed, reverting to its scaly gray form, her pink fingers transforming into taloned daggers. Casey tore at the tentacle, ripping it in two. With an ear-piercing cry, the thing fell with the platform, sliding out of view. Its screams died in the darkness.

Casey dangled over the ledge. Reaching up with her clawed hand, her talons dug into the concrete, pulling herself up. Her limbs heavy and her chest heaving, she lay on the floor, catching her breath. Too exhausted to worry about her arm, she clambered to her feet and lumbered toward the exit.

Outside, carnage awaited. Plodding wearily through open doors, she found blood-covered bodies strewn about, soldiers, many of them missing limbs. Stopping at the closest body, Casey recognized the frail shape lying in a crimson mess. Prewitt, his eyes wide and his hands clutching his bloody throat. Casey couldn't help but hope he'd died screaming.

The blood pooling around him darkened, as did the ground around it. It was as if the sunlight had been muted. Perhaps, Casey thought, she'd been down there longer than she realized. As she peered up at the sky, however, the answer became obvious.

A familiar, hulking monolith was floating overhead, speckled by blinking green lights. Fully formed and seemingly healed, it blanketed the horizon, stretching farther than she could see.

The ship hung silently, waiting for her. Only then, standing in its shadow, did Casey realize that all of her efforts had been for nothing. There was no escape. There never had been. Not really. For all her fighting and running, every moment had inevitably led her here. Back to the ship.

Instead of cowering, Casey's back straightened, and her eyes narrowed to slits. Her gray arm transformed back to normal, though the nanites within her remained active and ready.

Alright, here I am. Come and get me.

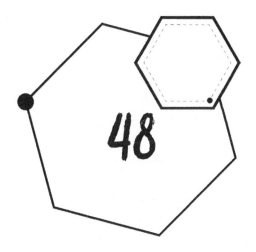

48

*B*etter to kill him now than to leave this poor bastard to *starve down here,* Harold decided.

The sweaty man fidgeted with his rifle, struggling to keep it level. Plucking a stray thought from the seeker within him, Harold was able to attach a name to the man's pale face: *Donovan*. Neither of the seekers seemed particularly concerned by Donovan's rifle as it wavered back and forth between them. *And why should they be?* Harold thought. The bodies they possessed were mere dressing. Even if Donovan calmed his nerves enough to pull the trigger and hit one of them, the seekers would simply take his body instead, leaving Harold or the clone to bleed out down there. While Harold hated being someone's puppet, he wasn't eager to die either.

Eyeing Donovan, Harold wanted to snatch the rifle away. Instead, the seeker within him tilted their view, focusing on a distant sound overhead. The platform was returning. Had the seekers summoned it? Was Casey returning? Harold counted the long, silent seconds as a faint glow from the platform's bottom inched into view. When it finally stopped before him, an oily nightmare awaited. Roaring, the abomination lurched forward. Yet, now with a severed tentacle and steadying itself with a limp, the black shape was slow to attack. Weary, even.

Not hesitating, the Prime lunged first. Tentacles swarmed around him as if trying to gather the clone within its flailing appendages, but the Prime was too fast and too strong to be stopped by an injured prey. Soon, Harold entered the conflict as well, watching helplessly as his own hands pummeled the beast. Its sickly flesh squished beneath his assault. When they'd faced the thing before, above ground, the battle had ended in a stalemate. This time, however, the abomination was weak, its attacks slow, and its defenses almost non-existent. Harold couldn't help wondering if the beast knew it was about to die. Working in unison, the Prime and the seeker controlling Harold tore the thing apart, piece by chunky piece. Black ooze splattered about, drenching them. If he'd had control over his body, Harold would have vomited. Undeterred, his master pressed on until, at last, the oily shape dripped to the floor, gurgling its last breath. Once destroyed, the thing's body broke apart into a liquid mess, dripping into crevices along the floor.

Eager to get out of there, Harold was thrilled to see himself step once more onto the lift. The Prime did the same. It wasn't until Donovan approached, leveling his weapon, that Harold even remembered the man was there. His eyes wide and seemingly full of hope, Donovan planted himself squarely on the platform.

"Geettt off," the Prime hissed, looming over Donovan.

In response, Donovan shoved the rifle's muzzle into the clone's chest. "We had a deal."

In a blur of sparks and shattering metal, the Prime snapped the rifle in two. Agog, Donovan backed away, but he still didn't leave the platform. Harold watched himself lunge, grabbing Donovan by the shoulder and tossing him off the platform like a rag doll. Noting his enhanced speed and strength, which the seeker provided, Harold wondered what kind of toll such exertion would wreak on his body when this was all over. If, that is, it was ever over.

"Wait!" Donovan scrambled to his feet as the platform lifted. "You can't just leave me here!"

"Weee keepppt oouuur end of the baaargaaain," the Prime replied. "Weee leeet yooouuu liiiive."

As the platform continued its swift ascent, Donovan's sobs vanished from earshot. Harold wanted to rage, to scream at the thing inside him, but he knew it would be of no help. The seekers had gotten what they needed. Harold assumed it was only a matter of time until he faced the same fate as Donovan.

Above, daylight poured into the tunnel, cascading over him, but Harold didn't feel any warmth.

Once outside, his eyes scanned the blood-covered facility. Twisted, broken bodies littered the courtyard, many of whom had died by his own hands. He'd seen their eyes bulge, first with fear, then sadness, as he tore out their throats with inhuman strength and speed. One after the other, young men serving their country had died in front of him. To them he'd been a monster, the stuff of nightmares. He wanted to vomit, but he wasn't even allowed to do that. Cursing the thing inside him, Harold knew he had to find a way to bring an end to all of this, no matter the cost. But how to do such a thing still eluded him. Without any control over his own body, he needed to find some way to force the creature out of him. He'd momentarily gained control once before, back in Casey's office. It had been a brief victory but a victory nonetheless.

Since then, though, the creature was aware of his consciousness fighting back and had been able to keep Harold contained like a child, trapped in a closet of his own home.

If only I can find the door handle . . .

Ahead, a green light stretched down from the ship's belly. Within the beam, Casey's feminine silhouette lifted off the ground, floating upwards. *They finally found you.*

Without a backwards glance, Harold's body followed the Prime into the light. Engulfed in emerald, they floated off the ground, toward the waiting ship.

Now what? he wondered. What exactly did they plan to do with her? The seekers had hinted at taking her back to the future, but to what point in time and for what outcome? Once this was all over, would they discard Harold as they had tossed away Donovan? As the ship swallowed him in its metallic hull, Harold's thoughts raced for some way to break free before it was too late.

The green light died, and darkness consumed him.

Moments later, he found himself standing face to face with Casey. The *real* Casey, not some fake, placid thing, like the one the ship had offered up earlier. She paced back and forth, her fists shaking and her teeth bared, as if she were spoiling for a fight. Harold couldn't believe what he was witnessing. Even now, trapped inside the ship with nowhere to run, Casey was defiant. Harold wanted to be proud of her, impressed even, but the reality of the situation stole his hope.

Poor girl. She thinks she can still win.

In his mind's eye, he saw a flash of Prewitt's cocksure smirk moments before Harold ripped out his throat. Like Casey, Prewitt had also seemed so confident, so unaware of how much danger he was in. Until he died. Desperate not to let the same thing happen to Casey, Harold shouted for his master's attention, begging it not to harm her. As always, his pleas went ignored.

Harold's body lunged forward and grabbed Casey by the throat.

Donovan's flashlight flickered, its bulb's illuminance a dim, pale yellow. Unable to see more than a few feet ahead, he had remained crumpled on the dusty floor, waiting for the inevitable darkness to consume him. He knew there was no way out.

When the last vestiges of light flickered and died, Donovan didn't scream or cry. He was beyond that now. Trying to remember the last time he'd eaten or drank anything, Donovan calculated how long he might survive down there. A couple of days at best, he assumed. At least those creepy spider things seemed to be gone. The shadows that consumed him were still; nothing moved in the silence. His own shallow breath was the only sound he could hear. Death wouldn't arrive in a violent, sudden rush; it would be slow and agonizing.

I should have let those things kill me. Prewitt, you bastard. You got off lucky.

Something warm touched his left shoulder, like a gentle breeze where there shouldn't have been one. Pushing down any last pangs of hope, Donovan turned slowly, spotting something in the distance. A tiny glow, barely visible, so faint, in fact, that if not for the complete blackness that otherwise surrounded him, he doubted he would have noticed.

Tossing his flashlight and rifle aside, he lumbered to his feet, following the light. Passing through the cloning chamber's torn doors, the crimson glow grew brighter, like a beacon. All the way in the back, the flickering light seemed to give off more and more heat the closer he approached. His breath grew humid while fresh droplets of sweat drenched his face and chest.

At last he was standing above the glow's source, an octangular hole in the ground. Some sort of ventilation duct, he assumed, though where it led, he couldn't begin to guess. They'd never discovered anything below the cloning chamber. If there was an antechamber or another level down below, Donovan would never have cared before that moment. He'd always hated that place. Nothing from the future, he decided, should be buried in the past. The whole thing was unnatural to the point of uncanny. "Revolting" was a more precise term.

Kneeling beside the opening, Donovan's hands searched the edges, trying to decide if he could fit inside. Even if he could, did he want to? He needed to go up, not down, he reminded himself. Still, this was the only option.

Fuck it, he thought, chuckling faintly. *What have I got to lose?*

Dangling his feet over the edge, Donovan dropped into the crimson light.

And fell out of this world.

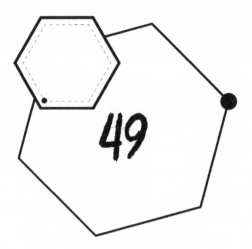

49

Through an aura of pale color, Casey perceived Harold's trembling fear even as his arms grasped her neck, pulling her toward his blazing red eyes. Though his face was a blank, expressionless mask, she felt the turmoil raging behind it. Somehow, he was still conscious in there. She needed to find a way to help him regain control. Instead of fighting his steely grip, she welcomed it, allowing herself to be pulled closer. She projected her thoughts outward.

Harold! Can you hear me?

No reply. Though she could smell his sweat bubbling up from the conflict within, his visage remained unchanged. Harold's eyes swiveled to the clone beside him. The Prime. Its red-and-black stained visage formed a nightmare, looming over her. If anything, the damaged clone appeared even stronger and more menacing than their normal gray forms.

Ruthie was right. I created a monster.

By injecting it with a dozen different poisons and vaccines instead of finding a way to kill such creatures, Casey had instead made something even stronger and more dangerous. All her hard work to find a cure had blown up in her face and was now staring back at her through bloodshot white eyes. In contrast to Harold's blank, seemingly emotionless face, the Prime's rage was plain to see. Its mouth opened, revealing sharp teeth as it bent over her.

"Yoouuuu deeeestroooyed uuuus," the thing said with a serpentine hiss.

Casey didn't flinch. Locked in Harold's grasp, she met the Prime's hateful gaze. "Not all of you, apparently."

A red-and-black taloned finger ran up her cheek. "Whhhaaat waaas done caaan nooot be uundooone."

Casey matched his glare, her eyes full of defiance. "Good."

The Prime took her from Harold's grip, shoving her forward down a long gray hall.

"Nooot aaaalll iiisss looooooost," the thing hissed. "Weeee haaaave yooouuu."

Casey frowned, her head drooping. Although she'd defeated the ship before, the last time it had been alone without another pilot. Now there were two others. Her feet felt heavy, each step dragging down the long, straight corridor, Casey doubted her enhanced abilities could save her this time. She needed a new plan. No more running or hiding; she had to destroy the ship and its creators once and for all.

Reaching inward, she attempted to activate her nanites. They didn't respond.

Her gut twisted. The ship, it seemed, had once again dampened her abilities. Stretching outward, she again tried to sense the conflict raging within Harold, but this time she felt nothing. It was as if invisible blinders had slid over her senses, blocking her vision. Realizing how powerless she was, her footsteps grew even slower.

Suddenly, she felt tiny, impotent, while the figures beside her seemed larger. Terrifying. Casey shivered, dreading whatever fate might await her at the end of the hall.

Like a faint echo reverberating through his skull, Harold had sensed Casey's consciousness probing his, only to be silenced as if someone had hit a mute button. Possibly the seeker inside him or maybe the ship. Either way, the effect was the same. He had no way to respond. Trudging behind her, Harold tried to recall how he'd gained control the last time, back in Casey's office. He'd taken the seeker by surprise. The creature hadn't expected Harold to regain consciousness, and that momentary amazement had given him an opening—an opening that was now solidly shut. Harold needed to find another way to surprise the thing that was controlling him if he ever hoped to help Casey or himself.

Ahead, the tunnel offered two arched doorways. He knew Casey had some control over the ship, if only he could get her away from the Prime. Even a few precious moments might offer her a chance to escape. To do that again, however, Harold would need to regain control of his own faculties. But how? Last time he'd pushed outward, using his emotions to flood the invader's senses. What if this time he pulled in the opposite direction?

As the split tunnels approached, Harold knew it was now or never. Pulling his thoughts further inward, Harold wrapped a mental projection of a dark cloak over himself, diving deeper and deeper into his memories. He needed somewhere safe. Somewhere to trap a monster.

A single image came to mind. Colored windows and arched walls sprang up before him, and rows of wooden pews lined up behind. Above, a giant cross emerged. Harold was standing in a church. What better place to contain his own personal demon? He just needed faith that this could work.

You're making a mistake, he thought as "loudly" as he could, hoping the seeker might hear. Through his physical eyes, like openings into another world, he could see Casey, now mere feet from the twin tunnels' entrances.

She wanted to be taken! Harold shouted. When still no response came, he raised the volume, his voice echoing through the cathedral. *It's a trap!*

Red mist swirled through the church, dancing around Harold until it solidified into a singular shape. A mental projection of a gray clone loomed uncomfortably close. Harold fought the urge to step aside and instead met the creature's inky black stare.

"What trap?" the thing asked with thin, imaginary lips.

"Do you really think she simply walked up to the ship and invited herself in *for no reason*?" Harold shrugged. "Casey wants to be here. She's going to bring the ship down and all of you with it. For an advanced race, you're really kind of stupid. In fact, you're what my mother would call 'stupid-smart.' Smart in theory, dumb in practicality."

The creature tilted its head as if replaying the events that had led them to this point. Distracted, it didn't notice the church growing smaller, shrinking, containing him inside wooden walls. Once the movement registered, however, the gray thing shifted its gaze. Walls pushed down, pews slid across the room, and the giant cross tumbled from above, locking the thing in place. The structure only needed to hold for a few precious moments.

Harold's consciousness slid outward, filling his physical body as one might slip into a pair of shoes. All at once, air stung his lungs. He winced from the fiery pain blazing along his skin's nerve endings, His body, it seemed, had been pushed beyond its physical limits. His limbs grew heavy and difficult to control from the sheer exhaustion dragging him down, but the hallway's frigid air jolted him enough to focus on the job at hand. He clung to that feeling, using it to stay alert, awake.

Ahead, the twin archways loomed. He needed to act. Now. With mere seconds at his disposal, Harold grabbed Casey by the shoulders and tossed her into the left doorway.

"Run!"

Stumbling to keep her balance, she spun, glancing back at him. Eyes wide, she appeared shocked by the sudden turn of events. When the Prime lunged for her, Harold threw himself in its way, shouting at Casey to flee while she could.

Nodding with silent understanding, Casey ducked around the corner and out of sight.

The Prime was too strong for Harold to contain, and he could already feel the seeker within him regaining control. Using these last precious moments, Harold dove into the Prime's gut, holding the wretched thing at bay.

As Harold struggled, inner shadows pooled around him, dragging him back into a mental abyss. The seeker inside had regained control. Trapped once again behind windowed eyes, Harold watched the Prime bolt past him, racing down the winding hall.

But Casey was gone.

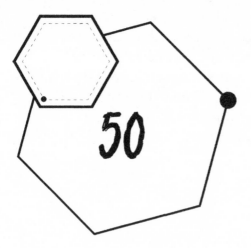

50

Walls crinkling, the ship's interior shifted, reconstructing its labyrinth of winding tunnels ahead of Casey, but she was unwilling to slow her rapid pace. She already knew where each turn would take her. After studying the ship for so many years, it held few secrets for her. Still, racing through one hallway after another, she felt foolish. Working together, Casey had believed she'd created some sort of fragile bond with the vessel. In truth, it had simply been biding its time. Waiting for the moment when the tables turned. For this moment.

Even the Prime had turned on her. Injected with countless poisons and potential cures over several years had simply made the damnable thing stronger. Now Casey couldn't help but wonder if the idea of the Prime experiment had secretly been given to her by the ship, like a whisper in a dream. Either way, the result was the same. She'd grown overconfident in her abilities, and that confidence had led her down a path of dangerous choices, such as trying in vain to cure herself in the hopes of having a child. Selfish choices. Casey had told herself over the years that everything she'd done had been to stop the seekers from returning or even existing in the first place. Out of breath and trapped once again within the ship's shimmering tunnels, Casey faced a cold reality: she'd done it all for herself.

Her experiments on the Prime, her continued connection with the ship, none of it had served humankind. It had all been to help herself. To find a cure, not simply for the nanite infection within her but more specifically to be able to safely have a child. *To be a mother, like Ruthie*. Her thoughts drifting, she wondered what had happened to Ruthie. Had she gotten out before Prewitt blew the underground base? Casey hoped so. She couldn't bear to add another name to the list of the dead. So many gone so that she could be saved. Their sacrifices couldn't be in vain. Her legs shaking beneath her, Casey's steps slowed. Panting, she gulped in metallic-tinged air, making a final, fateful decision. No matter the cost, it was time to end this.

It is already over, Casey, a slithering voice said, snaking through the back of her skull. *I warned you. Confidence in your abilities would be your undoing.*

Behind her, Casey heard pounding footsteps. The Prime was closing in. Gathering her strength, she snuck around another corner. Casey knew precisely where she was headed.

Unfortunately, so did the ship.

It won't work. Not this time.

Despite its words, Casey detected a slight tremor in its tone. "Let's see," she answered and then sped down the hall, heading for the ship's heart.

The ship's hypersphere hovered within a giant domed construct, interlaced with tubes running along curved gray walls. In the dome's center, the enormous hypersphere spun slowly, glowing crimson. As Casey entered, the sphere's light painted her skin blood red. Her trembling legs slowed. The last time she stopped the ship, bringing it down in a fiery crash, she'd done it in there. Casey could only hope that, even without her abilities, she might be able to do it again. Lingering directly beneath the spinning sphere, she reached out with her hands, feeling its warmth. Starting at her fingernails, the heat trailed down her chest, through her groin, and into her legs and toes.

It felt like a lover's embrace. Familiar, warm, and inviting.

Once again, she spoke the same command that had brought the ship down before: "Crash."

This time, nothing happened. The ship remained upright, the room still humming with invisible energy. Even the hypersphere remained unchanged. For whatever reason, her command had gone unanswered.

"It haaas aaa neeeew piiilot," an all-too-familiar voice answered.

Exhausted, Casey's head drooped, and she turned to face the Prime once again. The red-and-black creature loomed behind her. She had been so desperate to execute her plan, she hadn't heard its approach. Standing a few feet behind the monstrous clone, Harold lingered, like a pet on a leash.

"Nooowheeeree too ruuun," the Prime said, its thin lips spreading into a sneer.

Without another word, it lunged forward, its mouth wide, revealing rows of needle-sharp teeth. Stumbling backwards, Casey tripped over the floor's piping and fell, tumbling into the hypersphere.

Red light swallowed Casey. Burning brightly. Blinding. Closing her eyes, the light shone through her eyelids, too hot and luminous to block out.

The Prime vanished from view, its furious roar fading along with it. Red heat turned frigid. Encased in sudden, absolute silence, Casey exhaled, calmed by the tranquil quiet. Releasing frosty breath, she opened her eyes, finding herself standing in what appeared to be a football stadium.

Below a gunmetal sky, a banner read, "Portland State. Go Vikings!"

Her gaze dropped farther, stopping on the field around her. Thousands, perhaps tens of thousands, of beds stretched across the field. Dotted amongst them, doctors and nurses dressed in yellow hazmat suits tried to attend to the overwhelming mass of patients. Casey walked down an aisle, glancing left and right. She saw people of all ages and races, each in various forms of transformation: oval black eyes, scaly gray skin. Semi-conscious, the patients seemed completely oblivious to her presence.

A shadow slid over the endless number of beds, blanketing the field in darkness. Shivering, Casey glanced up. Her jaw slackened, and her legs nearly gave out. Thick, dark clouds broke apart, revealing a dozen enormous ships that filled the sky. The closest one, hovering over the stadium, swept the ground with emerald light. Blazing across the bed's occupants, as if searching, the light slid over Casey. Her mouth turned dry, and her stomach soured.

Dear God, is this the future?

The green light turned to red. Blinking, Casey suddenly found herself floating in a crimson sea, dangling weightless within the sphere. A voice echoed, distant and inhuman. Whatever it was, she knew it wasn't the ship. It was something else.

"Help us," the voice said. Its tone was both masculine and feminine, an intertwined chorus.

Casey glanced around at the brightness, unable to perceive anything beyond the light's glow. "Who? What's happening?"

"We're prisoners," the voices replied. "Like you."

"The hypersphere," Casey said, gasping as she tried to wrap her mind around this new discovery. "You're alive."

"We exist," the hypersphere answered. "But not like you or our captors."

"Captors," Casey repeated. "I thought you were a machine. The seekers told me there was no other life in the universe."

"Not in yours, perhaps."

"Another dimension," Casey replied. The answer now seemed so obvious, she wondered how she'd missed it all these years. None of the seekers' technology had ever resembled the hypersphere. Her mind turned back to the first time she'd touched it, so long ago. The sphere had shown her a way out. While standing on a snowy mountain, it had taken her directly to her fiancé, Arthur. Her thoughts bouncing from one encounter to another, she recalled all the things the hypersphere had shown her. The past, the future. All of them had been warnings. Both within the ship and the tower, the spheres, it seemed, had been attempting to communicate. Casey had simply never truly listened. Never understood. But now she did. The seekers had taken what they needed both from humanity and beyond. Like her, the sphere was a prisoner.

"Help us," the voices said again, its pitch growing shrill.

"How?"

Abruptly, Casey tumbled out of the sphere, crashing to a metallic surface. She was back inside the ship. Staring up at the spinning hypersphere, she didn't understand what to do or how she could help it. Then, as the Prime and Harold lurched forward, she realized she couldn't even help herself.

Yet, as the figures approached, their movements seemed slow, languid, as if they were wading through an invisible barrier. It took an eternity for the Prime to come around the sphere, making its way toward her. Casey stood, watching the thing's steady approach, its elongated arms inching upwards. The image was almost comical. It seemed the hypersphere had dislodged whatever block the ship had placed over her abilities. She could feel the nanites activate within her. This time instead of fighting the change, Casey welcomed it. Her skin turned ashen, hair slid from her scalp in thick chunks, and her eyes bulged and blackened.

No more running, she promised herself. *No more hiding.* A grin creased her gray mouth.

Casey raced forward, meeting the slowed Prime head on. In a blur of movement, she swung, her fist smashing into the thing's sickly cranium. Time reverted to normal as the creature flew backwards.

Harold was next. She didn't want to kill him, but she had to immobilize him long enough for her to deal with the Prime. Bent low, she kicked out, sweeping his legs, before hammering a fist into his gut. The red-eyed Harold fell without a sound.

Behind her, she sensed the Prime's recovery. Too late. It rushed forward, grabbing her. Flailing in its steel grip, she kicked and punched wildly. In a frantic frenzy, most of her attacks missed, but a few landed on its face and chest. They weren't enough to stop it from raising her over its head and heaving her across the room. Focusing inward instead of on the outward fight, Casey used the nanites to once again slow time. Dangling in the air, she struggled to reposition herself. It was a brief pause, but it was enough so that when time snapped back to normal, she landed on her feet and was able to lunge at the creature.

Surprised by her newfound strength and speed, the Prime matched it with blinding rage. There was no hint of the seeker's great intelligence within that sickly red-and-black shell. Whether maddened by the effects of all the poisons in its system or by Casey's continued efforts to thwart its plan, the creature swung its taloned fingers high and low, wide and maddeningly wild. Casey dodged the attacks with ease.

Time to finish this, she decided. Thrusting both arms outward, she used all her heightened strength to hit it square in the chest, hoping to shatter its ribcage. But, once again, her overconfidence was her undoing. As if anticipating the attack, the creature grabbed her arms and tossed her against the wall. Too sudden for her to slow time, the thing was already on her, pounding Casey with a barrage of flailing limbs. She kicked it off, attempting to create some distance between them and regain her edge.

And then the ship intervened.

Tubes around the room sprang up like snakes, trapping her against a slick wall. None of her strength or speed was enough to fight against the ship's overbearing power.

Slowly and cautiously, the Prime approached, watching her writhe in vain.

The last thing she saw was its bloodshot white eyes glaring above rows of needle teeth. Then the Prime's fist came shattering down onto her skull.

Casey had lost.

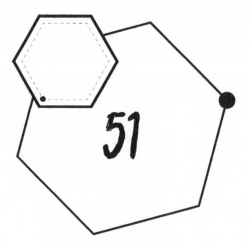

51

It was a beautiful dream, warm and inviting.

Emerald-green eyes gleamed up at Harold while the not-Casey's supple white legs slithered behind, locking his pelvis in place. He knew, of course, that she was no more real than the Roman Colosseum surrounding them. She was a mere figment of his perverse imagination, created by the ship to keep him docile while the seeker possessed his body. However, the warm breath inches from his lips and the moist, full breasts at his fingertips made it difficult to concentrate on anything beyond the vision at hand. It was a prison that Harold no longer had the strength or the desire to escape. Staring down at the naked not-Casey beneath him, he didn't *want* to be anywhere else. Didn't want to *feel* anything else. He just wanted *her*.

Tangled blonde hair draped his face as he kissed her neck. His penis hard, she pulled him inside of her.

The sensation was all Harold could have hoped for and more. After wondering for so long what it was like to be inside a woman, the reality lived up to the fantasy—or unreality, as it were. Harold didn't concern himself any longer with details about what was real or not real, true or untrue. Her body felt real enough, and nothing could stop his motion now.

The not-Casey's moans filled his eardrums, and her heartbeat pounded against his chest as her long, wet curves undulated against him. The sensations were too much to bear. Harold wanted to hold back, to extend the moment for an eternity, but he knew he couldn't. Pressure built to a crescendo within him. Then she whispered, moaning: "Harry . . . "

Harold's pelvic thrusts ceased abruptly. Something was wrong. His penis still throbbing inside her, his mind whirled as he struggled to recall if the not-Casey had ever called him that before. But, no, he knew it hadn't. The ship's visage of her had always lacked the Cheshire grin and the cocky arrogance that often accompanied the real Casey when she called him "Harry." Until now.

Like lights coming up at the end of a show, the Roman Colosseum melted away. Harold suddenly found himself on a platform inside a round, metallic room. He was lying, naked and prone, on top of Casey. Her eyes were closed, and her breathing remained slow and steady, as if sleeping. Harold had been raping her. Horrified, he tried to pull out, but it was too late.

He ejaculated inside her.

Harold stumbled backwards, disgusted by the sudden realization of what had transpired. Sobbing, he struggled to pull his pants back up. Hoping and praying that this was simply another fantasy in his twisted imaginary world, he spun around, only to find the Prime glaring back at him. Cold, grimy hands of dread crawled up Harold's spine. This was not a dream; it was real. Unfortunately, so was Casey.

Sobbing uncontrollably, he pushed words out through trembling lips. "Wh-why? Wh-what-what did I do?"

When the Prime offered only a faint sneer in response, the true magnitude of what Harold had done sank deeper and deeper into his consciousness.

"What did you make me do?" he screamed.

Glaring silently, the Prime drew closer. Harold stumbled in his bunched pants, falling over Casey's naked form. The feel of her skin now suddenly repulsed him beyond measure.

Scrambling off her, as Harold fell over, a red mist poured from his mouth and nose. The seeker within him snaked through the air before vanishing inside the Prime's gaping mouth.

After everything Harold had seen and done, after all the times he'd prayed to be set free from the seeker's control, now he felt empty without it. The seeker had manipulated him, but the physical action, the rape itself, had been Harold's own work. Trembling, unable to speak or move, his eyes watered, his gut twisting inside him as if it might burst. Through peripheral vision, he could still see Casey's bare, spread-eagled form on display. The guilt was like liquid fire burning through his every nerve. It was all consuming, overwhelming. Worse, the true horror of why he'd been kept alive immediately came crashing down. The ship had stoked the fires within him from the very start, teasing and manipulating him, first with the slave girl, then with the not-Casey. It all made grotesque, even logical, sense to him now. Erections, after all, were created by something the seekers couldn't reproduce—human emotions. Desire. Passion. Love.

The ship had needed him aroused. It needed his *seed*.

As the Prime drew closer, raising its taloned fingers toward his head, Harold didn't protest. With no more fight left, he knew the seekers had won. The end came all too quickly. Having served his purpose, the Prime twisted Harold's head around, snapping his neck.

Crumpling to the gray floor, Harold died, his body twitching. Casey's bare leg dangled over the table, swaying in front of him as his vision faded into nothing.

While pools of shadow engulfed him, Harold's mind drifted back to his mother. Her voice was the last thing he heard, quoting James 1:14: "Each man is tempted when they are dragged away by their own evil desire. Then, after desire is conceived, it gives birth to sin. And sin, fully grown, gives birth to death."

It was a beautiful moment, Casey thought, making love to Arthur in their cabin.

When he erupted inside her, she pulled him closer, hoping that this time, finally, they might bear a child. It was all she'd ever wanted. With Arthur's diploma less than two years away, Casey dreamed of what their life would be like once they escaped the small town of Blackwood with its small people and their even smaller dreams. Collapsing beside her in bed, Arthur's chest heaved rhythmically from the brief workout. The sound of his loud breathing was comforting to her. Twisting closer, she rested her head against his chest, feeling it rise and fall.

Smiling, Casey felt the moistness of his deposit within her. Maybe this time she'd get pregnant. She prayed as much. A first step toward leaving Blackwood and all the bad things she'd endured there.

An image of her pedophilic father bubbled to mind, accompanied by the stink of whisky and cigarettes. Rubbing her head against Arthur's chest, she quickly squashed the memory.

It was time for a new beginning.

A new life.

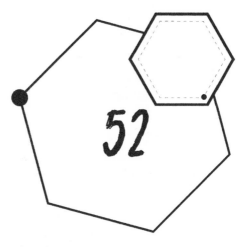

The future

Engulfed in warm sunlight, Casey lay peacefully. Her eyes fluttering open, she saw black green monoliths arching above, smelled fresh pine, and heard birds chirp in the distance. Closer, the sound of gently rushing water bubbled and gurgled.

As she rolled onto her back, dry leaves crackled beneath her. Groggily, she sat up, glancing about. She knew this place. To her left was Marsh's Creek, and to her right, just over the hill, lay the cabin that she and Arthur had rented for the year. Still, as she turned this way and that, Casey grew concerned.

Why am I lying in the dirt?

Her head throbbing, she struggled to focus on how she'd gotten there. It had been Friday night. She'd watched *Miami Vice* while Arthur finished his homework. Then a dog had howled outside. She'd opened the door, and a light blazed above, neither natural nor phosphorescent. And then . . . and then . . . ?

She was lying in foliage.

Casey stood, her body swaying. Her muscles ached, and her calves felt like they were on fire. Had she been running? Glancing down, another shock came just as quickly.

She was naked. Immediately, her peacefulness shattered while bile rose in her throat. Something bad had happened; she knew it. Only, she couldn't remember what. Brushing loose leaves and grass from her skin, she checked herself for wounds or bruises. When she didn't find anything, she sighed slightly, though she felt no relief. Inhaling a sharp breath, she clambered over the hill, making her way back home. With a gust of wind, the clouds obscured the sun, sending a chill through her body. Pine needles along the ground stabbed her bare feet, though she didn't slow her pace. She needed to get back to Arthur.

Where the hell is he?

Rounding the hill, stepping over frozen rocks that bit into her heels, she stopped at the edge of a gravel road. At its end, a broken structure lay hidden under an overgrowth of plants and weeds.

Home.

It couldn't be, she thought, glancing about to make sure she was in the correct place. But the road was right, and the mountainous landmarks spread upwards behind the broken cabin were the same as before. Only the building itself was wrong. Another shiver ran across her naked flesh, this time not from the wind.

Crossing the twisting gravel, she no longer noticed the stabbing pebbles and rocks underfoot. As she approached, her eyes never left the dormant, broken structure. *Home.* The word spun around in the back of her mind like a wheel that wouldn't stop.

Somehow the structure seemed to have aged decades in a single night. With her nakedness still a concern, she went to the door and shoved it open. Hinges whined, and wood splintered at her touch. As the door swung loosely aside, she assumed it might fall to the ground and shatter. Instead, the door banged against the wall with a hollow *thud*, announcing her return.

As she viewed the jumbled remains, half covered in dirt and grass, Casey's stomach felt as hollow as the cabin. Stepping inside, her eyes scanned about, looking for something to throw on. A few steps in and she'd already given up on finding her clothes, though perhaps she could locate a blanket or a towel. As Casey made her way through the debris, her mind whirled with possibilities about how the place could have grown so decrepit in such a short time. How long had it actually been? Obviously, she'd been gone much longer than a single night.

As Casey passed the kitchen, she was reminded of the last time she'd stood there, flirting with Arthur.

Arthur?

With a sudden recognition of just how dire the situation might be, Casey ran to the bathroom. The door was gone, and a tree trunk had fallen through the roof, exposing greenery outside. Casey's breath caught in her throat when her eyes landed on a dusty, fractured mirror leaning against the once-tiled walls. Though partially shattered and caked in dirt and dust, it revealed enough. She felt air escape her lungs as she struggled to breathe, and her legs threatened to give out beneath her. Her chest heaving, she peered closer at the naked reflection staring back. Age lines creased the skin around her mouth and under her eyes. Her face was rounder, fuller, and her breasts drooped slightly. Even the shape of her arms and the length of her hair were wrong. She'd aged, ten years at least.

Arthur . . .

His name tumbled through her thoughts as she clutched the dirty sink for balance. *What happened?* She wiped her watery eyes with her wrist, sniffing back tears. As she dropped her hand to the side, something caught her eye in the dingy reflection. Turning, she found a pink shower curtain dangling from broken rungs. Casey remembered when they moved in, how much Arthur had hated that color. He said he felt like he was pooping in the ladies room. She'd laughed, promising to change it, but she never did. Reaching down, Casey tore the curtain off the rusted pole and wrapped it around her exposed body.

Glancing back toward the front door, Casey steadied herself both outwardly and inwardly before leaving. She knew she couldn't find any answers, or comfort, in that place.

By the time she made it down to the main road, the sun had begun to drop, along with its remaining warmth. Huffing frosty breath, Casey tried to ignore the growing numbness in her feet and arms. She needed to get to town before sundown. It was a five-mile hike, one she'd done a dozen times but never in the evening, and never wrapped in a shower curtain. She might have assumed this was simply a dream, a nightmare if not for the thundering in her chest and the growing nausea in her belly. No, this was all too real.

After another half mile, headlights blazed behind her. Spinning, she waved her arms, gesticulating wildly. Casey could only imagine the sight on offer for the driver: a crazy naked lady wrapped in a shower curtain, waving like a mad woman.

A blue Ford pickup truck pulled over. Flinging the passenger door open, she found a handsome young man in his early twenties, offering her an odd grin.

"Jesus, ma'am, are you alright?"

Ma'am? Wow, I must really be old. Thirty, at least.

Casey climbed in without permission and shut the door. "No," she replied, her voice breaking. "I don't think I am."

He flipped switches, igniting the car's heater. "Here, let me warm you up." The young man reached into the back and pulled out a blanket. "And put this on. You must be freezing."

Putting the truck into drive, he headed down the road toward Blackwood.

Casey didn't say anything for several minutes. Glancing around the cab, she was careful not to make eye contact with the young man. Not up for a conversation, she wanted to just sit quietly, trying to silence the noise in her mind.

On the dash, propped next to the steering wheel, an odd rectangular shape illuminated the truck's cabin. Bright squares and text covered the glass surface. Noting her interest, the man pulled it out and handed the strange object to her.

"Did you need to make a call?"

Casey shook her head. Was that thing a phone? She'd never seen anything like it outside of something like *Star Trek*. Still, she couldn't find anything to say. Too scared to ask what year it was because she knew from looking at that phone that she wouldn't like the answer, Casey pressed her lips together and grunted a noncommittal response. Had it been *more* than ten years?

Interrupting her thoughts, the young man held out his hand. She forced herself to reach over and shake it.

"Jacob," he said. "Jacob Anderson."

"Casey," she mumbled, her voice barely audible over the truck's purring engine.

"You from around here, Casey?"

She nodded.

"Me too," he said, as if determined to start a conversation. "Grew up in Blackwood, but now I work in Portland."

"What do you do in Portland?" she asked in a thin, wispy voice, hoping to keep the conversation away from herself.

"Reporter," he said, shrugging. "Nothing big. Mostly agricultural reports. Feed prices, grazing fees, that sort of thing. But I hope to write bigger stuff soon."

When she didn't ask a follow-up question, silence returned, but not for long. Unfortunately, the young man didn't seem to get the hint. "How about you?" he asked. "Work around here?"

"I think so," she said, huffing. "Used to, at least. I'm a waitress. Or at least I was." Her voice sounded wrong to her own ears. Shallow, lower. Casey assumed her voice had somehow aged along with the rest of her. Fresh tears exploded from her eyes, and this time she couldn't seem to stop them.

Jacob didn't respond, keeping his focus glued to the road as if he didn't notice. It was the nicest thing he could have done. Casey knew she'd eventually have to ask to go to the sheriff's station and try to find some answers. However, for the moment, all she wanted was to sit in silence and be left alone. The young man seemed to finally understand that too. He was cute, but he was also a slow learner. Ahead, a sign read, "WELCOME TO BLACKWOOD, POPULATION: 1,340."

The town's population was over a third bigger than what she remembered, over a third as big as it had been when Casey saw the weird green light in the sky. Again, she wondered how much time had passed, and again she locked her mouth shut, terrified to hear the answer.

As they passed the signpost heading into town, a sharp pang jolted in her stomach. The nausea in her gut grew. Fumbling at the door, she struggled to find a way to open the window. Jacob hit a button on his side console, and the window slid down just before Casey threw up. Chunks splattered the side of the truck, both inside and out.

"I'll get you to the doc's office," Jacob said. "It's only a couple more miles."

Her face flushed, Casey nodded. "Sorry."

"Don't worry about it," he said with an aw-shucks grin. "It's my sister's truck."

Despite herself, Casey laughed. Then she felt the nausea return. "Pull over for a sec."

Jacob jerked the wheel, coming to a stop beside a cliff. Stumbling out, wrapped in the blanket and the shower curtain, Casey could only imagine how ridiculous she looked. As she bent over on the side of the road, her stomach churned, but nothing came out.

Then something in the distance caught her attention. As she peered over the cliff, she saw an enormous metallic structure jutting out of the earth. At least a hundred stories tall, it stretched toward the sky beside the mountain, threatening to overtake it. The last vestiges of sunlight sparkled along its curved surface, turning the strange object a fiery crimson. To Casey it looked like a broken tower.

Or a spire.

Clambering back into the truck, she pointed toward it. "What is that thing?"

Jacob shrugged. "No idea. It's always been here."

Casey shook her head. "No, it hasn't. I've never seen it before."

Jacob chuckled, turning the engine back on. "You sure you're from Blackwood?"

Casey didn't answer. None of this seemed right. As they drove away, another pang jolted her stomach. Jacob noticed her flinch.

"You sick?" he asked.

Feeling her stomach, Casey's gaze lowered. Eyes swiveling, she glanced in the side mirror. Her face was still rounder than she remembered. No, she decided, not round, swollen. Casey suddenly doubted she was ill.

Sucking air through clenched teeth, she shook her head. "I . . . I think I'm pregnant."

EPILOGUE

A strange mixture of grassy scents and acidic notes, combined with hints of vanilla, rose above an underlying mustiness. As light entered, the swirling smells gave way to a stream of light, revealing a seemingly endless row of leather-bound books. Donovan was standing in a library.

How he'd gotten there remained a mystery, though as he walked down the aisle, he had to admit that any place was better than the underground tomb he'd been trapped inside only moments earlier. Someone or something, it seemed, had plucked him out of the cavern and away from certain death. Having dropped into the lowest depths of the spire's ruins, he'd glimpsed one of those damnable hyperspheres just before a red light had consumed him. Now he was strolling along the longest bookshelf he'd ever seen. The aisle seemed to have no end. Glancing at the leather-bound tomes on either side, he noted that none of the books had titles. Instead, they had strange numbers marked along their spines. Stopping at a red volume, he read what he assumed to be a catalog designation: 000.456.762.45.6578

Hell of a title, he thought, pulling the book from the shelf. As soon as his fingers touched the leathery surface, however, he instinctively wanted to put it back. The ground beneath him seemed to sway, as if he were perched on a boat in a violent storm. Still, curiosity got the better of him, and he opened the book. Light, yellow and blazingly warm, erupted from its pages. It was blindingly bright, as if he were staring at the sun. Donovan shoved the book back onto the shelf and quickened his pace, putting distance between himself and the strange volume. Wherever he was, it sure as fuck wasn't Kansas—or Oregon, for that matter.

After continuing down the aisle with no end in sight, he turned his attention upwards. Light streamed through arched windows far overhead. It was a dome of some kind, vaguely familiar, not unlike a Catholic cathedral. Though, if whoever built the place was going for godly, they'd missed the mark. The façade, which he assumed was what it was, felt no more human than the ship or the spire or anything else connected to the hypersphere. Could he be inside the damned thing? If so, he doubted he was any safer than before.

His pace quickening to a full-out run, Donovan raced down the aisle until, at last, the end was in sight. Trembling from exhaustion, he slowed down, covering the last hundred yards at a slow, leisurely pace.

Let 'em wait, he decided. Whoever *they* might be.

Stopping at the end, he found himself surrounded by hundreds, perhaps thousands, of aisles spreading out like a spiderweb. Each one, he assumed, contained just as vast a catalog of books as the one he'd just escaped. Not eager to go down another pointless route, Donovan turned, making his way toward the library's center. The marble floor glistened with sunlight streaming from overhead, adding to the cathedral-like feeling he'd had moments earlier. But what awaited him at the center was no bearded man in white or angels with glowing wings. Instead, the universe itself spread out before him.

Spiraling slowly around, the somewhat transparent image abruptly collapsed upon itself into a singular point of light, only to expand once again into an enormous universe of countless blinking stars and rotating planets. Approaching it, Donovan reached out, waving his arm through the somewhat transparent projection. Just as before, the universe collapsed upon itself, then was reborn in a burst of light. The whole thing played out before him like a movie on a constant loop. Birth, expansion, collapse, death, and finally, rebirth. A more philosophical man might have found such a concept fascinating, but Donovan was no philosopher, and all he wanted at that moment was to find an exit, preferably to somewhere safe and sound, with a fully stocked bar.

No sooner had the thought occurred to him than the sound of clinking glasses broke the library's ominous silence. Spinning on his heel, Donovan's jaw came unhinged as he found himself staring at yet another uncanny sight. A ten-foot-long bar now stood smack dab in the middle of the already strange library. Adding to the scenery, a gorgeous brunette bartender with ample cleavage and an eager smile awaited him, drink in hand. As far as uncanny visions went, Donovan decided that he'd seen a whole lot worse.

Plopping onto a round barstool that spun gently beneath him, he wiped his dry lips while eyeing the display of liquor bottles. Aged whiskey, cognac, vodka, bourbon, everything he could imagine, and he could imagine a lot. Even though a whisper at the back of his mind quietly reminded him that none of this could possibly be real, at that moment, he didn't give a shit.

"Whiskey, sugar?" the bartender asked with a smoky voice.

"You read my mind," he said, smiling. She poured a glass and left the bottle on the counter. The first drink went down in a single gulp, stinging the back of his throat, burning him with a delicious, warm glow. Donovan didn't waste any time pouring a second. And a third. By the fourth his head was swimming, and his drinking slowed. Behind the bar, the alluring figure waited in a one-piece satin gown, which made her slender body look like one long curve. As far as hallucinations went, Donovan seemed to have hit the jackpot. *About time*, he thought. *No nightmarish visions of high school, black-eyed monsters, or spidery things crawling around. Just me, a pretty girl, and a strong drink.*

"And your universe," the woman finished, as if hearing his thoughts. Following her gaze, Donovan spun around on his stool, glancing back at the translucent mass of stars and cosmos.

"Oh, that," he said with a distant mumble. Turning back to the bartender, he smiled. "I'd rather concentrate on you. What's your name?"

She shrugged.

"How about I give you one?" Donovan let his eyes slide over her sultry curves and heavy eyes. "Daphne."

"Why Daphne?"

"I knew a girl back in Florida with that name. Sweet kid. You kinda remind me of her."

"Then," she said with a spreading smile, "Daphne it is." She offered her gloved hand.

Donovan shook it, and his lips curved into a wicked grin. "You feel real enough."

"Real enough for what?"

Stopping himself from uttering all the lurid responses that immediately sprang to mind, he simply chuckled. Wanting to change the subject, he turned back toward the spinning model of the cosmos. "So, *what about* the universe?"

"A place that has *before*, *after*, *then*, and *now*. All sorts of words with all sorts of meanings that we often struggle to comprehend," Daphne said. "For example, you say *yesterday* or *tomorrow*, but those titles are simply based on the spinning of your single world around a single sun. What is *today* or *tomorrow* on the other side of your universe?"

"Who gives a shit?" Donovan asked, finishing his fourth glass and starting on a fifth.

"We do," she said, her voice breaking. "Because we need to understand in order to escape."

Donovan put the glass down, narrowing his eyes. "Escape from where?"

She pointed toward the glistening universe. Donovan's mind slowly turned, clogged gears grinding, unsticking themselves. Daphne wasn't a seeker. And if he understood her correctly, she wasn't even from this universe. A chill shot through him, and he suddenly lost his taste for the drink. "Speaking of escaping," he said, standing, "how about you let me out of here?"

"There's no need to be frightened," she assured him.

"Uh-huh, I've heard that one before."

Daphne hesitated, looking at him long and hard, then withdrew a pencil and paper from below the bar. She drew a stick figure on the page, then took Donovan's index finger and placed it beside the image. "Imagine that little figure on the paper is you," she said, "living in a two-dimensional world, where all you see is what's on the page."

Feeling like he was stuck in a classroom, Donovan sighed, his head throbbing. "OK," he replied. "I'm the stick figure. So?"

"So," she repeated, pressing his finger harder against the page, "what would the stick figure in the two-dimensional landscape perceive of you?"

"Who cares?" he shouted. "Just let me the hell out of here!"

Donovan tried to pull away, but her grip was too strong. Huffing in frustration, he reluctantly lowered his eyes to the counter's surface, imagining what the drawing might see from such a skewed perspective. "The tip of my finger, I guess."

"The tip of something *larger*," she corrected.

The truth of her words landed in his gut like sour milk. He was starting to understand, though he wished he didn't. Recalling a long-ago conversation with Earl and Casey back in the ship, Donovan tried to remember precisely what they'd said. Something about the hypersphere being a three-dimensional representation of a four-dimensional object. At the time it had sounded like a B-grade sci-fi flick. Now, however . . .

Clearing his throat, Donovan found his voice. "The hyperspheres—"

"Are fingertips into your universe," she finished.

"What do you want with me?"

"The same thing you want, Mr. Daley," she said, smiling. "To escape."

"How?"

"We're both trapped in a causality loop that neither of us created. To break free, we must destroy the loop's source."

"You mean the seekers?"

She shook her head. "No."

"Oh," Donovan replied, catching her meaning. "Casey."

Daphne nodded. "We had hoped to save her, but now that path is closed to us."

"Sure thing," he replied, holding up a glass. "I've tried twice before, but here's hoping the third time's the charm," He took another gulp. "Just tell me one thing: why's she so damn important to everyone?"

"It's not her that's important," Daphne answered. "It's her child."

"Must be mistaken," he said, sighing, "she doesn't have one."

"Again," Daphne replied, "the concept of past and future is a confusing abstraction to us, but she does indeed have a child, a daughter."

"Wait." Donovan paused, grasping her meaning. "You want me to kill 'em *both*?"

Daphne's expression hardened. She didn't answer; she didn't have to.

Donovan finished the bottle. He'd done plenty of terrible things over the years, including murder. But not a kid. Never a kid. Clamping the bottle down with a hollow *thump* on the bar, he stood.

"Sorry, sweetheart," he said with a humorless smile, "you'll have to find someone else."

Suddenly, the bar and the library dissolved, engulfed in red light. Donovan stepped forward, finding himself at the top of a dead world. He knew that place; he'd been there before. Wind slammed him against a railing as he peered down at the enormous crimson spire stretching up from below. He was back, after all this time, back at the end of the world.

Only this time it was different. *Changed.*

Looking across the distant horizon far below, he glimpsed an endless ocean, dotted by thousands of enormous spires, stretching through the clouds. Where once there had been only a single, last visage of the seekers' home, now there stood an entire civilization. Beneath the sprawling ocean depths, he knew, lay the remnants of humanity and its long-dead cities. Pushing himself away from the ledge, he spun around, finding Daphne waiting for him.

"I'm afraid you don't have a choice, Mr. Daley!" she shouted over the rushing wind. "Not if you hope to save your world or yourself."

Donovan hesitated, glancing back at the barren remains of Earth, covered in crimson spires. His stomach twisting in knots, he finally turned back to her. "What's the kid's name?"

THE END

WANT TO KNOW WHAT HAPPENS NEXT?

Go to ALIENSKYPUBLISHING.COM
to be among the first to find out!

AND –

If you enjoyed THE SHIP'S REVENGE
please leave a review on AMAZON!

DOUG BRODE is the author of The Ship, as well as the creator of HBO/Cinemax's sexy sci-fi series Forbidden Science. He has also been a storyboard/concept artist on such popular films as Star Trek, Iron Man, Thor, Looper, Van Helsing, Planet of the Apes, MIB: International, among many others. He lives in California with his wife, Pamela, and their two little monsters, Leia and Hayden.